Turn Left at September

by
Dennis Collins

For Don

Behler
PUBLICATIONS
California

**Behler Publications
California**

Turn Left At September
A Behler Publications Book

Copyright by Dennis Collins 2005
Cover design by Sun Son – www.sunsondesigns.com

All rights reserved. No part of this book may be reproduced or transmitted in any form or by any means, electronic or mechanical, including photocopying, recording, or by any information storage and retrieval system, without the written permission of the publisher, except where permitted by law.

This is a work of fiction. Names, characters, places, and incidents either are the product of the author's imagination or are used fictitiously. Any resemblance to actual persons, living or dead, events, or locales is entirely coincidental.

Library of Congress Cataloging-in-Publication Data is available
Control Number: 2005920483

FIRST EDITION

ISBN 1-933016-25-6
Published by Behler Publications, LLC
Lake Forest, California
www.behlerpublications.com

Manufactured in the United States of America

*To my sister Diana,
who convinced me that I could write this book.*

CHAPTER 1

All of the stars were present tonight, none absent, none tardy. It was New Year's Eve, eleven forty-five to be exact, only fifteen minutes left in the year. The northern Michigan winter had been colder than normal and tonight in this remote timberland it seemed to be the clearest and coldest so far. Michael O'Conner stood outside his "fortress" in his thermal underwear, pissing in the snow. He was taking advantage of the holiday season for a vacation from his private detective business, a little well deserved time to himself. Tonight was his night to drink beer and watch the giant screen as the big red ball in Times Square descended to welcome in the new year. In a few minutes all of the horses in the world would be celebrating their birthdays.

It would have been a little more enjoyable if McCoy and Otis, his two good friends from the Detroit Police Department could have been here. They'd come a long way together in the ten months he'd known them. He had learned so much from these two mentors who taught him the skills he needed to survive in the world of the private investigator. Michael's first investigation had very nearly got him killed when the man he was shadowing laid an ambush and worked him over with a two-by-four. McCoy found him unconscious in Receiving Hospital and had sort of adopted him. A friendship blossomed as Michael recovered from his injuries and he was able to assist McCoy and Otis Springfield in solving a very complicated case. "Yeah," he said aloud. "Woulda been a great chance to let 'em know how much I appreciate all they've done." But Michael had spent other New Year's Eves alone, he could handle this one too.

With the moon reflecting off the snow, the beauty of this pristine hideaway never ceased to stir a sensation of awe in Michael. And it was all his, the deed inherited from his father. But the soul of this land chose its own partners and Michael knew that he belonged here. The concrete block building behind him may have looked out of place when the Army first built it as part of the war effort back in the forties, but nature has a way of overwhelming and absorbing intruders. The ivy had done its job, slowly climbing the sheer concrete walls until the building had lost its harsh shape and surrendered to the power of the forest.

Any mechanical sound in this desolate woodland has to be considered unusual and the faint hum that Michael was hearing was definitely a man-made noise. At first he thought it might be the mammoth Pelton-wheel hydroelectric generator that magically converted the fast-moving river into enough electricity to power a small village. But after listening for a few seconds, it became obvious that the ringety-bang sound in the distance was that of a two-cycle gasoline engine and it was getting closer.

Michael was beginning to feel the bite of the five degree temperature through his long johns and turned toward his lodge. He was thinking that he would illuminate the place with the floodlights in case the snowmobiler, or whoever it was, needed a beacon to follow. It might be Harley Charlie. Charlie Whitepigeon, the Chippewa biker lived over in that direction, but Charlie wasn't the type to go joyriding on his snowmobile in the dark.

Michael concluded that it must be someone lost or confused, probably from the new casino/ski club resort six miles away on the other side of the hills. Nobody would come this far off the groomed trails on purpose, especially at night. As he reached for the door, he heard the pitch of the engine change. It was gasping, sucking in air devoid of any fuel. The machine was running out of gas.

He looked in the direction of the asthmatic sound and saw the hesitant, uncertain flicker of a dimming headlight among the naked trees at the top of a hill about a half a mile away. The scene reminded him of an old movie, like the flame in a lantern dancing as some spirit carried it through an obscure and forgotten graveyard. He hurried back to his "fortress."

It took the rest of the year for him to wiggle into his snowmobile suit and get the cutter hooked up behind his Polaris. Clancy, the two-year-old Llewellin setter was already sitting in the cutter in anticipation of one of his favorite activities, a moonlight ride through the jack pines, birch, and scrub oaks, his big tail wagging so hard that it rocked the sled.

The search took almost three hours. There were no real roads or trails in the area and choices could get pretty random when all the terrain looks the same, even with the bright moonlight.

He found the abandoned Ski-Doo midway through the second hour but there were no footprints leading away from it. Maybe they faded into the deep track left by the snowmobile. Michael had criss-crossed the same general area four times, stopping every few hundred feet to sweep the landscape with his powerful flashlight.

Finally, he parked the snow machine and killed the engine so that he could hear any sounds of distress or calls for help in the still night air. Clancy got up off his haunches and sniffed all the points of the compass, as if wishing for even a slight breeze to bring him a scent. After a few moments, he seemed to get excited and jumped out of the cutter.

The big dog doubled back down the path, following his nose and ignoring the meaningless tracks. He stopped suddenly about fifty yards back, his head moving rapidly in frantic, jerky motions as he sniffed the pockmarked snow for a few seconds then disappeared into the trees. It took Michael at least five long minutes to get his rig turned around and by that time he could hear the dog barking and yelping as if he had a coon treed, or was in some kind of pain.

Michael's flashlight lit up a bright blue snowmobile suit curled up at the base of an old sugar maple. There was no response when Michael called to the body in the snow so he grabbed the shoulder of the snowmobile suit and rolled the lifeless torso onto its back. It looked like a young boy, small and frail. The heat generated by the beam of the five cell Maglight produced diminutive vapor at the nostrils of the victim. At least he was still breathing. Speaking to nobody, Michael said aloud, "What's a kid doing all alone in a place like this?"

Michael picked up the small body and struggled through the knee-deep snow to deposit him in the cutter. The dog instinctively jumped in with the slight figure and curled around him in order to share his body heat. Michael fired up the snowmobile and cut a trail for home. He didn't want to waste any time.

Inside the lodge, Michael had an easier time handling the limp body. He carried it up the stairs from the garage and laid it on the guest room bed. The first order of business was to turn on the electric blanket and crank the heat control all the way to the ten. As he surveyed the scene, Michael realized that the insulated snowmobile suit would slow the warming process. He pulled off the boots and was surprised to see pink socks. For the first time he took a good look at the person in his guest room. It wasn't a young boy at all. It was a girl. More accurately, a young woman. He was a little gentler now, stripping off the outer clothing but carefully leaving the expensive looking, Victoria's Secret, undergarments untouched. There wasn't any evidence of frostbite that he could see and though the breathing was still shallow, it seemed to be regular, as if she were just asleep. He pulled the covers up around her chin and hurried back downstairs to his living room to look up hypothermia in his medical encyclopedia.

The book wasn't as much help as he had hoped it would be. The body temperature is lowered, metabolism is slowed, and the blood flow to the brain can be interrupted. One statement caught his attention. "Internal warming may be necessary." *How the hell do you do that? Chicken soup?* He considered trying to get her into town where a real doctor could treat her but the only ways out of here this time of year were snowmobile or down the river in the inflatable boat. Neither option seemed desirable.

Michael was wishing that his buddies, McCoy and Springfield, could have accepted his invitation to join him on this New Year's, but it seems that holidays are a particularly busy time for cops, especially in Detroit. Those two would know what to do, or at least be able to figure it out.

Tonight though, Michael was on his own. Perhaps he could call Harley Charlie, that ex-marine seemed to always have the answers, ever cool under fire. Michael had met Charlie quite a few years ago, back when Michael was young and his father had just bought this place. They hit it off right away, explored the woods, caught fish, hunted partridge, the way that unburdened teenagers do. As with most childhood chums, they eventually pushed on in different directions, Michael enrolling in college while Charlie enlisted in the Marines. It was only a year or two ago that they renewed their friendship. Charlie had developed a passion for motorcycling and had become Harley Charlie.

"Hell, it was a natural, the long hair, the leather fringe, the headband, they were all already a part of my culture. All I needed was the bike." The hearty smile made his huge size seem less threatening.

Charlie was also probably the best electrician in the county, running a successful contracting business. He had made some wise educational choices while serving in the Marine Corps.

But it wouldn't be fair to burden him with a medical emergency. Charlie was probably getting ready for his New Year's Day appearance at the big celebration at the community center, all dressed up in his traditional tribal gear. Charlie's muscular six foot, seven-inch frame and classic chiseled native features could be quite imposing in war paint and feathers.

Maybe Michael could get a doctor to come out here. He picked up the cellular phone and tried to dial the sheriff's number but nothing happened. The battery indicator told him that he was running on empty. Michael couldn't remember when he last charged it and he didn't have a backup battery with him. He jammed the telephone into the charger on the kitchen counter. For now, he was out of business and completely cut off from the outside world. Happy New Year.

CHAPTER 2

Monica Wilson was born into a blue collar world. Her father came to Detroit from Scotland as a young man seeking work in the auto plants. He was a skilled tradesman and a labor rights activist. Within four years of his hiring at Dodge Main in Hamtramck, he became a union representative and worked his way up to the powerful position of chairman of the local bargaining committee. He spent all of his forty-plus years in the industry shrewdly fighting for worker's rights. As a union man he was without peer in his quest for justice and equality. At home it was a different story.

"A family is not a democracy," was his favorite answer any time his authority was questioned. His three daughters often discussed ways of dealing with their tyrant father, possibilities ranging from running away to murder. The two older girls escaped by getting married and moving away right after graduating from high school and leaving Monica, the youngest, all alone to handle the father's unreasonable need for control. Normally a cheerful and smiling young lady, she had developed a rebellious nature that led her into the world of drugs, sex, and rock n' roll. She had a natural talent for all three.

Monica had no idea what she was getting herself into when she began hanging out with the heavy metal bunch at the high school. She had no trouble being accepted by the boys in the crowd. Her fiery red hair, crystal blue eyes, and petite figure would have made her a popular girl in just about any group. After two and a half years as a high school honor student, Monica's grades began to tumble as her involvement in the subculture increased. At seventeen she had dropped out of school and been thrown out of her father's house. She was an "emancipated minor."

Left to find her own way, she learned that the quickest and easiest way to make money was by selling drugs. At first she wouldn't handle any of the hard stuff like crack or heroin but eventually she surrendered to the demands of the market and offered a full inventory to her loyal clientele. By her twenty-first birthday she had been robbed, raped, beaten, and arrested. Drug dealing is a tough business.

Her demeanor had become so antagonistic that she soon found herself unwelcome as a pal or a roommate. Most of the friends from her past wanted nothing to do with her. Only Etta, a beautiful, young computer programmer remained loyal to Monica, perhaps so that she would have a place to stay when the weather got cold.

Etta was a real loner. Still in her twenties and an ex-hooker, she had very little to do with men these days. She hadn't dated at all since moving in with Monica, not offering any explanations—and nobody seemed curious enough to ask. Etta knew that most prostitutes tell themselves that they're only in the business temporarily, until they can build a stake or get an education but she was one of the few who actually followed the plan. She went to school during the day and walked the streets at night, eventually earning an associate's degree in computer science. Now Etta had a real job in the data processing business. Her income was lower but at least she was in society's mainstream. Etta always said she was going to write an autobiography titled, "Bedsheets to Spreadsheets." She was enjoying life now, smoking an occasional joint and swaying to the music. Etta's former life had conditioned her to mentally block out unpleasant situations or surroundings. Nothing ever appeared to bother her. She seemed oblivious to Monica's tantrums and temperamental personality. They were a perfect match.

Among Monica's customers were a number of rock musicians, although not as many as she had expected. It seems that most of the struggling musicians were serious about their craft and kept themselves far too busy practicing and rehearsing to make time for frivolous pastimes like drugs. Still, she spent a lot of time hanging out with rock and roll bands. There had always been the dream of becoming a famous singer someday. Her pitch was nearly perfect and her voice was very good, perhaps even special, or unique, with a trace of raspiness.

On this pleasant autumn Friday night she found herself at The Aardvark, one of Detroit's more upscale gathering places out on far west Grand River, almost at the city limits. She was taking the night off just to listen to some music and relax. The music really helped. A mixture of oldies and moderate rock was just what Monica needed to get her mind off of the new lifestyle that seemed to have sneaked up on her and then entrapped her. "The leash," her pager, was home in the desk drawer.

The house band, The Nephewz, had just finished their first set and were taking a break, mingling with the crowd and being friendly. The bass player winked at her as he stood by the service bar nursing a tall Coca Cola. She returned his acknowledgment with a smile. "Nice sound. You guys been together very long?"

"All of our lives, actually, even though we're just getting started professionally. Been playing music together since we were kids, practicing just about every single day. We all still have day jobs. Are you in the business?"

"Well, not really. I'd like to think that I was a vocalist but I'm afraid I don't have any references."

The bass player laughed. "You're the first honest one I've run into. Are you here to see about the audition?"

"Not exactly. What're you talking about? What kind of audition?"

"We're looking for a female singer. I kinda figured that's why you were here alone; most of the unattached women that come in here want to try out for the band. Sorry if I pegged you wrong."

"Oh, don't apologize. It sounds like a great opportunity. Where do I go to sign up?"

"If your free tomorrow morning around, say ten-ish, we'll be getting together at my house."

She frowned. "I see."

"Don't get the wrong idea, lady. I got a little bandstand in the recreation room and you'll have my wife and kids for an audience. The other guys will be there along with about three more girls that we want to listen to. Whaddaya say, you interested?"

"What the hell, I got nothing better to do. Where is the place?"

The card he handed her said *Bud The Bass Man* in bold letters at the top. The address was in a western suburb, Livonia. "From the card, it's hard to tell whether I'm a musician or a fisherman. I wasn't thinking too clearly when I ordered them."

She spoke without looking up from the card, as if she were searching for some hidden message in the textured paper. "You guys do any recording or videos or anything like that?"

"Not yet," answered Bud. "But we're well connected. We're all related. There's me and my brother and two cousins in the group. Our fathers were both musicians back in the big band days, that's how we got our 'Nephewz' name. Our dads played with some of the best; Goodman, Dorsey, Shaw, bands like that. They're retired now but they still have a lot of friends in the business who owe them a few favors. As a matter of fact, that's one of the reasons we're looking for a singer. A couple of people from the 'Spirit' label said we could do a demo for them if we had a fresh sounding female vocalist." He glanced at the bandstand and noticed the rest of the group working their way back to the stage. He pumped down his Coca Cola in one big gulp that would have made Mean Joe Greene envious and said, "Time to go to work. Catch you later."

Monica listened a little more intently during the second set. It was a solid band, obviously schooled musicians playing complicated and crisp sounding arrangements. This looked like a serious opportunity. She was as excited as a ten year old with a new Barbie doll, fantasies streaming through her mind. "What should I wear? What should I sing? What will the other girls be singing? Are they pros?" She had visions of taking the first step in becoming one of the biggest pop stars in the country.

By the time she got home, reality had begun to set in. The odds of making it big were longer than the odds on the state lottery. Then there was the matter of her lifestyle. The drug culture would be a hard society to break out of. She knew too much about too many people and that could cause some anxious moments for some of those folks, especially the bikers. They were the ones she feared the most.

Billy Bones scared her more than anyone in the world. She had never met anyone as evil as Billy. He only seemed to smile when he was causing pain, or about to. He was the President of Satan's Disciples, a tough outlaw biker gang from the Warrendale area of Detroit. Their income was derived from the drug trade and from extortion, and Billy was both the brains and the muscle of the outfit. His story is the stuff legends are made of. Born along the banks of the Scioto River in Columbus, Ohio, he moved to Detroit the day he bought his first motorcycle and began wreaking havoc immediately. Barely eighteen years old, he quickly gained the reputation of being the best, and dirtiest street fighter on the west side of the city. He did nothing to discourage the rumors about his past that included the story of a triple murder in the Cincinnati area. A guy's rep was everything on the streets. The kindest way to describe Billy was "absolutely worthless." The thought of living a decent, productive life never even entered his mind.

Billy was Monica's connection, her uplink to the supply line. Monica had never gotten too close to Billy Bones but that wouldn't stop him from considering her as his personal property. That was the way it was with Billy. He had been her drug hookup and that was enough for him. Breaking his hold would be a real problem.

CHAPTER 3

Monica couldn't help feeling intimidated as she sat in Bud's recreation room. The entire basement of his ranch home had been transformed into what appeared to be a stylish nightclub, complete with a bandstand, spotlights, and sound system. There was also a professional looking video camera being set up by Bud's wife.

The three other girls who auditioned ahead of her were very good, obvious pros. They had all brought their own music and discussed the arrangements with the band before they sang a note. Their movements and expressions looked to be carefully thought out and well rehearsed, even the facial expressions were choreographed. Monica wanted to slink out the door. Maybe this had all been a mistake. She flashed back to the encouraging words from Etta as she was getting her makeup on this morning.

"Honey, you can be just as good as any of the others. I've heard you sing and you got every bit as much talent and your smile is a whole lot prettier than anyone else I ever seen."

When Monica's turn came to audition, Bud had to talk her into getting up on the bandstand. "Don't worry about a thing. Just be yourself, do what you do best and let it roll. We're here to have fun, nothing more."

Monica did three numbers, beginning with a song from *A Chorus Line*, building momentum with some hard-driving rock, and ending with a passionate rendition of *Me and Bobby McGhee*, the way Janis Joplin did it, full of emotion and raspiness. She was surprised at how comfortable and natural she felt in front of the small but attentive audience. The respectable applause at the end of her performance told her that it was well received. It had been her first time standing under a spotlight.

An older man, who had been sitting at a table in a dimly lit corner, got up and whispered something in Bud's ear. Bud turned to the four girls, who were clustered in front of the bandstand complimenting each other, and announced. "You were all great. It'll take a few days for us to go through the tapes and do some dubbing, so I can't give you our decision right now, but I would like to invite you all to lunch on Mr. Maxwell. He's our agent and he is very pleased with what he saw here this morning."

The lunchtime conversation at the Bodega offered no clue as to what the mysterious Mr. Maxwell was thinking. He seemed to grant equal time to everyone, chatting about his experiences and lengthy history in the business and revealing nothing of substance.

When lunch ended and they all went their separate ways, Monica returned to her apartment to find the message light blinking on her answering machine. The first message was from Bud. "I'll bet you didn't expect a call this soon," he began. "Get back to me as quick as you can, I have some news for you." Her heart was beating so fast that she almost missed the second message on her machine. It was from Billy Bones. "Where the hell you been? Call me, bitch."

Monica sat with her hands folded on the desk like a schoolgirl. How could she get out? Why hadn't she thought of this before she ever got involved? She should've known better. It would mean so much to her to be able to leave this dirty lifestyle behind. As she began to think more clearly, she decided to find out what Bud had to say first and then figure out how to deal with Billy Bones. Feeling great anxiety, she punched in the number of Bud the Bassman.

"Hey kid, Guess what? Mr. Maxwell is crazy about you. He says that you're the one. How about that?"

Monica stuttered. "I, I don't know what to say. What does it all mean? Are you sure you got the right girl? The others were so much more... professional."

"I got the right girl. It was your natural manner that impressed Maxwell. The other girls were very good but they also were very rehearsed. You were spontaneous, letting your emotion drive you and that's exactly what he'd been looking for. That beautiful smile of yours didn't hurt a thing either. He took our video and audiotapes with him and said to start getting an act worked out. He's got a promoter waiting on the west coast to look at our stuff. I told you we had connections."

"What do you want me to do next? I'm kinda new at this game."

"The first thing you have to do, if you're not already a member, is to join the musicians union. No major label will touch you if you're not a member. We're going to have a meeting at my house tonight around seven, you'll want to be there. We need to make sure that we get everything organized so there's no hard feelings on paydays."

"Okay, I'll see you at seven."

Etta had been standing behind Monica listening to half of the conversation and that was enough. She put her arms around Monica's neck and gave her a congratulatory hug.

Monica smiled and then frowned as her thoughts turned to the dilemma of Billy Bones. The best way to handle him was to feed his ego. It took the better part of an hour to make up a story to get him off her back. She made a lot of notes so that she wouldn't run the risk of tripping herself up. The last thing she wanted to do was get caught lying to Billy Bones.

"Hello Billy? This is Monica. I got your message."

"It's about time. Get your skinny little ass over here. I got all your shit for the next week sittin' here and you know I don't like keeping this shit around my place."

"I guess you haven't heard where I've been for the last twenty-four hours, have you?"

"No, and I don't give a damn. Just get over and pick this shit up."

"I don't think you want me anywhere near you for a little while. I've been in police custody since yesterday morning and they questioned me about you, wanted to know how often I had contact with you, that sort of thing. I'm hot right now and I'm sure I'm being watched. I didn't figure that you need me to lead them right to your front door."

"What did they pick you up for?"

"They wouldn't say. I guess they don't have to until they charge you with something."

"Sounds like they're just hassling you. It don't make sense to me. They usually get an undercover narc to make a buy, then bust your ass. You got any new customers?"

Monica thought for a moment. "Just the regulars. I haven't seen anybody new in over a month."

"This thing don't smell right to me. I'll tell you what. I'm gonna peddle this shit to someone else for now and take it day by day for a while. You stay out of trouble and keep me up to date on what's happening. Send me the information through someone we can both trust. Don't call me again until you hear from me direct. Got it?"

"Got it."

He hung up without saying another word.

She wasn't sure if Billy bought her story. He could be a hard guy to read and way too dangerous to take for granted. It wasn't a comfortable feeling, things were happening too fast. Yesterday she was headed nowhere, providing an instant high or maybe instant death to schoolgirls, peddling crack and shit at high school hangouts. Today she could sense a glimmer of hope. For years her worst nightmare was the distinct possibility that she would be the one who provided the lethal dose of something to someone's daughter. Drug dealers weren't supposed to have consciences, maybe that's why she wanted out so bad. The people that she met in the past twenty-four hours were from a different world than the one she had become mired in. She didn't fear them and that was a refreshing new feeling. She wanted to live in their world. Could she? Would her past life release her? When did she surrender her self respect and begin to stray so far from the values that she once believed in?

The clock on her dressing table said three o'clock. In four hours she would be going to a meeting that might help her get out of this nightmare that she'd made of her life. "Don't screw it up, girl. There's too much at stake," she said aloud.

A faint sound coming from her desk drawer startled her. It was her pager, one of the most important tools of the trade, if you happen to be a drug dealer. She always felt like a slave when she carried that damned beeper, like she was expected to come when she was called. She took the little gray pager out of the drawer and studied it for a moment, carrying it into the kitchen. It was time to destroy the first symbol of her servitude, time to reclaim her soul. She placed the pager on a cutting board on the countertop and pulled the tenderizing hammer out of the utensil drawer. Swinging the hammer with both hands, she shattered the electronic demon in a single blow and kept hammering until she was sure that it could not miraculously re-assemble itself and seek revenge.

Etta, standing in the doorway, smiled and shook her head. "You go, girl." she laughed.

CHAPTER 4

Monica arrived at Bud's house determined to suppress her feeling of anticipation. It seemed that she was the only one making an attempt to hide the excitement; everybody else was celebrating.
"What's going on?" she asked. "Just sell our first video or what? Everyone's acting like we've already got a contract."
Bud met her at the door. "It's almost that good. You know that guy you met earlier? Mr. Maxwell?"
Monica nodded.
"Well, he's a little more than just an agent. He's a vice president at Spirit Records. Maybe I'd better explain. About forty or so years ago, when he was new in the business, he was my father's agent. My dad helped him put together a production company. Dad was a better politician and knew a lot of influential types, so he introduced Maxwell to some of the higher-ups at the recording studios. You know, the guys who are too important to deal with agents. Anyway, Maxwell made the most of it and kept his hand in the production end of things. When Spirit made their move from Japan and set up shop in this country, he signed on as a consultant and worked his way up from there. Now he's their most powerful man on this side of the ocean.

I guess he always figured that he never would have gotten the break without my dads help and he felt that he owed my old man something. That's why he came out here, to repay an old debt. You gotta admit that it looks pretty good for us."
"Wow, I had no idea." Monica tried to sound calm. "It sounds like this man has an awful lot of clout but I'm sure we still have to deliver."
"We'll be all right. We have years of hard work and preparation behind us. I have no doubt that we're ready. What a group needs more than anything, is a big time promoter and we've got one of the biggest. Better yet, it's a personal thing with him. His staff will be busting their asses to make sure that we hit the charts. It's almost a done deal."

Monica hardly heard a word that was said at their impromptu business meeting. Her head was too filled with fantasies and wild dreams, and panic. What was she going to do about her past? Should she tell them now or try and hide it? And what about Billy Bones? Maybe he could be bought off. Not likely, he'd probably rather destroy her life than see her succeed. That's the way Billy Bones was.

The meeting ended at about eight-fifteen, the band had to play at the Aardvark at nine thirty and it was time to go to work. Monica agreed to meet the band at the club for the start of the second set, she needed to get a little work in front of an audience. She rushed home to change into something a bit more stylish for her big debut.

At the back of the freezer compartment of her old refrigerator there was a Tupperware bowl that held all of her cash and valuables. She fished it out from between the chicken nuggets and frozen hash browns to see how much she was worth. There certainly weren't any stockbrokers to contact or bank statements to total up. This was it, her life savings in a plastic bowl, her net worth in dollars and cents. Almost sixty-six hundred bucks. The ten year old Mustang was paid for and the rent was current through the end of next month. The only other liabilities were the phone and electricity; the heating bill was included in the rent. Billy Bones still owed her about four hundred dollars but she wrote that one off. The money ought to last until the checks from her new career started coming. Of course she would need some new clothes to wear on stage and she might have to move if Billy started harassing her but it looked like she'd make it okay. Etta had recently gotten a part time job at a boutique to supplement her current income and could probably contribute a little too, since she had been living here for five months.

The next few weeks proved to be very busy and anything but glamorous. There was a repertoire to memorize, including the choreography that went along with each number. And that would all change when the contract came through. They'd be needing fresh material. Rehearsals were grueling, no fun at all. The guys in the band were still working their day jobs and staying up until one o'clock or so every night to practice. She didn't know how they did it. The only bright spot was that she was beginning to feel comfortable on the stage at the Aardvark. That part was fun. At least she hadn't heard anything from Billy Bones. As a matter of fact, the whole biker gang appeared to be avoiding her. She was relieved about that. She still hadn't told her new circle of associates about her sordid past. Maybe they'd never find out. After all, why would they need to know?

When Bud arrived at the Aardvark that Saturday night, he was carrying a stack of big manila envelopes. "I got us some original material to work with," he announced, "we'll never get anywhere doing other people's stuff. We need something of our own."

Monica opened her envelope and began going over the music. It was complicated material, full of key changes and sophisticated chord structures and the arrangements had been written for a full orchestra. "I certainly hope you guys know something about transposing and things like that. We sure can't work with this until it gets translated."

Bud just smiled at Monica's confusion. "The whole score was written for a stage play, a musical. A buddy of mine from way back when I was in high school wrote it. He got it into the Birmingham Theater last year but it got canceled after less than a week. Critics killed it but they liked the music, said the score was Broadway quality. They couldn't understand why the composer wasted it on such a lousy play. Anyway, he gave it to me. Said to see if we can get it in front of the public. He knows I got connections. I figured we could see if it works for us."

Bring Him Down. It was a number written for the female lead in the play. She was supposed to be giving advice to a friend on how to deal with her two-timing husband. The song was assertive and strong, a driving, variable tempo and fit perfectly with Monica's jerky motions and raspy voice. After three weeks of rehearsal with countless revisions, and variations, they had a videotape that satisfied all of them. Maxwell had been asking for something original and now they had it. It went out UPS overnight to the Spirit studio.

In a matter of days, Maxwell began making arrangements for a taping in New Orleans. They were on their way.

The Spirit staff was already laying the groundwork at MTV and VH1 before anything had been recorded. The video started off slowly, only getting airtime in the wee hours of the morning. But there isn't any "Prime Time" for music videos. Soon the music networks were getting positive feedback on this new group known as Monica and the Nephewz, asking if they had any more stuff on tape. Maxwell had insisted that the band have enough quality material to produce a one-hour CD. They did almost the entire score from the flop musical that nobody could remember the name of and threw in a couple of rock standards for good measure. The CD was a reasonably big hit, not quite making the top forty but still showing strong sales.

Monica just hoped that Billy Bones didn't watch music television.

Success brought a few problems for the Nephewz. Maxwell wanted them to do a nationwide tour. Bud was able to arrange a leave of absence from his job as a pharmacist at St. Mary's Hospital but the other guys were faced with the prospect of quitting their jobs outright. A big decision when you have a family to support. Bud's younger brother, Kelly, the lead guitarist, couldn't bring himself to make the big and risky move. He was less than a year away from his masters at Eastern Michigan University and he and his wife had just opened their own business, a small music store in a busy little mall. Just too much to abandon for the "iffy" life of an entertainer.

Maxwell had wanted them to be booked on a tour as openers for Stanley Jordan and they would need to be free to travel. The opportunity evaporated while they auditioned new guitar players to replace Kelly.

After sifting through dozens of guitar players and listening to countless riffs and licks, Ronnie Murray became the new lead guitar for the group and that didn't sit well with Monica. There was something vaguely familiar about the long-haired kid. Something that made her uncomfortable, aside from the fact that she had him pegged as a crackhead, even if the others couldn't see it. He was a damned good guitarist though, she had to admit that. She kept her distance from him.

The delay in making everybody available actually worked in their favor. By the time they were ready to start doing the concert circuit, they had become an established group. It was a tour starring "Monica and the Nephewz." Maxwell had insisted that the vocalist get top billing.

Monica had outgrown her tiny apartment in Detroit and was ready to move on. She was making money now. More than she had made hustling crack at the high school hangouts. She notified Etta that she would be moving as soon as she returned from the concert tour and transferred the rental agreement into Etta's name. Suitcase in hand, she headed out the door to take the world by storm. She didn't notice the light flashing on her answering machine before she left.

"Hey bitch. This is Billy. Billy Bones. Remember me? You owe me, bitch. In a big way and I mean to collect. Think your pretty cool shakin' your ass on television for the teeny-boppers. You an' me got a little shakin' of our own to do. I wanna see what's so cool about that little ass of yours. Call me, bitch."

CHAPTER 5

Etta was a loyal friend. She had been Monica's "advocate" all along. From the first day she moved in with Monica, Etta had lectured her on leaving this sordid drug business in her past and getting her life on track.

"Try to think of one woman you admire who's a drug dealer. Just one. See what I mean? It's a dead end business and a dead end life. Get away from it, baby. Be somebody."

It finally looked to Etta as if Monica had turned that corner. There was a certain satisfaction in having been there, in the dregs, among the unwashed, and then finding the courage to reclaim your life. When you've done it, you just know. Monica was going to make it. Etta could feel it in her soul.

As a final boost, Etta decided to remove the last haunting demon from Monica's path. She picked up the phone and dialed Billy Bones' number.

CHAPTER 6

"She's been dead for at least twelve hours or so," said the patrolman. He looked at Detective McCoy. Noting the puzzled look on McCoy's face, he added, "I've been taking some forensic classes, we all gotta take 'em, y'know. We're studying how to interpret and evaluate the effects of rigor mortis right now."

"I'm sure you're right but I hope you don't mind if we have the Medical Examiner confirm that." McCoy winked at his partner Otis Springfield.

Aside from the headlights of a handful of cruisers, the scene was now being lit with the cool flush of an autumn sunrise. The pretty young lady lay fully clothed, just off of the shoulder of a busy Detroit expressway. She was flat on her back with her arms outstretched, the sash cord still cinched tightly around her neck.

Otis was making notes on the little pad he always carried in his shirt pocket. "I think I might know her. She kinda reminds me of a hooker that I busted a few years back. Ain't seen her since, though. Sorta dropped out of sight."

"Maybe she moved on to some new place and just stopped back here to visit relatives or something," offered McCoy.

Otis Springfield turned to the patrolman. "Who found her?"

"I did. Just driving along, looking for whatever. You know, abandoned cars, pedestrians, stray dogs. And there she was. It was still pretty dark and she's a little ways off the road. I saw her foot first, thought it was just a tennis shoe. I had to really jump on the binders when I seen there was a leg attached."

McCoy had been squatting next to the body to get a good look at her face. He was standing with the other two cops now. He fumbled with his wallet until he found a couple of his business cards. "Here, give these to the forensic guys and whoever else shows up out here. Tell 'em that McCoy and Springfield out of the first precinct have got the case. We need to start with an I.D. and go from there. This one could be domestic but not necessarily, doesn't look like anything sexual happened. Her face is swollen pretty bad, too, but I don't see any bruises.

She's got some pretty good marks on her wrists too. I'm curious to find out what that's all about"

The powerful beam of Otis's police issue flashlight was dancing over the grass along the shoulder of the highway. "Make sure you guys check out this ditch real good. At least a half a mile each way. Whoever pitched her coulda been throwin' shit outta the windows."

"Another one dumped on an outbound e-way," McCoy muttered as they walked back to the car. "It's always the outbound side. It seems like they must be suburbanites who visit Detroit, murder somebody and then dump the body on the way home."

Driving back to the station, McCoy broke the silence commenting, "Y'know, I could have been up north at Michael O'Conners place this weekend. Bird season is open and he invited me up to shoot a couple of fool hens."

Otis's brow furrowed. "Fool hens?"

"Yeah. Partridges. Fool hen is an old nickname that kinda describes their autumn behavior. I guess they must feed on fermented berries or something at this time of year and they start acting a little drunk. They'll sit absolutely motionless on a branch and you won't even notice 'em. Then, when you get about six inches away from them, they take off like a Concorde and give you a heart attack."

"Fermented berries?" asked Otis.

"Yeah. This time of year, they freeze at night and then thaw out when the sun comes up. After a couple of days of that, I guess it starts a chemical reaction or something."

Otis chuckled. "So you and Mike were figuring on stumbling through the woods with shotguns, looking for drunk birds to shoot, eh? What a couple of sportsmen you guys are."

McCoy started to answer but changed his mind. He figured that Otis was setting him up. Experience had taught McCoy that it wasn't always prudent to let Otis Springfield lead the conversation when he was in one of his mischievous moods, and this discourse certainly seemed to be going in that direction. McCoy decided on silence for the rest of the trip.

CHAPTER 7

The girl in the ditch had been easy to identify. The crime scene guys had found a purse, complete with all of the normal identification items; driver's license, health care card, social security... even nine dollars in cash.

Her name was Etta Kremer. There was a short record on her with no new entries in about the last three years. Otis's memory had been correct; he had arrested her for soliciting but it was one of those incidents that never made it to court and no one would remember why. The medical examiner's report said that all of her teeth had appeared to have been broken off just prior to her death. Both wrists bore deep cuts and bruises from what was obviously a pair of handcuffs. She had been tortured before she was murdered. This case was beginning to look more and more like a message killing, where the murderer wanted the body to be found in a very public place so that it would be sure to make the news.

Last known address was an apartment on Detroit's northwest side, out near the Rouge River where the amusement park used to be, only a mile or so from Mike O'Conner's private detective office. The pay stubs in her purse showed her working for a small accounting firm.

McCoy leaned over Otis's shoulder to scribble down the street address. "I guess her apartment and her place of employment are all we got to start with. Ready to roll?"

Otis nodded.

The apartment building was Second World War vintage, a four-story brick structure still in pretty decent shape but showing a little age. There was even evidence of a once-upon-a-time lawn in front. It was the sort of place that didn't have a lot of turnover—mostly factory workers and a few retirees because the elevator still worked. Some even thought of it as home.

The super remembered Etta affectionately, said that she had recently taken over the lease from the other girl, Wilson was her name. Yeah, Monica Wilson. Seems Monica had run off with a circus or had gone into show business or some other dumb thing like that. But Etta, now that girl has a head on her shoulders. Good job, all that stuff. "Etta is gonna be just fine. What do you guys need with her anyways. She ain't the type to get into trouble."

"Not anymore," answered Otis.

It was one of those investigations that cops hate. The victim seemed to have been invisible in life. Her employer claimed to know nothing of Etta outside the office, said she came to work, did her job, and went home. She kept her nose in the computer all day, didn't socialize with either of the partners in the accounting firm, not even at the water cooler. Always carried her lunch and stayed at her desk to share her sandwich with the latest People Magazine.

It was pretty much the same story from the neighbors in the apartment house. They said that there was never a sound coming from Etta's place so they never knew when she was home or away.

Etta's mother was dead and her father had been out of the picture for so long, he seemed to have fallen off the earth. She had been an only child and McCoy and Springfield uncovered no other living relatives.

For all of her anonymity, Etta seemed to have found a way to annoy somebody sufficiently to the point of commiting an extremely violent murder.

"She doesn't seem to be the type to provoke," observed Otis. "I figure that somehow, she must've got herself into some sort of situation where she either witnessed something or had some kind of information that made somebody nervous."

"I guess that about 'somes' it up," commented McCoy. "Maybe the ex-roomie would be able to shed some light on Etta's activities. What did the landlord say about her? Circus or something? You got her name, right?"

Otis scanned his notebook. "Monica Wilson. Feel like goin' for a ride?"

"Sure, lemme grab my hat."

"You don't wear a hat."

"Oh, yeah. That's right." McCoy grinned.

Otis tried to re-open the "fool-hen" conversation during the trip back to the apartment house. "I've never been up to Mike's place. Been invited a couple of times, but could never get away. How do you get there, anyway?"

McCoy seemed to sense where the conversation might be headed and appeared determined not to fall into another "Otis trap." "Well, you start in Detroit around the fourth of July and you begin walking north. When you get to September, you turn left."

Otis let it drop with a smile. It seemed that McCoy wasn't going to let himself become the butt of all of Otis's jokes today. There would be other opportunities.

"To begin with, I ain't the landlord, I'm just the super." The little man with the three day stubble, filthy t-shirt, and Jack Daniels breath stood defiantly in the doorway, hands on his hips, trying to look like General Patton but about a hundred pounds too light and not nearly handsome enough. "Second, we don't do background checks or ask for references. The place'd be empty if we did. We get the first and last months' rent up front and it's a month-to-month deal. You miss a payment, you're out. That simple."

"Did this, uh, Monica always pay her rent on time?" Asked McCoy

"Ain't you been listening?" The disheveled hair seemed glued in its out of place style as the skinny old man shook his head. "If she'd have missed I'd have turned her out."

Otis stopped snickering long enough to ask, "Do you have any idea where Monica is now?"

The super looked serious for a moment, possibly contemplating the risk of alienating both officers. "I really can't say. I know that she was doing some sort of job that had something to do with show business, coulda been a circus or something, Etta mentioned that one time. I think that she either moved to another town or maybe just a nicer place. Like I said, we don't keep track of our tenants. We just collect the rent. Oh, and no pets."

McCoy took his turn. "How about visitors? Did you ever notice who was stopping by to see them?"

"That's an easy one," the super shot back. "Nobody. Never. I don't think I never saw nobody go in or out of that place except them two girls, all the time they lived there."

Neither detective said another word. Otis waved his hand and they returned to the car. It was a somber ride back to headquarters. It was looking more and more like this would be one of those cases that would stay open for years. Perhaps the only hope rested with the forensic crowd and their DNA magic

"The torture thing really bothers me," Said McCoy "Somebody's trying to send a message, leaving the body on the expressway like that. We don't know who they're trying to reach, but there's not much confusion about what they're saying.

Otis added, "I think I would have heard if she was still turning tricks on the street. Looks pretty much like she was out of that business. Having a regular job sorta bears that out too. The key is gonna be finding out who the killer is trying to get at. No doubt, this one's gonna take some time."

CHAPTER 8

The tour was a resounding success. Fifteen cities in twelve weeks, a mixture of concerts and club dates. Mostly sell-outs and a couple of standing ovations. Road work was hard though. Monica couldn't believe how tired she was at the end of every performance. She longed for the sanctuary of a real home. The hotels she stayed in were always the nicest places in town but they were so impersonal and so temporary and even in the best of them there was the occasional sticky-fingered staffer. She had to re-orient herself when she woke up every morning just to find the bathroom. This would be okay every couple of years but she sure wouldn't want to live the rest of her life this way.

Ronnie, the new guitar player was becoming a real pain in the ass too. Always hitting on her, like he had something new to offer. Try as she might, she couldn't avoid him. He kept showing up in the most unlikely places, like in the ladies room. The rest of the band treated her like a kid sister. Why did this jerk have to come along and screw things up? She wanted no part of him and thought that she had made that clear a number of times but he kept coming back for more. He was like the flu.

Things seemed to be getting better after she mentioned it to Bud. Ronnie backed off a little, at least his comments were becoming somewhat less lewd. Bud must have said something to him. It didn't matter, as long as he left her alone. Always looking happy on stage was a hard enough chore without the added burden of a creep constantly looking over your shoulder.

Ronnie Murray had bounced from one rock band to another ever since he dropped out of Denby High in his junior year. He had studied classical guitar in his innocent youth, seemed to have been blessed with an abundance of natural talent and soon became quite accomplished. The talent was wasted on Ronnie though. Music wasn't his life. Drugs and women were his life. For a while he owned an old Harley and ran with a gang of bikers but eventually sold the bike and returned to playing his guitar. After all, the groupies that followed any band or entertainer in their town provided him with all the drugs he wanted and more sex than he could handle. He had struck gold with the Nephewz. The money he was making was substantial but it meant very little to him. Always careful to hide it from the others, it was the steady flow of cocaine and broads that drove him. There was something about Monica that intrigued him though. As if he knew her from someplace. He wished he could get in her drawers but that didn't look too likely at the moment. He'd have to figure out a new approach, a different angle. Something had to work.

Ronnie took great pains to conceal his passion for drugs. The rest of the band never suspected, he was sure of that. Monica was the one he wasn't sure of. He felt that she knew, even though the subject never came up. And, for some reason, she seemed to hate him. There was just something, some unseen force that stood between them repelling them like magnetic poles. He had to find a way around it. If only he knew why she looked so familiar. It was a haunting feeling.

As the tour went on, Ronnie began to falter. He was blowing a lot of the licks that used to flow effortlessly from his guitar. Sometimes he would show up late and he rarely put any effort into rehearsing, although he needed it much worse than the others. The band was trapped. They had to keep him at least until the tour was over. Bud felt guilty for hiring him in the first place.

Ronnie kept trying to cover his mistakes with crazy gyrations on stage. The more mistakes he made, the wilder he got. He was becoming an embarrassment to the band. They all tried to talk to him about his amateurish attempts to hide his blunders but he insisted that the crowds loved it. He was doing it for them. Who gives a shit what you assholes think. Every time the subject came up, he would end his night back in his room doing a couple of extra lines, just to help convince himself that everything was cool. He wasn't doing a damned thing wrong. Nobody understood him.

The critics didn't seem to waste time writing about Ronnie, even though he didn't exactly fit in with the rest of the act. They were content to give all the ink to Monica. Refreshing, innocent, they called her. If only they knew. And Bud proved to be a very polished PR man. His years of dealing with little, blue haired, old ladies at the pharmacy counter had taught him to listen with a sympathetic ear and smile a lot. But smiles just came naturally to Bud anyway; he was that kind of person. The reviews remained solid throughout the tour. The stuff scrapbooks are made of.

Maxwell met the band in Phoenix. They were performing at Firebird. "Things are going better than I ever dreamed," he said. "Every big name songwriter in the business wants to get on the bandwagon. Pardon the pun. I've got a ton of new songs for you to choose from." He opened his suitcase and showed them volumes of sheet music. "Go through this stuff when you're rehearsing and see if there're enough good songs for a couple more CD's and maybe two or three videos. You guys have become a hot property. You better think about getting yourselves an accountant and maybe an investment counselor too. Your price is going up substantially after this tour. We have a few lingering dates locked in at 'bargain basement' figures, but after they're out of the way, you'll be doing nothing but recording sessions and big concerts." He was talking directly to Bud, even though the whole band, except Ronnie, who always seemed to be absent, was in the motel room. Monica might be the star but it was clear that Bud was the boss.

Bud was glad that Maxwell hadn't said anything in front of Ronnie. He had already made up his mind to dump the kid as soon as they got back to Detroit. He'd try to talk his brother, Kelly, into coming back with the group. That would make it easier to explain to Ronnie. What the hell, he'd deal with it.
  Maxwell had to catch a plane for Los Angeles that afternoon so the group treated him to a quick lunch at the motel restaurant. Then Bud drove him to the airport. The mood was subdued during the short trip.
  "Something's bothering you, Bud. What is it?"
  Bud wanted to tell him about the problems with Ronnie but decided against it. "Nothing's wrong. I was just trying to think of a way to say thanks for everything you've done for us. There's no way we could have gotten this far this fast on our own."

Maxwell was looking out the window, avoiding Buds eyes. "It's really kind of a shame, but that's the way damn near everything in the world works. A guy can't even get a job as a bus driver unless he knows someone. Connections. That's what it's all about these days. Maybe it's always been that way."

"Well, thanks just the same."

"There is one thing that bothers me, though." Maxwell was changing the subject. "That new guitar player you got, that Ronnie. I'm not too sure of him. He doesn't seem to fit in. Is he okay?"

Bud didn't answer right away. He needed a minute to think. "We've talked about him, the rest of the group and me. He's not working out the way we hoped. Full of talent and not an ounce of common sense. I'm gonna replace him. Try to get my brother to come back with us. Now that there's the prospect of making some decent money, he might change his mind."

"I'll leave it up to you. You know them both better than I do."

They were both silent for the rest of the drive.

The band had two nights off before they had to head for Reno, and decided to stay in Phoenix and enjoy the western hospitality. All but Ronnie. He had heard that prostitution was legal in Nevada and wanted to spend his days off in a whorehouse. Bud squelched the idea without listening to the whining that Ronnie had been doing so much of lately. What the hell was wrong with that goofy kid anyway?

Reno was the last stop on the tour. Everybody had a hard time concentrating on the music that last night on the road. All they could think about was getting home. All but Ronnie. He wasn't thinking of anything. He was higher than a Georgia Pine by curtain time. His crazy antics during the performance just about ruined the first set.

Bud fired him during the intermission. "I don't even want you on stage for the rest of the program. Now I see what the problem's been all along. There's no way I'm going to let you screw things up for the rest of us. I'll have your instruments shipped back with the rest of our stuff, you can pick everything up in Detroit. You got any money?"

Ronnie nodded. "Yah, I got plenty."

"Good, I'll see you in Detroit." Bud walked away without giving Ronnie a chance to argue...or plead.

CHAPTER 9

Ronnie had a strange dream that night, one of those disorganized, confusing, drug induced fantasies. He was sitting on the toilet in a public bathroom playing his guitar and motorcycles kept driving through the stall. The riders kept reaching out, trying to snatch the guitar out of his hands. But it wasn't even really a guitar, it was a broken ukulele. And the same girl was riding on the back of every bike. Over and over, the same girl. She was someone he knew but he couldn't remember her name. She had needle tracks all over both arms, a tattoo on her neck, and was smoking a joint and blowing the smoke in his face as she rode by. Ronnie didn't wake up suddenly, he kind of tossed around in a state somewhere in between sleep and consciousness. Drifting back and forth for hours. It was the constant ringing of the telephone that finally woke him up.

"Your wake up call. It's seven A.M." Click. Motels always did that. Hung up before you could say anything. Must've had some bad experiences.

Ronnie swung his skinny legs over the edge of the bed, still trying to put his thoughts together. Six hours of fitful sleep just wasn't enough time for his system to recover from the abuse he put it through last night. He would be sick for another couple of hours. He knew that from past episodes when he'd overdone it. The dream kept flashing in and out of his mind and he still wasn't sure what was real and what was imagined. His head hurt.

The phone rang again. This time it was Bud. "Just checking to see if you were up. We're leaving for the airport in about an hour."

"I ain't goin' back just yet. Gonna stick around here a couple of days. I don't work for you any more. Remember?"

"Suit yourself. You might want to get to the airport anyway, so you can cash in your ticket or whatever."

"Yeah, right. If I decide to go, I'll meet you in the lobby. About an hour." Ronnie headed for the bathroom to vomit.

Monica and the band were climbing into the rented van when Ronnie came stumbling through the revolving front door of the motel. He jumped in the back seat without saying a word and sat directly behind Monica, staring at the back of her head. Ronnie never spoke during the entire ride to the airport. He was thinking. She's the one. The bitch on the motorcycle. The one blowing weed smoke in my face while I was trying to pull my pants up. Weird dream; weird broad. The vision of Monica on the back of a motorcycle began to stir some memories for Ronnie. He had seen her on the back of a bike somewhere in his past. He thought back to the days when he ran with the "Disciples." Is that where he'd seen her before? Bits and pieces were coming to him but it was so hard to think clearly with his stomach rolling and his head pounding. He let it go for now.

The van pulled up at the terminal and Ronnie was the first one out, pushing his way all the way from the back seat. "Good riddance," said Monica as Ronnie disappeared into the crowd.

Ronnie sat in the upstairs restaurant overlooking the airport, nursing a tall glass of pineapple juice and eating a half of a honeydew melon. He sat by the window so he could make sure that the band boarded the airplane and waited until the plane took off.

Now he was alone and anonymous. It made him feel giddy. "I can do anything I want. Nobody knows and nobody cares." His thoughts turned to the hookers that hung around the casino. He had his eye on a little Asian one, maybe Vietnamese or something like that. Checking his funds, he counted almost four grand in cash plus the plastic. "I wonder how long it'll take to blow it all?" he thought. No gambling for him. Broads and booze. That's where it's at.

The Avis Car Rental at the airport kept a few exotic cars in their stable for the high rollers and Ronnie drove out of the terminal in a shiny red Jaguar XLS. If you're gonna live, do it.

He made a quick stop at a porno shop to pick up a few magazines to get him in the right frame of mind and then headed back to the motel to try to put his body back together. He was still feeling the effects of last night.

The hot shower helped quite a bit but he knew that a good long nap would give him the staying power he'd need for the big night he had planned. As he lay in the bed thumbing through his magazines, he began to think of Monica—and the motorcycles. Another face came into his mind. A big guy with tattoos. Bad son of a bitch. What was his name? Some kind of pirate name. "Billy Bones." That was it. Just like that, it all came back to him.

Billy was a self-declared feudal lord and nobody had ever successfully challenged him. Everybody seemed to be content giving Billy all the room he needed. If you wanted drugs or girls or anything illegal, Billy Bones was the guy you dealt with. Heaven help you if Billy thought you were trying to cut him out of his share. Billy had a number of dealers working for him and one of them had been Monica. Ronnie wondered how much Monica was paying Billy to let her perform on stage. It must be quite a bit. After all, she was becoming quite a big star these days. He drifted off so sleep. This time he didn't dream.

About four days was all it took for Reno to get sick and tired of Ronnie Murray. The casinos had barred him. Labeled him as a troublemaker, always trying to score with someone's wife or girlfriend. The motel had asked him to leave after he trashed the room, like all big rock stars were supposed to. And he had been arrested and held briefly for causing an accident with his shiny, red Jaguar.

Time to move on. This town wasn't so exciting after all.

Ronnie entertained thoughts of visiting California but gave up on that idea when he realized that he was running out of money. Besides, he would have to establish new drug connections out there. Then there was the business of Monica. He could hardly wait to get back to Detroit and talk to Billy Bones. He was sure that he could provide some kind of service for the biker gang leader that would guarantee a lifetime of drugs and women. What more could a guy ask?

Maybe he could even work out a deal with Monica. That thought brought a smile to his face. She might not want anyone to know about the things she'd done. Just how far would she be willing to go to protect her new career? The thought of her being his love slave was getting Ronnie all worked up.

As a matter of fact, the whole band could be in the palm of his hand if he played it right. He could destroy all of them. The feeling of power was overwhelming. He'd need to think this out, come up with a plan. The prospects for the future were becoming brighter by the minute. He was really looking forward to seeing the expression on Bud's face when he dropped the bomb.

He had planned to wait until his clothes came back from the laundry before catching a plane back to Detroit but now he said, "Piss on the clothes." and headed the Jaguar for the airport.

The girl at the Avis counter was cute but not very friendly. Especially when she found out that Ronnie had done over six thousand dollars worth of damage to the pride of the fleet.

"What do you care? It's not your car. Besides, it's insured." Ronnie couldn't understand why she was upset.

"This car has been reserved for one of our most loyal customers. He's expecting it to be ready for him to pick up in a couple of days and there's just no way it can be fixed that fast."

"Tell the boss to buy another one. You guys got plenty of money, shit." Ronnie picked up his receipt and walked away, tossing the receipt in the trash can by the door on his way out. "Bitch." he said.

Ronnie made a thorough pain of himself all through the flight home. The flight attendants were drawing lots to see which one had to endure his smart-ass comments next. When Andrea, the little blonde, waited on him, he said. "Next time send me the black haired girl, she has bigger boobs."

Andrea was almost in tears when she went to the captain. "There must be something you can do. Can you talk to him or anything?"

"We have to set down in Memphis," the Captain said. "We'll see how he likes walking home from there."

So Ronnie lost his seat in Memphis after a highly animated argument with the pilot and airline officials. The rest of the passengers cheered as he was booted off the plane. Good riddance again. He never understood why people got so pissed off at him.

He spent the night lost in the red light district of Memphis, drinking like it was his last night on earth. His mood had become so bad, he couldn't even score with the hookers. It was like he had two heads. There was enough coke left to do a couple of lines and then crash in a second rate motel room. He woke up the next afternoon out of drugs, out of money, and out of options. He spent his last fifty bucks for a bus ticket home.

Six days ago he had been the lead guitarist in an up and coming rock group and now he was nothing but another jerk riding a Greyhound with the rest of the losers who couldn't afford airfare. What a way to end a tour. That would all change after he talked to Billy Bones, though. People would have to start treating him differently, with respect.

The bus rolled into the downtown Detroit depot just before daybreak. The city looked very different. When Ronnie had left to go on tour, the trees were still green. Now it was the week after Thanksgiving, the temperature was right around the freezing mark, and the oaks and elders were naked. The early birds were already on their way to work, beginning to clog the streets looking for parking places. Ronnie picked up his overnight bag and walked to the corner to catch a City Transit bus for the rest of the trip home to his mother's place. A City Transit bus, the final insult. There would be a lot of people that would pay for this. He shivered in the chilly breeze. Nobody shits on Ronnie and gets away with it.

CHAPTER 10

Monica and the Nephewz had been home about two weeks, working out new numbers and rehearsing. They were putting in twelve hours a day, seven days a week. It was exhausting, but they were beginning to show some results. Kelly was working out with the band and that made things a lot easier—no tension, no arguments. Now that the band was having some real success, there would be enough money to hire someone to help Kelly's wife run the music store. A big problem was solved by Kelly's return to the band. A producer from Spirit had been working with them day and night, blocking a new video, hiring dancers, and contracting special effects. It seemed as if there were endless details.

The entertainment business is merciless. If you can't keep up with the demand, your fans will move on. As long as they keep asking for more, you'd better be able to deliver. The band knew that fame could be short-lived and they wanted their share. If they could keep it up for just a few years, things were bound to get easier, then maybe ride a nostalgia wave for another six or seven years. For now they would have to concentrate on recordings and videos, with a few TV dates scattered over the next three months.

Monica had said that she wanted to spend some time with Etta while she was back in Detroit but apparently, Etta must have moved. There was a new young couple in the old apartment and they said that they had no idea what happened to the former resident. The apartment super might have a forwarding address but it seemed like he was never home, so Monica figured she'd try again some other day.

Bud appeared preoccupied when he showed up for rehearsal today. He wasn't full of his usual jokes and chatter and seemed less tolerant of the little mistakes that everyone made, though he made a few of his own. They always took a break around ten and went out for coffee. Bud grabbed Monica's arm as she was leaving and hollered to the rest of the gang, "She'll catch up with you guys later. I want to go over something with her."

Monica was caught off guard. She wasn't aware of any problems other than the normal glitches that are part of any new material. "What'd I do?" Her voice displayed her bewilderment.

Bud got right to the point. "Maxwell called me last night, said he's flying in tomorrow for a special meeting with you and me. He was quite emphatic about you being there."

"Why? What's it all about? Am I being fired?"

Bud smiled a little. "I don't think it's that bad but he said we've got a potentially serious problem on our hands and he wants it cleared up right away."

"What kind of problem and what's it got to do with me?"

"He wouldn't tell me but if he's flying all the way from the coast, you can bet he's taking it seriously. Now go catch up with the rest of the gang. And bring me back a large coffee."

Monica shuffled out the door, looking at the floor all the way. Could Maxwell somehow have found out about her past? No, there had to be more to it than that. He wouldn't fly in from California for anything like that. Or would he? It's hard to think straight when your mind is flooded with guilt.

They met Maxwell in his suite at the Metro Airport Ramada Inn. He seemed relaxed, almost happy. Always the gentleman. "Come on in. We've got a few things to talk about and then I've got to get back on a plane for Boston. You're not the only ones with a busy schedule." His laugh helped to put them at ease.

"This business about your guitar player, Ronnie Murray. I understand you let him go while you were still out west. Is that right?"

Bud answered. "Yes that's right. I found out he was taking drugs. He got stoned out of his mind before a performance and I canned him between sets. I just couldn't see taking a chance. He was really screwing up bad."

"I see," said Maxwell. "Anyway, he's demanding some pretty stiff severance terms. First of all he wants to be paid a full share of the profits for the next five years and then he wants a third of my commission on all your activities for as long as I continue to represent you." Maxwell wasn't smiling anymore.

"Where did he come up with that shit?" asked Bud. "He signed on for one tour, that's all. You've got a copy of the contract. We don't owe him a damned thing more."

"His manager claims that they have all the ammunition they need to put you out of business." Maxwell turned to face Monica. " The manager tells me that you're a drug dealer and that you were the one that was supplying the stuff to Ronnie. He also says that Ronnie will swear that he saw you dealing to kids in the crowd, your fan club. Pretty strong allegations, I'd say."

Monica couldn't answer; she was stunned.

Bud jumped in. "Did you say 'manager'? Ronnie never had a manager that I know of. He never even mentioned one."

Maxwell fumbled through his attaché case. "I got his name in here somewhere. Funny name...Ah, here it is. Billy Bones, ever hear of him?"

Monica let out a sigh and shuddered. Both men were staring at her now.

"I'd better tell you the whole story," she said softly. "I know Billy. He's not a manager, he's a gangster. There's not an ounce of decency in him. I used to run with his crowd, a biker gang. It's true that I sold drugs for him at one time but the stuff Ronnie is telling you is all lies. I haven't been near any drugs or any of the people involved with any of that stuff since the first day I met Bud and the guys. I swear." She began sobbing, gently.

Maxwell went back into his attaché case and pulled out a fax sheet with a telephone number on it. He handed it to Monica. "I've already contacted these people. It's a law firm that handles this sort of thing. I'm going to ask you to set up an appointment with them and get something worked out. They're waiting to hear from you."

Monica took the paper in her hands and stared at it, remaining silent.

"One point I think I should make is that I have no intention of giving this Bones guy a goddamn cent of my money." Maxwell's voice rose only slightly but it was obvious that he was angry at being hustled. "I don't know who all's in on this and I don't care. I just don't want to hear another thing about it until it's settled. You're too hot a talent for me to lose, so I sure hope you can get this matter behind us—and I mean soon."

Bud held Monica's arm as they left the motel. She was still in shock and he could tell her mind wasn't functioning. "I'll help you with the lawyer thing. You'll need somebody to keep you from falling apart. It's really nothing more than extortion. I know that you've been straight, at least as long as you've been with the band. The rest of the guys will back you up. You can count on all of us."

Monica was trying to dry her eyes with the back of her hand. "Bud, you don't understand. Billy only makes one offer. He'll never settle for anything less. He'll do whatever it takes to get his way. The threat of exposing me was just Billy's way of saying that we'd better give him what he wants or he'll start killing people. There are no rules for Billy."

"Hey, don't let your imagination run away with you. This guy's just another loser trying to cash in on someone else's good fortune. We'll blow him away in court."

Monica shook her head furiously. "I'm telling you that he won't consider a courtroom to be a boundary. You'll never see him in court. He figures that he's the one who makes the rules. He's vicious enough to start murdering people if he doesn't get what he wants."

Bud stood silently for a full minute and then spoke. "It has to be handled. You got any ideas?"

"I'll need some time to think. You have to be very careful of anything you say to Billy. He has a way of interpreting things that doesn't always make sense to rational people. I'll contact him as soon as I can gather the courage, but don't talk to the lawyer till you hear from me."

Bud nodded. "Better make it soon, Maxwell wants it taken care of right away."

Monica sighed. "I'll do it tonight."

CHAPTER 11

Her hand was shaking so badly that it took three attempts to punch Billy's number into the keypad on the pay phone.

He answered so quickly that it made her knees go weak. "Yah, it's Billy."

"Hi, it's me, Monica." It was all he gave her a chance to say. "I haven't seen any money yet. What the hell's the hold up?"

"Billy, can't we talk about this?"

Billy laughed on the other end of the line. "You know me better'n that. I don't negotiate. I tell you what I want and you give it to me; that's the way it works."

"I'll give you whatever you want, Billy, but please leave Mr. Maxwell alone. Can't I meet you someplace and talk about it?"

"Look, bitch, I told you how it works. Talking won't change a damned thing. Just start paying up. I'll be generous—you got until New Year's Day. And I mean the stroke of midnight to get the cash flow started, then I'm coming after you and all your little friends."

Monica cringed as she heard the phone slam down on the other end. The sense of panic was overwhelming. She cried hysterically. There seemed to be no way out. What was she going to tell Bud? She didn't dare let this thing get into civil court—it would be disastrous. The images of things to come flooded her mind. Ordinary people could never fully understand the ferocity of a sociopath like Billy Bones.

By the time she stumbled into her motel room, she had regained a little composure. She had somewhere around three weeks to try to work something out. Maybe she could strike some kind of a deal with Ronnie Murray. He might be able to persuade Billy to back off, although it didn't seem too likely. She'd have to come up with some kind of a plan.

Billy smiled at Ronnie Murray as he slammed the phone down in Monica's ear. "Looks like we've got her right where we want her—scared shitless."

Ronnie giggled. "You know what? I'm probably gonna make about as much money this way as I would've if I'd stayed with the band. I love it."

"You bet. Finding me was one of the smartest things you've ever done, kid. I'm gonna make you happy for the rest of your life. As a matter of fact I've got a down payment for you tonight.

CHAPTER 12

It was good to get together again. Detectives McCoy and Springfield of the Detroit Police Department were working with each other for the first time in over a month, and it would probably be their last time ever working together as partners.

After more than two months of investigating the murder of Etta Kremer, the probing and searching had produced nothing. No evidence, no clues, no suspects, nothing. With no pressure from a family or an outraged community, it was easy for the hierarchy of the department to suspend the investigation due to lack of progress. It left a rancid taste in the mouths of two very good cops.

Both detectives were slated for promotion and that would almost certainly send them in different directions. Otis Springfield would likely be the first to move up. He had a couple of months more time in rank than McCoy and had actually scored one point higher on the exam than his old buddy. Otis never missed a chance to mention it either. Ever since the two cops first met some twenty...no, thirty odd years ago, there had been a friendly, healthy competition going on between them. The mutual respect that these men shared served as a tribute to their character.

At first McCoy had been somewhat cool to the prospect of promotion so late in his career, but Otis soon convinced him that all he needed to do was put in the required time at that level and let it fatten the pension check.

"And then," Otis pointed out, "we can both retire and form that partnership we talked about with Mike O'Conner's private detective agency. O'Conner, Springfield, and McCoy."

"Right," nodded McCoy. "O'Conner, McCoy, and Springfield."

They had been assigned to investigate a possible homicide. The request had been made by the Coroner's Office.

It seems that there was something unusual about the latest John Doe. He'd died from a drug overdose like so many others, but it was the enormous concentration and mixture of drugs that alerted the coroner. Nobody would need that much to get high, and most dopeheads would never have access to such large quantities of the high-grade stuff.

McCoy and Springfield walked into the Coroner's Office and were both a little surprised by what greeted them. It was the second week of December and the season was right, but it still was unnerving to see Christmas decorations hanging from the walls in such a funereal place.

Ray Walters, the coroner, noticed their reaction and offered, "I got a new secretary." The detectives both nodded and smiled. "Captain Bice sent us over, said you had a John Doe to check out."

The coroner opened a file folder as he spoke. "Oh yah, the guitar player."

"You know who he is?" asked Detective Springfield.

"No, I just know what he is, or was. The fingertips of his left hand were calloused the way they get from playing a steel stringed instrument. I'm guessing it's a guitar because of his age and the way he was dressed. Here's a list of what I found in his system."

Otis Springfield whistled as he scanned the document. "Man, this looks like the list they hand out at the academy, got damned near everything on it. He should have been dead before he even finished takin' all this shit."

The coroner nodded. "The toxicologist was most certainly impressed. Must've started with the uppers and worked his way into the depressants. It's the only way he could've remained conscious. This isn't your garden variety O.D."

McCoy pulled out his note pad. "Anything get started yet? Prints or anything?"

"Yah, they did all that stuff this morning, about two hours ago. Those reports ought to be on your desk pretty soon. They got some pretty good prints. You'll probably have an I.D. before lunch. I'll have my report done in a few minutes. You can take it with you."

McCoy and Springfield waited alone in the office while the doctor retreated to his workroom to complete his paperwork.

Otis Springfield spoke first. "I hate working homicide this time of year. Especially a young guy like this. It's so tough to tell the parents."

"I know what you mean," said McCoy. "Your son is dead. Merry Christmas."

The coroner returned to the office and handed the detectives a manila envelope. "Here it is. I sure hope it helps."

McCoy and Springfield walked into First Precinct Headquarters and stopped at the coffee machine on their way back to their desks. There was a coffee pot in the squad room and the vending machine sat in the hallway to serve private citizens. McCoy liked to buy his coffee from the machine just to irritate Brady, the coffee cop who was always watching to make sure you dropped your fifteen cents in the can when you poured from the community pot. At one time or another, it seemed as if Brady had accused every officer in the precinct of cheating on the coffee fund. McCoy raised his cup and smiled as he walked past Brady's desk. Brady didn't look up.

Otis sipped his coffee as they walked. "If the doctor was right about the fingerprints, we should have an I.D. pretty quick and then try to figure out what the hell happened. We might wrap this up before Christmas."

McCoy shook his head. "Don't get your hopes up, Bubba. Whoever iced this guy must've known that there'd be an autopsy. It may be another one of those message killings. You remember those, don't you?"

"Why don't we just wait and see what we have to work with?" countered Otis.

McCoy checked his desk and saw an envelope from Support Services. He shook out the contents and began sorting through the papers. "Looks like they got quite a bit of information on this guy. Let's see what we got here. Ronald Murray; age 21, arrest record: three arrests for possession of controlled substances and two B&E's. Here's another for larceny and one more for receiving stolen goods. Lots of arrests but it looks like they were plea bargained down to misdemeanors. Never served any real time. It says here that he was a member of Satan's Disciples."

Otis's ears perked up. "That's Billy Bones's gang. We been tryin' to bust him for a couple of years. He's about the baddest bastard on the streets. If he's involved in this, we're gonna have our hands full. Man, I'd sure love to nail him."

"Billy Bones?" mused McCoy. "His parents must have had a real sense of humor. Ain't that the name of some pirate or something like that? Seems I read that name back in about the fifth grade or so."

"It's not really Billy," answered Otis. "As a matter of fact it's not Bones either. His real name is Kenneth Koscielski. Not nearly as romantic sounding is it? Needless to say, nobody on the street knows his real name, at least nobody that's still alive."

"You make this guy sound super-human," said McCoy. "What's so special about him? He must've made mistakes. Seems to me you could've got him on something by now."

Otis became animated as he began to explain. "To begin with, he's the ultimate intimidator. Anybody knows that it's sure death to cross him. He's known for backing up everything he says. He makes major demands on everybody around him and nobody ever stands up to him. I heard that there was one guy who could handle him. Some big guy from way up north somewhere's, but he's not around these parts any more. To top it off, he's a bona fide genius. Has an IQ of 170 or so. He keeps that a secret though, like he's ashamed of it or something."

"In that case, maybe we can use his brain against him. Know what I mean?"

Otis looked puzzled. "No, what do you mean?"

McCoy leaned back in his chair and folded his hands on his stomach. He looked like a philosopher about to say something profound, something worthy of quoting. "Smart guys always pride themselves in being able to stay one jump ahead of everybody else. If we know how he thinks, we can feed him little tidbits of erroneous information and see where he takes it. If he's the guy who did this, he must have had a motive. Right now we're completely in the dark. Maybe he'll light a few things up for us. I love playing mind games with his type, it makes the job interesting."

Otis shrugged. "We sure don't have much else right now. I guess we could try it. I know how to find him. Let's give it a whirl. Maybe it'll be him leading us."

"Right after lunch." said McCoy.

"Amen," answered Otis.

CHAPTER 13

The detectives pulled up in front of the clubhouse on West Chicago Avenue a little before one o'clock. The building looked like the last holdout against urban renewal. It had been some sort of a neighborhood drug store at one time and then probably a shot and a beer bar, but now the big windows were bricked over and protected by thick iron bars. An equally foreboding iron gate guarded the front door. The rest of the building was stark cinder block, painted flat black. A silver emblem was lag-bolted above the door bearing a silhouette of the grim reaper and, in Old English letters, the words *Satan's Disciples M/C*. A mat paradoxically proclaiming "Welcome" lay on the stained sidewalk in front of the door. The building had once been part of a busy corridor, but it stood alone now, the only one on the block to defy the wrecking ball.

McCoy noted that there were no motorcycles parked on the street. After all, it was December. There were two rusty vans parked in the tall, dead weeds in the vacant lot along the side of the building. It was hard to tell whether they were abandoned or if they just looked that way. One of them had a pair of shiny new handcuffs hanging from the rear view mirror. McCoy stepped around behind the two vans and scratched the license numbers into his notebook, then rejoined Otis in front of the clubhouse. The absence of a padlock on the massive hasp of the front gate told him that someone was inside. The two detectives scanned the street without speaking. It was a well-rehearsed routine. Finally McCoy looked at Otis and they approached the front door together.

As McCoy raised his hand to knock, the door suddenly flew open, revealing two well- muscled young men in black tee-shirts, jeans, and motorcycle boots. The taller one displayed several exotic tattoos on his forearms and biceps, with one particularly disturbing looking representation of a rat crawling up his shoulder, its head stretching up the man's neck and sniffing at the back of his ear. The other man had no visible body decorations at all. They were both smiling broadly and the bigger one looked at Otis and spoke, "Hello, Detective Springfield. How nice of you to drop by. I see you've brought along one of your little playmates."

"Good afternoon, Billy. We'd like a few moments of your time. This is Detective McCoy."

For a moment, it was standoff time in the doorway. Billy, still smiling, looked McCoy up and down, then finally took a step backward to allow the two policemen to enter the clubhouse. The other man had retreated to the old bar across the room and stood there with a beer in his hand, one foot up on the brass rail, near the end of the bar.

It was the first time either cop had been inside the Disciple's clubhouse and they both glanced around, making mental notes. The odor was mildew mixed with some sort of incense and a faint hint of cannabis. The place had the look of one of those 1950's working men's bars, complete with the embossed tin ceiling. A narrow building with a long bar against one wall, a few booths with tattered upholstery along the opposite wall and a pool table in the middle. There were a couple of odd tables with mismatched chairs that seemed randomly placed. The wooden floor had seen better days and exhibited at least four nailed down sheet-metal patches highly polished by years of foot traffic. A cubicle in the rear corner was obviously the restroom. An old, rusty motorcycle frame complete with fenders but minus the wheels was leaning against the back wall near the door. The room was surprisingly well lit and featured a larger than life poster of a bikini-clad model astride a vintage Harley as the lone wall decoration behind the bar.

Billy took a seat on one of the barstools about halfway down the bar, leaned back and waited for Otis to speak. Otis moved slowly toward the bar while McCoy remained near the doorway. McCoy didn't make a sound and he didn't change his blank expression. This was Detective Springfield's show and he was welcome to run it. Instead of walking down to where Billy was seated, Otis stopped in front of the first man. "You're Mace, aren't you?

The shorter, curly haired man stiffened and looked at Billy as if to seek permission to confirm his identity. Billy's nod was barely perceptible. "That's what some call me. I guess it'll do." The voice was swollen with arrogance. "You here to see me?"

"Not your turn yet, you can relax." Otis turned his gaze back on Billy and said, "It's him I want and I'm getting closer every day."

The movie star smile never left Billy's face. He held his arms out with his palms up and shrugged. "I've been right here. It's winter, man. Too cold to ride and I ain't into cross country skiing so you can find me right here until spring. Any time, day or night."

"I'm here to talk about Ronnie," Otis's voice rose slightly.

"Ronnie?" echoed Billy. "Ronnie who? That name ain't taking me anywhere. Can't think of anyone by that name. That all you got for me?"

"Try Ronnie Murray, guitar player. He's a Disciple." Otis was staring directly into Billy's eyes now.

Billy shook his head and laughed. "Oh, that guy? He was never a Disciple. He was just one of those wannabe bikers. A hanger-on. I don't even think he ever owned his own iron." Billy was looking at the floor now and his smile was gone. "I don't like it when guys claim to be something they're not. When did he tell you he was a brother? You got him up on some kinda charges? He hasn't been around here in at least a year."

"I don't believe you. I think you've seen him quite recently, say two, three days ago." Otis shifted his weight.

Billy's head jerked upright and defiance filled his voice. "Think whatever the hell you like. You can't prove a thing and we both know it. Wanna dust this place for fingerprints? Go get yourself a warrant. If all you want is to harass me, you better bring along more intimidation than that meathead over there." Billy pointed his chin in McCoy's direction.

McCoy stood motionless, looking disinterested. Only Otis noticed the trace of a smirk that swept across his face.

Otis straightened up and held up his hands. "Don't get yourself all worked up, Billy, and don't figure you can bait me or my partner. We both been around too long. I'm far from being done with you. You're as dirty as they come and dirt is my business." Otis turned and walked toward the door, joining

McCoy as they prepared to exit the clubhouse. "You'll wish I never entered your life."

"I already do," snorted Billy. He didn't offer to open the door. He held his hands on his hips as McCoy fumbled with the latch.

And then they were outside in the blustery December wind. Otis was smiling. He had accomplished his mission. Billy was upset. Otis always smiled when he got the best of Billy Bones in a match of wits. The two cops jumped back into the cruiser and headed for the precinct headquarters.

McCoy was silent for a few minutes and then asked, "Who was the other guy? What'd you call 'im… Ace?"

"Mace," Otis corrected, "real name's Ed Caruso, he picked up the nickname from the tear gas. Same stuff they issue to us, not that junk that you buy in the sporting goods stores. He must have a connection in the department somewhere."

"Somebody use it on him or something?" McCoy looked puzzled.

"The other way around. He gets into a fight with some guy in a bar, maces him and then kicks in the fellows face while the poor creature is squirming on the ground. Done it three, maybe four times. Always wants to take out a few teeth."

"Nice guy."

Otis shook his head. "Yeah, nice guy. They're both nice guys."

CHAPTER 14

Back at headquarters, the detectives were sorting through the personal effects that were found on the body and saying silent, skyward thank yous that someone else had already informed the next of kin.

Otis was reading the preliminary. "Says here, they found the body on the expressway shoulder."

McCoy looked in his direction. "Inbound or outbound?"

"I-75 north near Seven Mile Road"

"Outbound. I knew it. And just inside the city limits. These guys... Geez." McCoy was shaking his head.

"This makes it our second in a row, with the e-way thing. I sure hope we do better on this than we did on the last one. It didn't seem as if Ronnie had much of a life. I don't see any evidence of a real job anywhere. No paystubs or anything like that in his personal stuff. Ever hear of 'Monica and the Nephewz'?" queried Otis.

"Seems like I've heard them or seen something about them somewhere. Why, you like their stuff? I thought that kind of music was mostly for kids," McCoy was straining his eyes to read the manufacturer's name on a nylon guitar pick.

"If I'm interpreting this right, this Ronnie guy had something to do with that group at one time or another. Here. What do you make of this?" Otis handed McCoy a tattered newspaper clipping.

An article from *The Dallas Morning News* proclaimed, "Billy Bob's Texas rocks to 'Monica and the Nephewz'." The article was complimentary, pointing out the refreshing innocence of Monica and the disciplined musicianship of the band. The word "disciplined" had been highlighted with a yellow marker.

He examined the clipping for a very long time before commenting. "I knew that Monica and company were billed as a Detroit group but I don't know if any of them still live around here. Monica, Monica, Monica—why is that name so familiar?" McCoy scratched his head.

"I'm sure it will come to you, McCoy. It always does."

"You really think that this Bones character is the key here? I mean, it's obvious that you dislike him and maybe you just wish he were the bad guy. Know what I mean?"

Otis shrugged his muscular shoulders and held out his hands. "Right now, I don't know what else we got to look at. You saw those two today. Don't you think they're hiding something?"

"Well, you're probably right, but if this guy's as smart as you say he is, maybe they just want us to think they're guilty. Okay, let's go ahead and call 'em the killers, put together some scenarios and see what it all looks like. We might as well be doing something."

Otis was writing on a legal pad, listing possible motives, scribbling questions for the medical examiner, and the uniforms who were first on the scene. "The problem here is that he seems to have been such a nothing kind of person, who would want him dead?"

"Somebody who figured he knew too much. And it had to be tied to drugs. That's another Billy Bones connection. Billy ever been busted for drugs? I could smell the shit in his clubhouse earlier."

Otis knew this gang. He had investigated them for months without a single break. "We know that the Disciples as a gang are all suppliers but we haven't had a good collar on any of them yet. They're a tight group and they don't do the street level business. They have their dealers so intimidated, none of them would dare go against 'em. The penalty wouldn't just be death, it would be extreme torture and, eventually, death. And death would be the easy part."

McCoy changed the subject, "Oh, by the way, Mike O'Conner called and wants to get together with us at Eddie's tonight. You up for it?"

Otis countered, "Oh yeah. I haven't had one of those heart stopping greaseburgers in about two weeks. I'm even starting to feel healthy. Not having heartburn is a scary situation for a guy like me. You can count me in. That new waitress at Eddie's, what's her name? Ruby, that's it. You kinda got the hots for her, don't you?"

McCoy seemed slightly embarrassed. "Well, she is a sweet looking thing. Friendly too."

"Yeah. Especially friendly to you."

"You think so?"

CHAPTER 15

Michael was waiting at their favorite table when the two detectives walked into Eddie's Bar but it was the guy sitting across from him who grabbed the attention of both McCoy and Otis. It was his size more than anything. Cops are trained to assess threat factors in people they encounter and this fellow had all of the characteristics of an extremely formidable specimen. This was one big dude. Though he was seated, it was obvious that he easily cleared the six and a half foot mark. There was no awkwardness in his movements either. Even under a long sleeved shirt, there was no hiding the enormous biceps and the rest of the body would have made a template for the perfect professional football defensive end. The shoulder length jet-black hair could signal a rebellious streak. He was looking at Otis as if evaluating the athletic presence of the agile looking cop.

When he stood to welcome the two newcomers, it was obvious that this was a man who could intimidate just about anybody. It was the genuineness of the friendly smile that served to relax Otis and McCoy.

None of the effects of the brief mini-drama were lost on Michael, as he remained seated with a smug, amused grin on his face. "Welcome guys. This is Charlie, my neighbor from up north. Charlie, meet Otis Springfield and Albert McCoy, the two cops I've told you so much about."

The big man's handshake confirmed the evaluation that had been mutually formed by both detectives. Otis was the first to speak. "You look like you've got some Indian blood in you."

The infectious smile broadened on the handsome, tanned face. "All of it. Anishinaabeg. Want to see my pedigree?"

"Huh? How do you spell that?" came the reply, Otis reaching for his notebook.

The Indian didn't lose his smile. "Just say, 'Chippewa.' People seem to be more comfortable with that."

Michael motioned toward the two empty chairs, "Sit down guys. Charlie hasn't been to the city in a few years so I thought

I'd bring him down with me. We've been friends since we were kids. He's the busiest electrical contractor in my area but I convinced him that he needed some time off."

McCoy looked Charlie up and down and commented, "I would have pegged you for something a little more physical than electrical work. You just don't look like the type."

Charlie just smiled and shrugged. "I like to stay in shape. Play a few sports, nothing serious though, just a little of this and a little of that. I've got a couple of dirt bikes and a big Harley. They help too."

Michael chimed in. "Charlie's just being modest. He was a hand-to-hand combat instructor for a while in the Marine Corps and still competes in martial arts tournaments. Tell 'em about your titles, Charlie."

"Aw, it's not that big. I've won a couple of tournaments, that's all. Just stayin' in shape." It was obvious that Charlie wasn't interested in bragging about his accomplishments.

Otis diverted the attention back to Michael O'Conner. "How's the private investigating business these days, Mr. Bloodhound?"

Michael ordered a round of draft beers from the waitress who seemed to magically appear, a cheerful and well preserved woman, late fortyish, who seemed to make an effort to stand very close to McCoy's chair. Otis smiled. Michael paused a moment, realized that he might be witness to a budding romance, and then returned to the conversation. "I'm not into anything right now. I just got done doing a series of background investigations on a long list of applicants for the State Corrections Department. You wouldn't believe some of the types who apply for jobs as prison guards. I found drug dealers, embezzlers, child molesters, even an ex-priest. It's getting close to the holidays so I decided not to take on anything new until after the first of the year. Besides, I'm looking into taking an educational leave from the business so that I can take a class or two in 'game biology.' I've been watching a pretty good size colony of black bears that live around my place and I'd like to learn a lot more about their habits and stuff."

"Better watch yourself or you might turn into a snack for one of those monsters," said McCoy.

Michael smiled knowingly. "Nah, they'll never bother a human unless you get between a sow and her cub or maybe get too close to them when they feel cornered or something. And they're all pretty much in hibernation right now."

McCoy laughed and offered, "It must be great to just pick and choose when you want to work, when you want to take time off for school, take a vacation, and Lord only knows what else. Don't you wish the Captain would grant us that luxury, Otis?"

Otis smiled and nodded.

"Well, I'm a one man shop," defended Michael, "When I'm into something that's really demanding, there's nobody around to share the load. Sometimes I'm forced to put in sixteen hours a day. It all evens out. After you two guys retire, I'm hoping that you'll accept my offer to join my agency. We'd make a great team. There's all the work you ever wanted out there. And the hours are flexible."

"Thanks, but that's still a couple of years away," responded Otis

Michael took a sip from the frosty mug that the waitress had just deposited in front of him. "The reason I wanted to see you guys is to invite you up north to my place for my Annual New Year's Day football overdose. Twelve hours of non-stop pigskin, all the shrimp you can eat and all the beer you can drink. It's the kind of day that they had in mind when the term, 'Guy Thing' was coined. Charlie here can't make it because he's involved in one of those pageants. You know, the tourist thing."

Otis said. "Now you know that I'm a huge football fan and all that shrimp sounds terrific, but McCoy and I just got this new homicide that looks like it's going to tie us up at least through mid January. I simply don't see us getting the time off."

McCoy bowed his head in agreement as Michael looked over at his friend Charlie who was wearing an "I told you so" look on his face.

"Doing a murder case, eh?" Michael tried to appear indifferent. "What kind? Family? Mob? Drug war? I know that some are a lot harder to figure out than others. Maybe you'll get lucky."

"Not likely." answered McCoy. "This one might fit into any one of those pigeon holes that you just mentioned and you can throw in 'Outlaw Biker Gang' to spice it up a little bit. It's a real puzzler. So far we got no motive, a few really weak leads, and no standout suspects."

"Got the murder weapon?" queried Michael.

"I don't even want to talk about that one." McCoy shot back.

Otis jumped in. "All we've got to keep us entertained right now is Billy Bones"

The big Indian stiffened at the mention of the name. "Billy Bones?"

All three of the others turned and looked at Charlie but it was Otis who spoke. "You reacted like it's a familiar name. You know him?"

"I might," returned Charlie. "Pretty good size, curly hair, lots of tattoos, lots of muscle tone, good looking? If it's the guy I'm thinking of, I seem to recall that he runs some sort of biker gang "

Otis was on the edge of his chair. "Satan's Disciples. That's him. What do you know about him?"

"It was about five years ago. I was by myself in a bar on the west side, just minding my own business. I was down here to visit an old leatherneck pal and I stopped for a drink. This guy singles me out. It happens to me a lot because of my size. Guys looking for a rep. I always try to avoid confrontations and usually I can get them to cool down and eventually laugh about what a dumb idea it was. But this guy wanted me and he wouldn't let me walk away. I had to put him on the floor. He was a handful though."

McCoy glanced over the table at Otis. A smile crawled across his face and then he looked at Charlie. "So you're the one."

Charlie didn't speak he simply threw his hands in the air in a "Hey, I'm innocent" gesture and leaned back in the chair as if he was trying to withdraw from the conversation.

Otis explained. "In this city, nobody goes up against Billy. It's suicide. He rules the streets, virtually unchallenged. I keep waiting for somebody to cut him in half with a twelve gauge. From behind, of course."

"I feel kinda left out," said Michael. "I'm the only guy here who has no idea who you're talking about."

"Just another hood." answered McCoy. "A nobody."

As though sensing that there might be some questions, Charlie offered, "I don't know anything else about the guy. One little skirmish and that was it. I didn't even know who he was. The bartender followed me out the door and told me what the guy's name was, but it didn't mean anything to me. He said that I should get on my bike and ride, get as far away as possible and never come back. I took his advice. I've never been back to that neighborhood."

"Case closed," said Otis, "But it sure is good to see, in the flesh, the only guy who ever got the best of Billy Bones. Did he know your name?"

"I don't see how he could," said Charlie, "I'd never been in that place before and I didn't talk to a soul when I was there except Bones, and I sure as hell wasn't wearing a name tag."

McCoy reached over and slapped Michael on the back. "Good boy. You're getting better every day. Maybe you can drop some more answers in our lap before Christmas. I'd sure as hell like to be able to get this one put away."

McCoy motioned the waitress, who had not taken her eyes off of him, to the table. "How you doin', Ruby? One o' these days, what say we get together for dinner or something?"

The pretty waitress was clearly embarrassed by the stares of the other men at the table. "Someday. We'll see."

"Sounds like a yes to me," said McCoy "But for now, I just want a burger and fries and get these guys whatever they want. On me."

Otis checked his watch. "Hey gang, I'm outta here. Seein' as how I'm the only one in this crowd with a family, I'd like to keep 'em."

"You do that," said McCoy. "And give my best to Marla and the kids."

A quick wave, a friendly smile and Otis was gone.

CHAPTER 16

It was normally about a twenty minute drive from Eddie's Bar to Otis's house but a light snow was beginning to fall and it would take just a few minutes longer this evening. Otis fiddled with the radio, searching for something that he could enjoy, some kind of music that wouldn't offend his taste. All this heavy metal. Awful stuff. A smile crossed his face as a strange thought occurred to him. He said it aloud. "Remember when they used to refer to classical music as 'Longhair'? Hah."

He didn't even know what station he was listening to or why he didn't skip right through the talk format and continue his pursuit of real music. The voice said that it was an interview that had been recorded earlier in the day. "And you, Miss Wilson, you're a native Detroiter?"

"I most certainly am," responded the innocent sounding feminine voice. "Whittier High School and the Norwest Shopping Mall. Those were the two places where I spent most of my younger days." There was a little scattered laughter in the background.

Otis reached for the radio knob but stopped short. He sensed that he was about to hear something important.

"The band. The name. Perhaps you can enlighten us, Bud. How did you arrive at a name like The Nephewz?"

A deep male voice answered. "That was really a no-brainer. There are four of us and we're all related. There's me and my brother and our two cousins. Since my dad is their uncle and their dad is my uncle, that makes us all nephews. Simple."

The moderator laughed and broke away for a commercial saying, "More from Monica and the Nephewz right after this from our sponsor."

Otis sank back into the seat to absorb what he had just heard. Ronnie Murray had a newspaper clipping that referred to "Monica and The Nephewz" but there was something else bugging him. The interviewer called her by her last name. Otis was sure there was something important about the name Wilson. He seemed to remember that McCoy was haunted by the name

"Monica" too. There was a meaning to this, a connection somewhere. It was just a matter of putting it all together.

Almost immediately after he got home, gave his wife a hello kiss, and hugged each of his three children, Otis was on the phone to Eddie's Bar.

"Hey, Eddie. This's Otis. McCoy still there? Good. Can you put him on?' Otis fumbled with his notebook until he found a blank page and then dug the stub of a pencil from his shirt pocket.

One word came from the receiver, "McCoy."

"Hey, I'm glad I caught you. Do you recall saying that the name, 'Monica' was kinda nagging on you?"

"Haven't thought about it much but yeah, there's something about that name."

Otis supplied the solvent. "How about Monica Wilson? Does that help?"

There was an uncomfortable silence on the line while McCoy put the thoughts in order in his mind. When he finally spoke, it was in a very restrained tone. "Yes, yes, yes, I think I remember. Back when we were on that Etta Kremer case. Wasn't that the name that the super gave us? The apartment guy. She's the one he said joined the circus or something."

"Well" said Otis, "She's the one from 'Monica and The Nephewz,' the group that Ronnie Murray had the clipping on. Seems to tie the two cases together, don't ya' think?"

"Geez. You're right. And Christmas is only a few days away and now we're gonna get busy," McCoy shook his head. "Story of my life. Another holiday shot in the ass."

Otis jumped right back. "Think about me, man. Three kids and a wife at home and I'll probably be spending the whole time between now and New Year's at the precinct. We've got lots of figuring to do here. I know Billy Bones is up to his eyeballs in it, too. I just know it. But it sure feels great to have something finally begin to make some sense. You coming in early tomorrow?"

"Yeah, I'll meet you in the office about an hour before the start of the shift. We're gonna have to have it all organized to show the Captain when he comes in so that he doesn't get any big ideas about moving us on to something else. This thing is so low profile, he's liable to want to drop it, don'tcha think?"

"Not really," answered Otis. "He knows we've been digging in. I figure he's going to give us a good shot at getting it wrapped up."

Otis could hear another voice on the line, this one was much fainter. It was Michael yelling at McCoy from across the bar room. "Hey, McCoy. Your burger's getting cold. C'mon."

"I gotta go," said McCoy. "Let's just keep this amongst us girls for now, eh?"

"Whatever you say, guy. I'm at home and I'm sure that my wife and kids wouldn't care anyway. You're the one out pumping down the beer with your friends. Can you keep a lid on it?"

McCoy just grunted and hung up the phone. When he returned to the table, his hamburger appeared undisturbed but Michael and Charlie were finishing up the last few French fries on McCoy's plate.

"If the fries seemed a little soggy, it's because I spit all over them before I went to answer the phone." said a poker-faced McCoy.

His two friends looked at McCoy, waiting for him to crack a smile but his expression never changed as he enthusiastically polished off the remainder of his hamburger. Nobody spoke as he picked up a napkin and wiped his mouth and then inspected the napkin to see if there were traces of mustard. McCoy then casually dropped the napkin onto the empty plate leaned back and looked at the two faces staring at him. He looked at one and then the other, raised his eyebrows and said. "What?"

CHAPTER 17

"Got all your Christmas shopping done?" asked Otis.

"I don't do any," replied McCoy as he thumbed through the reports. He seemed to be feeling slightly superior this morning because he had been sitting at the desk when Otis arrived. "Nobody to buy anything for since my mom died. I sure as hell hadn't planned on buying you anything. By the way, I thought you said you were coming in early this morning."

"Been here about an hour," countered Otis. "I was digging this up for you." He deposited a three by five card on McCoy's desk. "Oh, and I'll bet you will do a little Christmas shopping. At least for one gift."

McCoy smiled, looked at the address on the card and glanced up at Otis. "Monica?"

"Close," answered Otis. "It's the bandleader. I'm sure he'll know how to find her. We need to talk to him about the Murray case anyway." Otis glanced at his watch. "They're show business types so there's no point in trying to catch up with them much before noon."

"I know what you mean," said McCoy. "Most rock bands ain't through pukin' until at least eleven. Any plans for this morning?"

Otis smiled. "I was thinking of an encore at the Disciple's clubhouse. I'm not too concerned about Billy's beauty sleep. I'm thinking about our old, 'let's see just how tough you really are' routine."

"Great idea. Let's go." McCoy was already on his feet.

It wasn't quite daylight when the police cruiser pulled up at the clubhouse. It was impossible to tell if there were any lights on inside because all of the windows had been bricked over. A solo rusty van was stationed in the vacant field next to the clubhouse, the frost on the windows testifying to the fact that it had not moved last night.

"What's it look like to you?" asked Otis.

"Well," pondered McCoy. "The other day, there were two vans outside and two guys inside. My guess is that there's one person here besides us and it probably ain't Billy 'cause his van isn't here."

"Brilliant deduction," agreed a cheerful Otis Springfield. He was out of the car and half way to the door before McCoy even had his seatbelt undone. This time, he had a chance to knock on the door. Considering the early hour, both detectives were surprised how quickly the big door swung open.

"What do you need?" It was Mace.

"Where's Billy?" asked Otis.

Mace stared at him without replying, but Otis was very good at this eye contact game. They stood like two prizefighters in the stare-down as the referee recites the rules. Finally, Mace blinked. He had lost round one. "He don't report to me. He's his own man. I don't ask where he's going and he don't tell me."

"Hey guy, that's okay," chimed in McCoy. "We just wanted to drop off some information anyway. It's something that you oughta know too."

Apparently feeling like he had regained the upper hand, Mace demanded, "Well, just drop it off and leave."

"Ain't that simple," said Otis. "This requires a little interaction. We tell you the rules and you acknowledge that you understand."

Mace condescended. "Whatever."

"Okay, let's get started," said McCoy. "Do you understand that if I come here to arrest you and you decide to resist, I am authorized to use whatever force I consider necessary to affect that arrest?"

"What?" Mace tried to look defiant.

"Just answer. Yes or no." said an unsmiling Otis.

"Yeah, yeah, okay. What next?"

McCoy spoke more slowly now. "There is a possibility that the force may be lethal. Do you understand that?"

"What's your point here?" Mace's voice lacked authority.

"What I'm saying is that sometimes cops, in the line of duty, have to kill people. People like you, Mace. I'm saying that there is always the outside chance that I'll have to stick my Glock right in your face and blow your brains all over this clubhouse. When it's over, all I need to do after I wipe your blood off my shoes, is to fill out a report saying that you came after me. Nobody will question it and I'll be at the drive-up window of the Kentucky Fried Chicken place, ordering my lunch about the time the coroner is opening up your chest cavity. That's the way it works."

"Why you guys giving me all this? I ain't done nothing." There was the whine of fear in Mace's voice and that is exactly what the cops had wanted to hear.

Otis broke his silence. "It's just something that could happen. You're hanging with some bad company. My guess is that the absolute best thing that might happen to you will likely be a conviction as an accessory to murder one. Twenty in Jackson if you're lucky. Think it over. Where do you want to be at this time next year? Prison? Graveyard?"

Otis stuck his business card in Mace's shirt pocket and the detectives turned and walked out the door without saying another word.

The sun was playing tag with the high clouds as Otis and McCoy strolled back to the car.

"Whadda ya' think?" asked McCoy.

Otis glanced skyward. "They're closing in. Enough storm clouds up there to give the kids a nice white Christmas."

"Don't remind me. Shoveling snow is not one of my favorite pastimes."

Back in the Police cruiser, Otis glanced over at McCoy and said, "He's ours."

The sudden, unexpected, thinly veiled death threat that they had just delivered had had a dramatic impact. Every time they used that routine it always produced the desired result, unnerving the toughest of the tough guys.

"Body and soul," smiled McCoy. "Let's go visit this bandleader."

CHAPTER 18

It was shortly after eleven o'clock when the patrol car pulled up in front of Bud's neatly kept brick ranch in a long row of neatly kept brick ranches.

"Hardly looks like a rock star's home," commented McCoy. "I've always had this mental image of either a mansion or a dumpy room in a flop house."

"I guess I never really thought about it," answered Otis. "I suppose everybody's got to live somewhere."

They were at the front door now, McCoy leaning on the doorbell. A boy who looked to be about ten years old opened the inner door and stared at the two huge men on the front porch. Without taking his eyes off of them he yelled, "Dad."

The man who responded to the young boy's cry for help certainly didn't look like a rock musician. It might have been his neatly trimmed hair or his clear eyes, but he carried the look of a typical businessman, dressed in GQ style and impeccably neat. "Yes? How can I help you?" As he looked past the detectives he immediately knew that the unmarked cruiser at the curb was a police vehicle. The look on his face was more curiosity than fear. He held the door open for the two men to enter and then led them into the kitchen without speaking. The detectives followed Bud, McCoy commenting that cops are very accustomed to doing interviews in kitchens.

"We're here about Ronnie Murray," said Otis.

Bud just shook his head. "That guy. What a piece of work. He back in town? I left him in Reno after I fired him from the band a couple of weeks ago. What's he into now?"

"The morgue," replied McCoy. "He died of a drug overdose."

The news seemed to hit Bud like a hammer in the chest. He had to sit down before he could respond. "Dead? Ronnie? You sure?"

Otis gave it a minute to sink in and then added. "We're sure about the dead part, we're sure about the morgue part, and we're sure about the drugs. What we need to find out is how it all came about, the circumstances. We have reason to believe that someone deliberately spoon-fed him lethal doses of drugs until his system simply shut down. We're treating it as a homicide until we're convinced otherwise."

"I see," said Bud, his voice slightly shaky. "But how can I help? The last time I saw him was about three weeks ago and he was fine then."

"We need all the information that you can give us on his associates," advised McCoy. "Up until just now we weren't even sure that he ever played in your band. Before we can solve his death, we need a pretty good snapshot of his life. Did you ever know an Etta Kremer?"

"Um, no."

"How about a Billy Bones?"

Bud stiffened and looked up at McCoy. "Billy Bones? I know the name, that's all. Never met him. He's been causing trouble for us. Says he's Ronnie's manager and wants some ridiculous severance settlement because I fired Ronnie. He's been threatening to go public with information that can hurt the band. Nothing he's come up with is true but that won't matter if the tabloids get hold of it."

Otis let out a low whistle. "The connection. Now we've got it. I knew that bastard was involved. What did you tell this Bones guy?"

"Well, I have never talked to him personally. Monica, she's our vocalist, wanted to take a shot at handling it first. She knows Mr. Bones. I guess she's had some dealings with him a long time ago, before I ever knew her."

The detectives exchanged glances and then McCoy said. "We need to talk to Monica too. How can we contact her?"

Bud looked up at the kitchen clock. It was almost noon. "She should be here in ten minutes or so. She's coming over to pick up some new arrangements. You can talk to her then."

The detectives nodded in unison.

When Monica arrived, Bud met her at the door and brought her directly to the kitchen and the waiting detectives. She visibly paled when she realized what was happening.

"What's going on? Is something wrong?" As if she couldn't think of anything else to say, she looked at Bud with an expression of disbelief. A look that said she felt betrayed.

Otis spoke first. "Good afternoon Miss Wilson. I'm Detective Springfield and this is my partner, Detective McCoy. We have a few questions for you about some of your former associates."

Monica swallowed and nodded.

McCoy began, "Let's start with Billy Bones. What can you tell us about him? Did you ever belong to the Disciples or have any dealings with Billy?"

"Am I being arrested? Don't you need to read me my rights?"

McCoy sat down across the kitchen table from Monica. "Miss Wilson, we're here to investigate a possible homicide. Maybe two homicides. You are not currently a suspect in those cases and so no arrest is anticipated. You may be worried about some past doings that may have been illegal but I can assure you that those are of no interest to us at the current time. All we want from you is information that might help us in the homicide investigation. We will not ask you any question that might serve to incriminate you."

If McCoy's words were intended to relax Monica, they were clearly insufficient. She remained stiff and colorless as she replied, "I'll do anything you want as long as you can guarantee that you can put Billy away for the rest of his life."

"I wish I could make that promise and it's certainly what I'm striving for," replied McCoy, "But there simply aren't any guarantees in my business, no matter how much I want there to be."

Otis spoke up from his position next to the breakfast bar, "Did you know Etta Kremer?"

Monica's eyes closed and a tear streamed down her cheek. The detective asking the question had just referred to Etta in the past tense. She didn't want to know more. It would be too much for her. She simply nodded.

McCoy motioned for Otis to follow him out to the front porch. Bud seemed to understand and moved to Monica's side to comfort her.

"Well?" McCoy shrugged

"It's certainly emotionally charged and I really feel sorry for her, but we've got to get some answers. I think we've found our motive and our perp. All we need from here on out is evidence. Lots of solid, irrefutable, conclusive, airtight evidence, and she's most likely our best source right now. She's the center point, the only one linked to everybody else. She's got to be the key here."

McCoy voiced his observation. "You know, if it wasn't for the fact that Christmas is only two days away, we'd be into a cop's dream here. We've got the chance to link up an unsolved homicide to a current case and shut down a major drug operation in one major stroke, and without any special budget allotments."

"I'm sure the city council would be proud of us," replied Otis. "Unpleasant as it's gonna be, we'd better get back inside and get this done."

Monica appeared more composed when the detectives returned to Bud's kitchen. "Tell me about Etta. Is she alive or dead? I think I know, I just need to hear it."

McCoy moved directly in front of Monica, looking her in the eyes as he said, "Murdered. Tortured and killed and then dumped on the side of the road. It's still unsolved."

This time, Monica seemed prepared. "It was Billy. It had to be. Etta was the best friend I ever had. The only one who believed in me when everyone, everyone including my own family wrote me off as worthless. She stood by me and walked me out of the dark path that I had strayed into. I owe her my life. I owe her everything. What do you need from me? How can I help you? I'm not worried about incriminating myself anymore. This is much more important. I owe it to Etta."

The detectives looked at one another, surprised by the sudden strength and resolve in this young woman.

McCoy spoke first. "I'd like to set up an appointment for you to speak with a prosecuting attorney. Will you be available for the next few days? I know that it's almost Christmas, but I think I can set something up for tomorrow if I get on it right away."

Monica looked up at Bud, who answered. "We don't have any bookings until New Year's Eve at a Casino way up in the upper peninsula. We'll have to leave a day or two before that."

"I'll have everything done and out of the way by then," promised McCoy, "In the meantime, Miss Wilson, you will need to be thinking about all of your past dealings with Billy Bones and any connections that he may have had with Etta or with Ronnie Murray."

Monica's eyes flared at the mention of Ronnie Murray. "He's in this too. He's the one that started it. I want him put away too."

Otis broke his silence, "Ronnie has been put away, Miss Wilson. Permanently. Embalmed and put away in a drawer."

CHAPTER 19

"There's still a lot of day left," commented McCoy as the two cops finished a quick lunch at the nearest fast food place. "Anything else sound like it might be fruitful today?"

"I was just thinking." said Otis. "We know who we're after now. We don't have to pussyfoot around and play games any more. I'd like to run out to the Disciples' clubhouse again. Two visits in the same day just might get 'em nervous enough to do something."

"I second the motion." McCoy headed the cruiser to the southwest end of Detroit.

The vacant lot next to the clubhouse had two vans parked in it when the police car pulled up in front. Otis commented. "Billy has to be making a lot of money off of his drug operations. You'd think that he'd be driving something a little more flashy than an old rusted out van. I wonder if he's got another life with a different identity somewhere. It's been done before."

"You know, that's a thought worth chewing on. This guy is supposed to be really slippery and that's just the kind of thing we should be looking for." McCoy opened the door of the car without ever taking his eyes off of the clubhouse.

This time, McCoy had to knock on the door several times. He was beginning to wonder if anyone would answer when the door abruptly jerked open. It was Billy with his big Hollywood grin. "McCoy, ain't it? Bet you didn't think I'd remember. You stopping by to drop off my Christmas gift?" He looked past McCoy, focusing on Otis. "How about you, Detective Springfield? Bring me anything? Oh yeah, I forgot. It's Kwanzaa to you."

Neither detective responded and neither smiled, playing the mind game to the hilt. They waited until Billy took a step back and then walked into the clubhouse, scanning the scene for anything unusual as they entered, Otis checking out the right side of the room and McCoy, the left. They hadn't discussed the routine before they entered. They didn't have to. They knew what to do.

Mace was sitting at the bar, his back to the door. He didn't turn around and he didn't acknowledge the cops' presence. From the row of empty beer bottles on the bar in front of him, it looked like Mace had been drinking ever since McCoy had rattled his cage. The hesitant unsteady motion as he tilted his head back and took another swig from the bottle substantiated that evaluation.

Billy was clearly irritated by the intrusion and was making no effort to conceal his contempt for these two unwelcome troublemakers. "What is it? State your business. If you've got a warrant, let's see it. If not, say your piece and get out."

Otis stepped around Billy, putting him in the middle with McCoy on the other side. "Mace tell you we were here this morning?"

"Might have."

"Did he tell you what we said?"

Billy took a step back so that he could keep both detectives in his line of sight. "Maybe. That's between me and him."

"Just making sure," joined in McCoy

Billy glanced over at the bar where Mace was sitting. The beer had done its job. Mace was out of it. He probably wasn't even aware of what was going on. Billy let the silence hang for a few seconds and then asked. "That it? That all you wanted?"

McCoy moved in closer, stared straight into Billy's eyes and slowly nodded his head.

Billy walked briskly to the door, opened it wide and waited. The two cops leisurely strolled to the door, smiled at Billy and walked out. They heard the door slam behind them.

Otis looked up at the darkening sky. "Yep. Probably get an inch or two of the white stuff tonight so Santa will have easy going tomorrow night."

"Holy shit," yelped McCoy. "Is tomorrow Christmas Eve?"

Otis laughed. "Why certainly, Mister Scrooge. But that should mean nothing to you. After all, you're not buying any gifts. I'll bet you don't even have a tree."

"Aw, I got this one present I've been meaning to buy. Just never seem to have any time. I got a little tree too. Not a real one. It's only about a foot high. All I gotta do is take it out of the box, set it on top of the television and plug it in." McCoy wouldn't make eye contact with Otis.

"Get in the car and drive. It's just about time to wrap it up for the day. Got to get those reports done before we can go home. Well, I can go home. You need to head for the Mall." Otis was still smiling broadly.

The conversation got back to business on the ride to the precinct. Otis spoke first. "Y'know, I don't think that Mace said a word to Billy about us bein' there this morning."

"I agree," chimed in McCoy, "He might be more shook up than I thought. Maybe he's one of those types who's acutely aware of his own mortality and when he hears someone else suggest that they can control those sort of things…well, it can be enough to tip him over. He sure looked like he was, let's say, detached."

"If that's true, that's going to make it all the more interesting," observed Otis. "It's one of those twists I hoped for, but hadn't really expected—like getting a pony for Christmas. Think we should stop back there again tomorrow, maybe crank up the heat a little more?"

McCoy was concentrating on working his way through the holiday traffic and his answer was somewhat fragmented. "Tomorrow? Probably won't be time. I've got that interview set up between Monica and the prosecutor. I've already talked to the prosecutor's office. They're going to forego pursuing any charges regarding Monica. Her testimony is going to be way too important to jeopardize at this point. Besides, they'd never get enough for a conviction anyway. It could turn into an all day thing."

Otis nodded in agreement. "And don't forget. We got a little precinct get together over at Eddie's Bar after work. I won't be able to stay very long, though. I've got kids. Remember? Planning on spending the whole holiday with them. You ain't figuring on going in on Christmas Day, are you?"

"Well, no. But I guess I'm on call, so who knows. I'm on call every Christmas. It's one of the downsides of being single."

Otis was smiling again. "But that could all change by the time next Christmas rolls around, if that cute little waitress, Ruby has her way."

McCoy stifled an embarrassed laugh. "Just what I need. All my friends plotting my future. Thanks pal, but I'm quite capable of making all my own mistakes."

CHAPTER 20

On this Christmas Eve, McCoy picked up Monica at her hotel and headed downtown while Otis went on to Bud's house hoping to fill in some blanks on Ronnie Murray.

It had snowed overnight, depositing about two inches for the first significant dusting of the season. On the way to the courthouse, McCoy tiptoed the cruiser around at least three minor traffic mishaps, compliments of the first slick roads of the winter.

A very large woman wearing a Santa cap and ringing a bell stood next to the Salvation Army kettle on the sidewalk in front of the courthouse. She was singing "Hark, the Herald Angels Sing" and smiling at passers by. As McCoy and Monica approached, they noticed an old lady, at least eighty, slowly walk up and stand beside the Salvation Army woman. Tentatively at first and then in full song, she joined in the singing in beautiful harmony. There was a disciplined and trained quality to the old woman's voice that belied her age, the joy in her eyes remembering a time when perhaps she sang for gala audiences in gowns and black tie and, at least for now, stopped all foot traffic on this city sidewalk. People stood, respectfully listening and smiling. "Glo-o-o-oria in excelsis Deo."

Some, Monica for one, were moved to wipe tears from their eyes. When the song ended, Monica rushed to the kettle and stuffed a twenty-dollar bill into the slot. Most of the other observers moved in to donate as well.

McCoy remained silently in the background until Monica rejoined him. Gesturing his head toward the big gray building he said, "Well Miss Wilson, this is the place. Let's get it over with."

What surprised Monica the most was that the man from the prosecuter's office looked so terribly young. When he first entered the room, she thought that he must be an intern. He was a handsome, conservatively dressed African-American with what appeared to be a permanent smile on his face. Monica had always pictured prosecutors as old and dour looking. After all, wasn't it part of their job to look intimidating? Maybe this guy wasn't an attorney. Maybe he was just here to do the interview and wouldn't be appearing in court where any self respecting defense lawyer would eat a neophyte like this alive. Monica's bravado began to fade as she imagined Billy Bones holding this kid by the throat with one hand, while slowly opening his pocket knife with the other.

"Hello. My name is Robert Bowen and I know what you're thinking," said the young man. "I look too young and too innocent, right?"

Monica didn't speak at all but nodded as she slowly sank into the oak chair being held for her by McCoy.

"That's okay, Miss Wilson. Most people have that same reaction when we first meet, but I'm going to ask you to trust me. I'm not as virginal as I look. The judges all know me and so do almost every one of the trial lawyers who work in criminal cases. Last time I looked, I had the best conviction record in the office and they give me my full share of the tough cases."

McCoy spoke up. "He'll get the job done, Miss Wilson. I've worked with Mister Bowen on at least three other cases and we got convictions on all three. No plea bargaining either."

A stenographer with her funny looking little typewriter-like machine sat at the end of the conference table. She had left the room a few minutes earlier and returned with a large pitcher of icewater and a stack of plastic glasses. Setting the pitcher down and sliding it toward the others, she looked up only briefly and offered, "Don't pay any attention to me. I'm just a fly on the wall."

McCoy nodded his acknowledgement.

It took Monica over four hours to get her story out, not including the forty-five minute lunch break. Even though the stenographer was furiously typing away in her mysterious coded language, Robert Bowen took many pages of notes, frequently asking Monica to clarify this point or that.

The tale began several years ago during Monica's most confused time of life. She was just discovering the underground society in those days, stumbling her way through it and being routinely abused along the way. That was when Billy first showed up.

In the beginning, it was like he was a saviour. He was the perfect gentleman around her, never making any kind of advances, always asking what she needed and making sure that she had it. He even provided her with a place to stay when she ran out of girlfriends who had, one by one, grown tired of her surly manner. All he wanted in return was for Monica to run some errands for him from time to time.

Billy's presence made life considerably easier for Monica. The guys in the neighborhood stopped harrassing her. They just smiled and waved when she walked by.

Everything was simple enough in the beginning. She would pick up a grocery sack from one guy and deliver it to another, maybe twice, sometimes three times a day. The bags were always stapled shut and Monica never even considered opening one to look inside. She figured that it was something illegal, most likely drugs, but she didn't want to know for sure, thinking that if she was ever stopped or arrested, she could honestly say that she didn't know what she was carrying.

It didn't occur to her at the time but later she came to realize that Billy was never actually present when she picked up or delivered the bags, keeping himself separated from the action.

She remembered the day that she moved into Billy's inner circle and shuddered slightly as she told that part of the story.

Monica had spent about three months running around the city delivering these ominous bags, and then one day Billy sent one of his biker gang to summon her to the Disciples' clubhouse.

"Been doin' a good job out there," he said, "keepin' your mouth shut, not askin' questions, doin' what you're told. I like that."

Monica's only answer was a small, self-conscious smile. It was just her and Billy. Nobody else around. He was sitting and she was standing. Billy had not invited her to sit down.

"Know what's in the bags you been carryin'?"

Monica shook her head. "I never looked."

"You had an idea though, right?"

Monica nodded.

"Think you could handle movin' that suff on the street? Pretty big money in it."

Monica was shocked. "You mean selling it?"

"A guy will go with you for a week or two, whatever it takes until he's comfortable you'll be okay. The people we've got out in the street need to be people we can trust."

Monica shrugged and breathed a very weak, "'kay."

"Somebody will come by for you in the morning , just do what they tell you and you'll be fine."

Robert Bowen interrupted and commented. "In the last part of the story that you've just told us, you have never said that Billy ever acknowledged that it was illegal drugs in the bags that he had you delivering. Am I correct in assuming that?"

"I can't ever remember making any direct reference to drugs," said Monica. "Even later on. I don't think he ever did anything except hint around about it and let whoever he was talking to draw their own conclusions. Sometimes he would refer to the stuff as, 'shit' but he never used the word drugs or anything like that."

"At this point, Miss Wilson, were you still under the impression that he was a reasonable and fair minded man?" The prosecutor was beginning to assume his courtroom manner.

"I don't know exactly when my opinion started to change but I sure remember the day I saw the real Billy come out. I couldn't believe it. I still get chills when I think about it."

Bowen's smile returned. "I'd like to hear all about that." He poured a glass of icewater from the pitcher and nudged it over in front of Monica.

She took a long drink and sighed, "Well, I'd been dealing on my own for almost a year. I thought I was doing fine when all of a sudden this Mexican guy comes along and tells me to go find another neighborhood. He's taking over. I didn't know who he was and I didn't argue. I just went back home and sent out word that I needed to talk to Billy right away. I didn't have his personal phone number back then, so I sent the news about what happened with one of Billy's runners. The next day, I get a message to go to the clubhouse and see Billy. When I got there, Billy took me down into the basement. My eyes were burning because it was really smoky down there. Billy had a charcoal barbecue going full blast down in the basement. And then I see the Mexican guy who booted me off my corner and he's all stretched out with no shirt on, tied between two posts in the basement. That's when I first saw that look in Billy's eyes. It was like he wasn't focusing on anything in particular, just space. It wasn't the kind of look you get from drugs. This was more like he was possessed by demons or something. Something supernatural. It terrified me.

"Then he walks over to the grill and takes this long poker out of the fire. The point was glowing bright red. The Mexican guy could see what was coming and started praying and then crying. When he began to cry, it sort of moved Billy's excitement level up another notch, he even started to giggle. He took the poker and jammed it into the guys chest and started writing with it. The poker would cool down a little bit and not burn deep enough to satisfy Billy so he kept sticking it back in the fire and getting it bright red again. The guy was begging him to stop but Billy never even heard him. It took him close to an hour to write the word 'Disciple' across the guy's chest. By then, the poor guy was just barely conscious so Billy smiles at me and says, 'Let's wake him up,' and then pulls the front of the guys pants open and jams the red hot poker right down the front. I've never heard such a scream in my life. Billy smiled at me and said, 'I guess I'm done for now.' And then he cut the ropes, dragged the guy up the stairs, opened the back door and threw him out into the alley. The last I saw of him, he was crawling down the alley."

"Oh, my God," came from the stenographer.

McCoy and Bowen remained completely silent, waiting for Monica to regain her composure and go on.

Monica lowered her head and ran her fingers through her hair as though trying to erase the image that had just returned to haunt her. "From that day on, I've looked at Billy differently, like some sort of devil. The look on his face that day was definitely not human. I can't describe it. There was something in his voice too and I heard it again just a few days ago when I called him."

"Why did you call him?" asked the prosecutor.

"He's planning to extort money from the band and I was foolish enough to think I could reason with him."

"What's his ultimatum? What if you don't pay him?"

Monica's voice was trembling. "Well, It's all a big lie but he says that he's going to expose me as a drug dealer, selling to kids in the audience but I know Billy better than that. What he really means is that if I don't cooperate he'll begin killing people."

McCoy piped in. "Looks a lot to me like he's already got a head start."

"That's true," said Monica, "I don't mean to sound cold here but I think that those two murders are just Billy's way of telling me that he's serious. One time, oh, a year or so ago, Billy asked me if I'd ever watched anybody die. When I told him no, he said that I didn't know what I was missing. Now, he's given me until the stroke of midnight on New Year's Eve and then he says he's coming after us. It won't stop there though because it's not about money. It never was. Billy considered me his personal property and he's not going to let me walk away from him. Ever."

McCoy looked at Bowen, the boy prosecutor and said, "One week. One week from today is all I've got. We absolutely have to get enough evidence to bring charges. He's got to be locked up before New Year's Eve." Then he remembered the conversation with Bud, the bandleader. He turned to Monica, "Don't you guys have some sort of appearance scheduled for New Year's Eve?"

"We're supposed to be doing a gig that we booked way back in September, when I was still new with the band. It's some sort of combination casino and ski resort way up in the upper peninsula. I think it's called "Copper" something. It's up there where the copper mines used to be."

"Copper Sky," said McCoy. "I know the place. I've got a friend who owns a lot of property and a hunting lodge just a few miles west of there. It's one of the new Indian Casinos on tribal land. A really nice place."

Robert Bowen was studying his notes. The voice came from behind the legal pad that hid his face. "On the surface, I'm not sure if we've got enough to put out a warrant, at least not a murder warrant, but I'll give you every break I can. Just keep digging and stay in real close communication with our office. If it looks like you're going to be able to bring me what I need, I can issue an arrest order for something else and buy you a couple more days anyway. It's about the best I can offer. I don't want a murder warrant until I'm fairly sure I can get a conviction. I don't think any of us want to see this character walk."

McCoy tilted his head and raised his eyebrows in agreement. Monica sat with her eyes closed taking long, deep breaths.

For the next hour, Robert Bowen asked specific prosecutor-like questions, rapid fire, barely waiting for an answer before asking the next. He was doing this partly to fill in gaps in the story and partly to watch Monica's reaction to the type of grilling that she would face in a courtroom.

Parts of Monica's account brought tears to her eyes, especially when she talked about Etta. It was at these times when her firm purpose showed at its strongest. Both the prosecuter and McCoy were impressed with her intensity and determination. Her strong devotion pushed her fear aside. At this point she didn't care what happened to her as long as Billy was punished. Etta never deserved to die, especially at the hands of an evil creature like Billy. Monica kept having flashbacks of the day that Billy tortured that poor Mexican and the look on Billy's face. She imagined what Etta must have gone through just before she died. The terror, the pain. She imagined Billy watching Etta die and she imagined the smile on Billy's' face. It was too much to bear.

Robert Bowen recognized the level of passion in Monica and backed off, knowing that she was approaching a threshold that she dare not cross. He looked over at McCoy and said, "I think we're on the right track here. I'll give you a rough outline of what I need. It's probably all out there."

McCoy stood up, put his hands in his pockets and said to Prosecutor Bowen, "You know you're dealing with a certified genius, don't you?"

Bowens broad smile returned, "So is he."

CHAPTER 21

It was beginning to snow a little heavier about the time that Otis Springfield arrived at Eddie's Bar. He was surprised to find that McCoy was not there. It was December twenty-fourth, the annual precinct Christmas get together, something that McCoy really enjoyed. He lived just down the street from Eddie's so he usually left his car at home and then walked to the bar. That way, he wouldn't have to limit himself to just two or three beers.

"Where's your partner? He coming?" It was Ruby the waitress. She was wearing a red and green outfit and a red and green ribbon tied around a sprig of mistletoe in her hair. There was a trace of hope and disappointment in her question.

"I'm sure he'll be along any minute," answered Otis, "We were running in opposite directions today, trying to wrap up a few loose ends before the holidays, but he said he'd meet me here."

A look of relief filled Ruby's face as her pretty smile returned. "Okay, I was just curious. What kind of guy is he, anyway? You should know him better than anyone else, being his partner and all."

Otis seemed to think for a moment. "Well, we go back a long way together in the department. I guess I'd have to say that he's probably about the best all around partner I've ever had. Never have to worry about him doin' something stupid at the wrong time and he's the guy I'd want covering my back when things get serious. He's a lot of fun too. I guess we think alike. Good guy."

Ruby's smile never left her face. She didn't respond but her body language displayed approval as she winked and then turned to hurry back to the kitchen to grab the next order of steak sandwich and fries.

Otis too was hoping that McCoy would show up soon. He wanted to compare a few notes and get all of the serious business out of the way so that he could join in on the festivities. He could see that the party mood was taking control of the crowd. With the exception of a couple of young men in motorcycle jackets, they were almost all guys from the precinct including Captain Bice and even Brady, the coffee cop.

When McCoy entered the bar, it was obvious that he had gone home first, cleaned up and changed his clothes. He was also carrying a small, gift-wrapped box in his right hand. He spotted Otis and walked directly to him. "Anything earthshaking come out of your conversation with the bandleader?"

"Nothing negative. I guess he talked to their main contact at the record company and they agreed that the best thing was to offer us full cooperation. They say they got nothing to hide. How'd you make out with the prosecutor?"

"I've got to say that this Monica babe's got some guts. Looks like we're in good shape with the prosecutor's office too. They gave us Bowen, that really sharp kid with the good conviction record. I like him because he hardly ever offers a plea bargain. Does his homework and then goes for the win. One thing, though. We gotta make the collar before New Year's. I'll explain later." McCoy could see that the party was on the verge of consuming them.

"Hey, McCoy. Look what I found." It was Sullivan, one of the uniform patrol sergeants who had been with the department almost as long as McCoy had. Sullivan was dragging a reluctant and embarrassed looking Ruby and pointing to the mistletoe in her hair. "Gotta do it, McCoy. It's tradition and I know how you older guys are about tradition and shit."

McCoy reached out and took Ruby by the hand and she willingly moved to his side and nestled under his arm. "I sure hope you got a designated driver tonight, Sully. It'd be a shame if one of your own guys had to drag you in on a DUI."

"The missus has got that covered. She'll be picking me up around nine o'clock." countered Sullivan.

McCoy nodded and then looked down at Ruby. "Can you take a break from the tables for a minute? I'd like to wish you a happy holiday."

Ruby was eyeing the gift in McCoy's hand and seemed surprised. She hadn't been expecting anything. She wasn't even sure if McCoy was really interested in her, even if she herself were smitten. Ruby caught McCoy off guard by jumping up and kissing him on the cheek. "Sure. Anything for you."

There were no quiet corners to hide in at Eddie's Bar tonight. There wasn't even a vacant table. The couple had to settle for standing at the end of the bar, near the entrance to the kitchen. McCoy had hoped for something a little more intimate. He handed her the gift without comment. When she looked at him playfully, he shrugged and said, "Hey. It's almost Christmas. Go ahead. Open it."

Ruby's meticulously manicured fingers trembled only slightly as she carefully opened the present. She wasn't prepared for the splendid string of cultured pearls that met her gaze as he folded back the tissue in the handsome leather box. She gasped in astonishment.

McCoy heard a low whistle and turned to see Otis looking over his shoulder. "Lotsa beads there big fella. Had those oysters workin' overtime, didja? Must be somethin' serious going on here."

McCoy turned to Otis and said, "Michael O'Conner pulled some strings for me. He's still got a lot of connections in the jewelry business."

Ruby was shaking her head. "I can't. I can't. Oh Al, it's too expensive."

"It's what I wanted to do and I'm not taking it back. Gotta show my appreciation for all the great service I get in this place. And as far as I know, you never dropped a hamburger on the floor. At least not one of mine. Oh, and you might as well just call me McCoy. Everybody else does. I'm not used to hearing my first name."

Ruby threw her arms around McCoy's neck and gave him the biggest and warmest hug that he could remember. He even closed his eyes so that he could shut out the rest of the world and enjoy the closeness of Ruby. At this moment, that necklace was worth every penny that McCoy had paid for it. Events were moving along at a pace that McCoy hadn't expected. They had jumped the hurdle of uncertainty. In the last few seconds both of them had declared their intentions and feelings without saying a word. Yesterday, it was like a game of chess with Ruby making a tentative move and McCoy making a cautious countermove, neither showing their true purpose. That was over now.

Ruby returned to waiting on tables but her step had more bounce and her cheeks considerably more color. McCoy joined his old police buddies, telling stories and toasting memories, and stealing an occasional glance in Ruby's direction and making eye contact every time.

Otis was leaning against the bar, nursing his only drink of the evening and observing the crowd. He was paying special attention to the two men in motorcycle jackets. He had never seen them in here before. They seemed to be just having a quiet beer. Or could they be checking things out? Might they be Disciples sent by Billy Bones to spy on the enemy? Whatever their purpose was, it seemed to be finished now. They were headed toward the door, zipping up the leather jackets against the cold. He let the thoughts pass. "Way too much imagination," mumbled Otis.

CHAPTER 22

Christmas morning was a special time at the Springfield house. This was a loving family consisting of Otis, his wife Marla and their three young children. Otis had started his family later than a lot of people. He'd been in his late thirties before he married. His wife was ten years younger than he, fresh out of college and beginning a career as an elementary school teacher. Both partners had invested a lot of effort in making it a successful marriage and, after seventeen years it was paying off richly, in spite of the unpredictability of Otis's job with the Department. He often commented that he had married a remarkable woman and she would reply that it was him who gave her strength.

Like all kids on Christmas morning, the Springfield children were up at five o'clock and rousted their parents to begin the big day. By nine-thirty, all of the gifts had been opened, breakfast had been finished, and the family was getting dressed for church, another Christmas tradition in the Springfield household. Visiting would take place later in the day. Otis always made it a point to bring the family by his mother's house on Christmas Day. Her condition had deteriorated over the years and she didn't always remember the kid's names but she always had plenty of hugs to go around. Her youngest sister had moved in with her and become her caretaker.

Otis was staring out the bedroom window, watching the gentle snowfall as he tied his necktie. Marla was at her dressing table putting the finishing touches on her mascara when the ring of the telephone froze her. The couple looked at one another for a moment as if deciding whether to pick it up, although they already knew the answer.

"Hello" There was no Christmas joy in Otis's voice.

"Man, I really hate to bother you on Christmas," McCoys voice said, "I didn't want to even call, but can you spare a couple hours sometime today? Something's come up. I got called in earlier this morning and there's one thing that needs doing right away and I can't do it alone."

"What's up? Is it the one we've been working on? The two homicides?"

"Three," said McCoy, "they found your buddy Mace on an expressway shoulder this morning and you'll never guess which lane he was in."

Otis was caught completely off guard. He had never expected this. It took a few seconds for the shock to wear off. "What do you make of it?"

"I'm not sure," said McCoy, "but we've got to go visit Billy now. Today. We can't put it off. I wish we would have had some time to put a plan together but it looks like we're in it up to our knees and we don't dare let up. We might even want to haul his ass in here today. I don't know. We'll talk when you get here. Sorry."

"Yeah," Otis gently returned the telephone to its cradle.

Marla had been holding her breath throughout her husband's conversation. "They need you today, don't they." It wasn't a question.

Otis just nodded, unable to bring himself to look her in the eye. "I'll try to make it as short as I can. Gotta save some time to take the kids over to Mom's. At least I had the morning with you guys. I'm sorry, hon. It's this job." His voice trailed off.

"Otis, I married a hero. I don't regret it. Never will. I knew what I was getting into and the kids have lived with it all their lives. We've learned to appreciate whatever time we have together and accept the rest. Go. Take care of business. We'll be fine."

Before leaving the house, Otis stopped in the living room and spent a few precious minutes with his children. If he ever might feel any resentment toward his job, it would be at a time like this, but Otis was not prone to self pity. When he told the children that they and their mother would have to go to church without him, they only seemed mildly disappointed. It was an old story with them.

CHAPTER 23

Otis found McCoy sitting at his desk, notebooks and papers spread from corner to corner. McCoy waved his hand but never looked up. He seemed to be studying intently. "There's no doubt that we turned Mace into a liability when we shook him up the other day. That's your motive. I want to make sure we get this right," he commented, "cross all the T's and dot the I's and all that stuff. I only want to haul this guy's ass in here once. Honestly, I don't think we've got enough to pick him up today. Maybe we can get some DNA evidence or something. That'll take some time though."

Otis put his hands on his hips. "Got a cause of death yet?"

"Do we ever. We didn't need a medical examiner for this case. His throat was slit, and I mean it was an ear to ear job. This one's really got Billy's signature all over it too. The guys wrists are all chewed up from what must have been handcuffs. Looks like he struggled right to the end, like he saw it coming. The body was right on the shoulder of the road, just barely off the pavement and just barely inside the city limits. Two more blocks and it would have been Grosse Pointe's problem. Billy must have wanted to make damn sure that he was found right away, sort of a Christmas present for you and me. My theory is that Mace was another one of those guys that Monica Wilson had done some business with and Billy wanted her to see just how serious he is."

"So what are you thinking?" asked Otis. "Want to see if we can shake him up? Don't expect him to give you anything to use against him. I've been working on that for years. He'll be waiting for that, just playing with us."

"Any ideas?" McCoy leaned back in his chair.

"Well, I'm thinking that maybe we can try something he won't expect. We just gotta play by the rules, be careful that we don't hand him any sort of a free pass. I don't even want to be close to that. No matter what happens, we've got to be the ones in control. I know him. He'll be looking to turn it around so that he's the one in command. He's damn good at that game too. He will undoubtedly expect a visit today and he knows that we'll be after him for this homicide. Maybe we could temper our zeal a little bit and see how he reacts."

"Yeah," McCoy's eyes lit up at the prospect of playing a mind game. "Yeah, I like that idea. We can have some fun with this one. Just remember, we've got a deadline here. He's got to be locked up in less than a week."

There was a fully trimmed Christmas tree leaning up against the front of the Disciples' clubhouse; no stand, just the tree. Somebody would be wondering what happened to their yard decorations this morning. The two detectives stood looking at it for a few long moments and then looked at each other and shook their heads in unanimous disgust.

Billy made them wait this morning. McCoy knocked on the door four times, with a little more emphasis each time. When the door finally opened, it was a sudden and powerful motion, actually creating a perceptible vacuum in its wake.

"Ah. It's Santa Claus and one of his little elves. What did you bring me, Santa? A new wagon?" Billy was wearing his best patented Hollywood smile today. He stood aside to allow the pair to enter. "You guys never give up, do you? Even gotta come out here to hassle me on Christmas Day. I guess everybody's got their job to do. Okay, go ahead with whatever you got to say and then get out and leave me alone."

"We're here about Mace," said McCoy. "We've got a few questions."

Billy walked around behind the bar and picked up a hairbrush and began to run it through his tight curls. It didn't seem to make much difference. McCoy was thinking that you couldn't possibly mess up Billy's hair, it always sprang right back. He set the brush down on the bar and turned to the detectives.

"Yeah. Well in case you hadn't noticed, he ain't here." Billy shot back, "He's got an ex-wife and a kid somewhere around town and I expect he's probably over there."

"No, Billy. He was killed sometime last night." Otis moved to where he could study Billy's eyes. "We got the guy who killed him though. Picked him up within a couple of hours of the murder. We're just filling in details, trying to piece together his last few hours. We know that he was in this clubhouse two days ago. It's the time between then and midnight last night that we need some answers on."

If there was any surprise in Billy's eyes, Otis couldn't discern it. Billy ran his fingers through his curly hair and turned to Otis. "You got the guy? Already? How'd you catch him so fast?"

"Eye witness," said McCoy, "A minister. You know, a preacher was on the way to his church to get it all set up for Christmas services and he sees this guy standing over the body and a car sitting there, running and the door wide open. When the guy sees the preacher, he jumps in the car and takes off. The preacher got the license number and a good description of the guy. Couple of our people picked him up at his house. This guy is no stranger to our department. He's been busted quite a few times. It's open and shut."

Billy began pacing back and forth and then caught himself. He thought for a moment and then turned back to the officers. "I'm not gonna be much help to you guys. I haven't seen him in two days. He left right after you two walked out and that's the last time I laid eyes on him. Sorry."

"That's okay," answered Otis, "We were just trying to get any information we could. We'll have this one wrapped up in a day or two."

"Whatever," Billy sounded disinterested. "I guess I'll read about it in the papers."

"It won't be in the papers," answered McCoy. "All the reporters are home celebrating Christmas. Outside of his ex-wife, who doesn't want to talk, Mace doesn't have a family and neither does the killer. Who's gonna care? I sure as hell ain't gonna call the Free Press."

For the first time, Billy showed a trace of emotion. A stunned expression briefly flushed his face. "That it? Are you guys done now?"

"That should be all for today," said Otis, "But we still got business to settle with you, Billy. We're far from being done."

Billy stiffened. "You go ahead and give it your best shot, tough guy. You don't scare me. Never will."

The detectives left without saying another word.

"Great way to spend Christmas Day, eh?' Said McCoy as they drove back to the precinct.

Otis glanced at his watch. "That didn't take as long as I expected. It's not even one o'clock yet. I've got plenty of time to get back home, pack up the wife and kids and head on over to my mom's house."

"How's your mom doing anyway? Last I remember she'd had a heart attack or something like that."

"It was a stroke," answered Otis. "My Aunt Lucille has moved into the house to take care of her. It's the best thing for both of them. My aunt is twelve years younger than mom and she's in great shape. Studied nursing too, so she knows what's going on. She might even be an RN by now, I know she was studying for the test. My uncle died two years ago and Aunt Lucille has been going crazy ever since. She's one of those women who needs to take care of people. It's right up her alley. Mom doesn't mind having her there either. She says that she could manage alone but likes the company. I guess they've always been close in spite of the age difference."

"You've never mentioned your dad," observed McCoy

Otis didn't reply. It was as if he hadn't heard the comment. He had his notebook in his hand and was thumbing through the pages.

McCoy let the subject die without further conversation.

The cruiser pulled into its assigned spot in the underground garage at headquarters and as they were getting out of the car, Otis leaned over the door and asked, "What do you think of our chances of getting this guy in jail in the next five days?"

McCoy shook his head. "I don't see him giving us anything to work with. I think we're going to need those forensic guys to help us tie him to something. But even that doesn't look real good right now because the first two victims came up clean. Nothing on the bodies at all. It sorta explains why there was no sexual assault on the girl, doesn't it?"

"I told you Billy Bones was smart. He's not your garden variety hoodlum," said Otis. "This guy is gonna take some work.

Maybe we'll get lucky with the guy they've got in the morgue. By the way. Do you think Billy bought our story about busting somebody for the murder?"

"You know, I was wondering just how much of that stuff he would go for," said McCoy. "One thing's for sure. We surprised him. He never expected that. I just want to see what he's going to do next. Who knows? By this time tomorrow, we might have this thing all wrapped up."

Otis smiled, "Yeah right."

CHAPTER 24

Back at his desk, Otis made quick work of filling out his report. He wanted to get back to his family and resume his Christmas celebration. Resisting the temptation to cut corners, he was making sure that his report would include everything that could have even a remote connection to the case. It was then that he recalled something about last night. "Hey, McCoy, I just remembered something. Did you notice those two guys at Eddie's Bar last night? The two in motorcycle jackets over against the wall near the door?"

"I think so. One had a front tooth missing and a little goatee and the other one had a tattoo on the back of his hand." McCoy was letting Otis know that the button for his practiced vigilance was always in the "on" position.

Otis looked across the desk. "Well, I was wondering whether they were just neighborhood lads or if they might have been on a mission."

"After you left, I asked Eddie about them and he said that he'd never seen them in his place before. They came in just about ten minutes before any of our guys showed up. I got a good memory for faces so I figured that I might come in a little early tomorrow and run through a few mug shots."

"Not gonna do it today?" asked Otis.

McCoy had stood up and started walking toward the locker room but now turned toward Otis, mimicked an evil smile and answered. "Like you, I got better things to do right now."

Within twenty minutes, Otis had finished all of the required paperwork and was ready to head for home. He stopped by the locker room to wash his hands before leaving and he encountered McCoy, his lower torso wrapped in a towel and still dripping from the shower. He was standing in front of a mirror, his face fully lathered and very carefully shaving with a disposable safety razor.

"I figured you for an electric razor dude," commented Otis as he dried his hands.

McCoy stopped shaving while he talked. "I don't think they do that good a job, do you? If I want a good shave, I always do it the old fashioned way."

"I guess," answered Otis. "One of the worst things about getting older though is that it takes a lot longer to shave. Not only do you have to work around all those wrinkles but you gotta shave in places that you didn't have to worry about when you were younger, like inside your ears and like that."

McCoy looked at Otis but didn't say anything.

Otis continued to prod him. "But then, brushing your teeth can be a whole lot easier. You just pop those babies out and drop em' in a glass of that bubbly stuff."

"Champagne?" asked McCoy

Otis shook his head. It was no use. McCoy wasn't going to give him the upper hand today. Finally, he asked, "Headed over to see Ruby? You've got to have some reason to get all cleaned up like this."

McCoy bobbed his head back and forth before he answered. "Yeah, but it's not what you think. We aren't going to be alone anywhere. Michael O'Conner called the bar last night to see what I was doing today and Ruby answered the phone and set up a get together for the three of us. So it looks like a friendly little Christmas dinner party. I don't really mind though. I'm not sure I'm ready for any more surprises."

Otis had a huge grin on his face. He was enjoying McCoy's embarrassment. "If you feel you need a chaperone, far be it from me to argue with you. After all, the thought of that hundred and ten pound woman wrestling you to the ground just makes me cringe."

Before McCoy could think of a response, Otis hurried out of the locker room and back to his desk. By the time McCoy got to the office, Otis was putting on his topcoat and getting ready to leave. He turned when McCoy entered the room and immediately stuck out his right hand. "Merry Christmas, big guy. I wish you the best of everything."

McCoy shook his hand and quietly said, "Thanks, Otis. The same for you and for your whole family." His smile was warm and genuine.

As he opened the door, Otis turned and asked. "I thought Michael was going up north to his place in the woods. Did he change his plans?"

"No," said McCoy, "he's still going. I think he's leaving three or four days after Christmas. He just wants to be up there for New Year's. If we get Billy locked up before then, maybe we can join him."

"Sounds cool," Replied Otis. He waved and was gone.

CHAPTER 25

Ruby's house was a modest two bedroom bungalow on Detroit's northeast side, only a few short blocks from McCoy's place. Her home seemed to radiate a lot more warmth than his, though, and McCoy could feel it the moment he walked in the door. "Must have something to do with that mystical woman's touch," he thought.

"Mister O'Conner is already here. He's in the back, in the TV room," Ruby took McCoy's jacket and hung it in the hall closet. McCoy couldn't help wondering when the last time was that his jacket had actually been on a hanger. It sometimes hung on a hook near his back door but more often, it could be found draped over the back of a dining room chair.

"It was really thoughtful of you to invite him," said McCoy, "He's all alone, you know. Has no family at all."

"I think that makes three of us," smiled Ruby. "My husband was killed in Vietnam. I was pregnant at the time but miscarried when I got the news. Thankfully, I wasn't too far along. Only a few weeks. I was an only child and my parents are gone now too. You don't have any family either, do you, Mister McCoy?"

"My parents are gone too. I had a younger brother but he died in a traffic accident when he was seventeen. I've got a slew of cousins but they're all still over in Ireland. My dad was the only one in his family to come to the States."

"Oh? That's interesting. Do you stay in touch with your Irish family?"

McCoy was relieved that the conversation had switched to living relatives. "About ten years or so ago, a bunch of the family came over. I was still a uniform cop back then. They were really impressed when I got all dressed up for work. You'd have thought I was Chief or something. I always promised them that I'd come and see them someday too. I even went and got a passport but I've never gone beyond that. I don't really know why either, because I'd really like to see Ireland."

"What's stopping you? I'll bet you don't really have a reason for not going, do you?" Ruby's tone was playful.

"One of these days." McCoy was following Ruby toward the back of the house where he was surprised to find a relatively spacious family room, obviously an addition to the original structure. "This room sure adds a lot to your place. Nice."

Michael was sitting on the edge of a large upholstered chair in stocking feet, totally engrossed in a football game. "Usually, these bowl games aren't much good, but this one's been a real dogfight right from the opening kickoff. These kids are playing hard. Must be a lot of pro scouts in the audience." Michael looked up and smiled.

"Hi, Mike. I didn't see your car outside," said McCoy, "What'd you do? Take a cab?"

"Naw. I parked in the driveway. Came in the side door."

Ruby excused herself and hurried off to the kitchen, leaving the two men alone to watch their game and talk about guy things. Fifteen minutes later, she returned to announce that dinner was ready. Michael jumped up and shut off the television and they all headed for the dining room. Ruby had prepared a beautiful meal of roast turkey with all of the traditional embellishments like stuffing and cranberry sauce. There was even a home made pumpkin pie visible on the kitchen counter.

As they all sat down to enjoy the feast, Ruby was the first one to break the silence. "So, Michael. Tell me about this place that you have up north. I've heard little bits and pieces around the bar and it sounds fascinating."

"I guess it is kinda interesting. The Army Corp of Engineers and the railroad built it back during the Second World War with a whole lot of government money. It was supposed to be a secret place so they hid it way back in the woods. They used it as a storage yard and repair facility. Its main purpose, though, was to keep the rails open during the winter so that the copper mines could ship their ore. After the mines closed, the railroad pulled out and just abandoned the place. It'd been vacant for over twenty years when my dad bought the property to use as hunting land. He didn't even know it was there. Nobody did. We found it the summer after dad closed the deal. It's a pretty big building.

They used to bring trains right inside to work on them and there was a staff of about twenty men who lived there."

"My goodness," commented Ruby, "if it's way back in the woods, what do you do for electricity and all that stuff?"

"That's easy," said Michael, "There's a big hydroelectric generator that runs off of the energy from the river. It works great and my buddy, Charlie is an electrical wizard and he keeps it running in tip top shape for me."

McCoy added, "It's definitely not an easy place to find or to get to. It gets snowed in pretty good for most of the winter. You can't drive a conventional vehicle in there for at least four or five months out of the year. The only ways in are snowmobile or, if you're really adventurous, you can take a rubber boat up the river from town. Oh, and Michael's got an airplane too."

Ruby seemed impressed. "Oh really? You fly too? You two are just full of surprises. It makes me wonder if I can keep up with you."

For the rest of the evening the conversation remained light and lively. McCoy purposely avoided any mention of the case that he was working on and Michael had enough social intelligence not to try to take the discussion in that direction.

Ruby was glad to see everybody enjoying themselves. It made her feel like a successful hostess but most of all, she was happy to have McCoy in her home, sharing her laughter and having Michael O'Conner there was exactly what she needed to remove any awkwardness that could easily have been there during this early encounter.

It was about nine-thirty when the party finally ended. They were standing at the front door when Michael said. "Hey. Just remembered I took off my shoes when I came in. They're sitting by the back door. My car's out there anyway, so I'll just let myself out." He headed toward the back door.

"No problem," said Ruby, "it was nice to get to know you."

Being alone with Ruby for the first time, McCoy took the opportunity to steal a little good-bye kiss. It wasn't much more than a teenager's first smooch but he figured that he'd made his point. Ruby hadn't resisted and she didn't embarrass him by pushing for more. She seemed quite satisfied. As McCoy walked out the front door, not another word was said but the message was clear in their parting smiles.

Michael heard McCoy's car start and then saw him pull away from the curb just as he was getting settled into his driver's seat. While he fumbled in his pocket for the keys, he heard another engine start and watched a van pull out from a spot a few doors away. The van still had not turned on its headlights as it slowed momentarily in front of Ruby's house. Michael could see two men inside and one of them appeared to be writing something. From his vantage point, backed in the driveway and in the shadow of Ruby's house, Michael was fairly sure that the guys in the van hadn't noticed him. He watched as they reached the corner and then turned in the same direction as McCoy.

Michael had the advantage of knowing where McCoy was headed so he decided to take a little shortcut and head him off. He raced a zigzag pattern through the residential streets until he got to the main street that he knew McCoy would be using. He pulled up to the stop sign and waited. It wasn't very long before McCoy's dark blue Bonneville passed in front of him. Four vehicles behind McCoy was a beat up Ford van. Under the bright streetlights, Michael could see that the occupants were wearing motorcycle jackets and it looked like one of them may have had a small beard. They were both looking straight ahead.

"Well, I guess I'd better find out," Michael said aloud as he dropped in behind the van. He didn't want to get too close so he only moved in tight for long enough to read the license plate number on the van. Then he dropped back a respectable distance while he wrote down the number. When McCoy turned onto his street, the van turned with him. Michael was unsure about what he should do at this point. It might not be anything more than a coincidence, but then, it might be an assassination attempt. He couldn't take that chance. He wheeled the big Tahoe around the corner and fell in behind the van once again. Straining against the seatbelt, he reached around his back into his waistband and slid the Glock model 36 out of its concealment holster and deposited the heavy .45 into the pocket of his jacket. To his surprise, Michael's hand was steady and calm. There was no panic in him. In the past year, Michael had learned to be aware of the danger but to focus on the task.

In the van a silhouette of the passenger was visible as he turned his head to look behind him and then say something to the driver and look back again. The movements were jerky and nervous. They were spooked now. Whatever their plans might have been, things had changed so they were adjusting. The van sped up and hurried past McCoy's house just as he was pulling into his driveway.

Michael turned in behind McCoy's car, noticing that McCoy's right hand held his pistol as he stood behind his car and intently watched the van disappear.

McCoy remained quiet, listening to the sound of the van as it grew fainter. Satisfied that it was not doubling back for another pass, he turned to Michael and asked. "Did either one of them have a beard? Got a plate number?"

"You knew they were following you. How?' It was as if Michael hadn't heard the question.

"I've been around a while, Mike." answered McCoy. "I scanned the street before I ever left Ruby's front porch. I spotted two heads in that van and so I kept an eye on it in the rear view. As soon as I got to the corner they pulled out from the curb with no headlights. I had 'em in sight all the way home. I saw you join in about six blocks back. I figured that you must've had an idea what was going on."

"Is it something to do with that homicide you're working on? I'm totally in the dark here. Are you going to fill me in?"

"C'mon inside. I'll tell you all about it. You did get the license number, right?"

Michael followed the big detective into his house. "Yeah, yeah. Of course I got it. I've been hanging around you for the last year or so, haven't I? I should have learned something by now."

McCoy took the slip of paper from Michael, walked over and picked up the telephone on the small desk in the living room. Next to the desk, a joyfully lit miniature plastic Christmas tree on top of the television set was the only evidence of holiday spirit. "Yeah, McCoy here. I know it's Christmas but I need you to run a plate for me." Michael could only hear one half of the conversation but he listened intently as McCoy read the license plate number into the phone and then waited, impatiently pacing back and forth as far as the phone cord would allow. "Okay, okay. Here's what I want you to do. Get some of the guys to roust him. I'm ninety-nine percent sure that he's following me in connection with a couple of homicides I'm working on. Yeah, yeah. I know. I am being careful. Just let this guy know that he ain't the only one out there with muscle. See if he's got a rap sheet will ya'? And call me back as soon as you find something out. Got it? Bye."

McCoy turned back to Michael, gestured for him to have a seat and disappeared into the kitchen. He returned carrying two beers, handed one to Michael and then sat back on the corner of the desk.

"Okay, where do I begin?" McCoy lowered his head and thought for a minute. "Otis and me have pulled a couple of homicides that have been real nowhere cases. There's been no real physical evidence, no clear motive, and no primary suspect in either case. Then, a couple of weeks ago, we find a connection between the two crimes. You remember that conversation that we had with your Indian buddy Charlie about that guy that he fought with in the bar?"

Michael took a swig of beer and nodded.

"Well that guy, this Billy Bones character. He's the connection. He runs an outlaw biker gang called Satan's Disciples and they're nothing but a bunch of gangbangers and drug dealers. We don't have any hard proof of anything but there's no doubt that he's involved up to his eyeballs. There was another homicide last night and I'm sure he's responsible for that one too. Anyway, this Billy guy is a real intimidator and me and Otis have been breathing down his neck. He must figure that he can scare us off or something. I kinda figure that those two in the van are a couple of his soldiers."

"Do you think that they were ready to make some sort of move when I showed up?" asked Michael.

McCoy shook his head and seemed about to say something when the telephone rang. "Hello, McCoy here." He pulled a pencil from his shirt pocket and scribbled something on a small notepad on the desk. "Yeah, Okay. Thanks."

McCoy picked up the notepad and turned to Michael. "The registered owner of the van is a Joey Winters. He's identified as a Disciple."

CHAPTER 26

There were a lot of things to talk over with Otis today. McCoy had been putting it together in his head all the way to work this morning. It looked like it was going to be one of those brain busting days when you would consume reams of note paper and dozens of pencils. He had stayed up half the night writing out questions and topics. There certainly wouldn't be any time available to talk to newspaper reporters, but there was one sitting at McCoy's desk when he walked into the office.

McCoy tried to appear nonchalant as he hung his topcoat on the clothes tree behind his desk. "Ah, Mister Gregory Price, star reporter. And what can we do for you this fine morning?"

"Tell me about your latest homicide. Otis here says that he can't divulge anything without talking to you first because you're the lead investigator."

Otis had an amused smile on his face as he watched McCoy try to mentally form an answer that wouldn't sound terribly insulting. Finally McCoy asked. "How'd you get wind of this anyway? We haven't sent out any releases."

"Anonymous tip line. And it is anonymous. I have absolutely no idea who called it in."

Otis laughed out loud. "I love it. You guys hide behind that 'source' clause all the time. How come we can't get that kind of protection?"

McCoy wasn't as cheerful as Otis. "Tell you what, Greg. I'll put together a report with all of the information that I can share and I'll fax it right to your office. I'll make sure that you get it before anybody else. Guaranteed."

Gregory Price had a reputation for rooting out stories but he was also acutely aware of the value of keeping the police on his side. He had seen the devastating consequences of alienating even low-level officers and the look on McCoy's face told him that he was dangerously close to that line. He dug a business card out of his wallet and handed it to McCoy, adding, "One of those cases, eh? You can trust me. I'll only release the details that you authorize. When you get everything ready, use the fax number on here. It goes right to my desk."

McCoy accepted the card in silence and Price left the office with no further discussion.

As soon as the reporter was out of earshot, Otis turned to McCoy and asked. "What was this crazy business last night all about? Being followed? You sure it wasn't just too much eggnog?

"It was real, all right. The guy's a Disciple."

Otis waved a sheaf of papers at McCoy. "Joey Winters. I got his stuff right here. He's another bad one. I've never come across him myself except for seeing him and that other guy at Eddie's Bar on Christmas Eve, but from the looks of this ..." He waved the papers again. McCoy reached over the desk and took the file from Otis.

"Assault. Assault. Assault with intent. Sounds like he's a guy who likes action. Any weapons charges in here? Ah, there it is. Attempted carrying. He's done some hard time too. Oh well. It's good to know what you're dealing with."

Otis handed McCoy another page. "Here's a list of his known associates and Billy Bones isn't on there. I figure that it must mean that it's a pretty confidential relationship. Sorta like Billy's secret weapon. You know, his ace in the hole. We've had him identified as a Disciple for around five years."

"Y'know, that's another thing that's been puzzling me," said McCoy. "We've been to that clubhouse close to a half dozen times so far and there's never been any bikers hanging around. I wonder how many members he's got in that gang and where the hell they all are."

"I've chased them around for a while," commented Otis. "Last reports I saw, said there was about fifty known members and associates but we know that there are more than that. For example, we never knew anything about Monica Wilson and she said that she worked for him less than a year ago."

McCoy dropped Joey Winter's file on the desk. "You ever put together a picture of the gang? Who they are and what role they play? There's got to be some sort of hierarchy, some kind of a chain of command."

Otis just shook his head. "If there is anything like that, they're keeping it a big secret. As far as I know. There's Billy Bones, and the next layer is invisible. That's one of the reasons we've never been able to get to him. Some of the guys in the Disciples have never even met Billy."

"McCoy?" It was a young officer that McCoy remembered seeing over at forensics. He held an envelope in his right hand, waving it toward McCoy and then toward Otis and then back again. McCoy raised his hand and the young officer extended his arm to hand McCoy the envelope. "Forensic report. They told me to make sure that you got this."

"Thank you," said McCoy as he took the envelope. "Thank you very much." He sat down in his chair and read for several minutes before speaking. Eventually, he looked across at Otis and said. "They gave us something. Finally gave us something. It looks like something good too. On Mace's body. Unidentified human hair samples in his watchband. Something we can work with. All we gotta do now is get some comparison specimens from Billy. We might try to find this Joey Winters guy while we're at it."

"Seems like we're going to that damned clubhouse just about every day," remarked Otis. "We're going to start losing our effect. We gotta come up with something more original. I vote for going after Joey first. That'll give us some time to bounce around a few ideas on how we want to handle Billy. It might serve a dual purpose too. Billy will probably begin to wonder what we're waiting for. Might make him nervous. He'll be wondering why he's not seeing anything in the papers too. He must have called that anonymous tip line right after we left him on Christmas Day. That reporter was here at the precinct at seven o'clock this morning and he came right to our desks. If we put him off until after noon or so, it'll be too late for him to get anything in today's edition. I want to do everything that we can think of to unhinge Billy. Oh yeah, I even woke up a judge this morning and got him to sign a search warrant for the Disciples' clubhouse, just in case."

"Sounds like a plan to me," said McCoy. "Got any ideas on how to find this Joey Winters character? I'd sorta like to confront him in person. We've got a lot to talk about."

Otis leaned over to read the Joey Winters file. "I've got an address in a trailer park just north of Eight Mile Road. I suppose that's just as good a place as any to start."

The placard in front of the mobile home court said *Tranquil Estates*. McCoy pointed to the sign as they entered the driveway. "You gotta wonder who dreams up these names. Here this place sits with a factory on one side, used car lot on the other and a redneck bar across the street and they call it 'tranquil'. I wonder if it was one of the same characters who gets paid to think up names for cemeteries." He glanced at his watch. It was a little bit past nine o'clock. McCoy doubted that Joey Winters would be awake this early.

Otis was thinking out loud. "Let's see here. Number ninety-five, ninety-seven, ninety-nine. There it is, number ninety nine." There were two vehicles parked in the spots alotted to number ninety-nine. One of them was a badly dented Ford van and the other was a highly polished, bright red Mercedes S-500 sedan. From his days in traffic, Otis knew that it was not a standard Mercedes color, obviously a custom paint job. He drove past Joey Winter's modular home as McCoy scribbled down the license plate number of the Mercedes. Otis continued another five hundred feet to where the road dead ended at a trash dumpster, made a U-turn and waited there while McCoy called in the number for a trace.

The outdated radio in their unmarked car always seemed to insist on delivering enough static to make the messages extremely difficult to understand but the old girl was on her best behavior this morning and the information came through crisp and clear. "Registered to a Joseph Winters at Ninety-nine Serenity Drive, Tranquil Estates, in Harper Park."

"Hah, he owns both of 'em," remarked Otis. "I guess he has one for work and one for pleasure."

"Yeah," McCoy added, "and he parks his seventy-five thousand dollar car next to his ten thousand dollar house."

CHAPTER 27

Joey's eyes were not focusing very well this morning and the pounding on his front door was beginning to give him a headache. He stumbled his way from the bedroom pulling his jeans on as he negotiated the narrow pathway through the littered living room. The pounding wouldn't stop. For a moment, Joey froze and thought about returning to his bedroom to retrieve the nine millimeter Baretta hidden under his mattress. A quick glance out the window, though and he recognized the Black Ford parked out front as a police car. "What the hell do they want?" he muttered and fumbled with the deadbolt. The pounding on the other side stopped as soon as he began to open the door.

For a few moments, they just stood looking at one another, McCoy and Joey in a classic challenge game. Who would blink first?

It was Joey who broke the silence. "Yeah? What do you want with me?"

McCoy was ready for an opening like that. "I was going to ask you the same question last night but you didn't hang around long enough."

"Huh? What are you talking about? Whatta you guys want anyway?" It was the first time that Joey acknowledged Otis's presence. He looked back and forth at both detectives. "You gonna bust me? Get it on. I ain't done nothing and you can't prove nothing. I'll be out in under an hour."

Otis smiled at him. "Now don't go getting all excited, tough guy. We just want to talk and I'm sure that you'd rather do it here than in downtown Detroit."

"Then talk, damn it. I don't have time for this shit."

McCoy moved in close. "You'd better understand who's making the rules here, pal. You've got all the time I need and you'd better have some answers I like too. Cause if you don't, we just might do this every morning. Got it?" McCoy had his finger within an inch of Joey's nose.

Joey maintained eye contact to show his defiance but his tone mellowed somewhat. "Start askin', it's your quarter."

"First of all," McCoy began, "Who was the other guy with you last night and two nights ago when you guys were at Eddie's Bar?"

"I don't know the guy's name, they just call him Gizmoe. He's just someone to talk to, that's all. Don't even know where he lives. I either run into him at the bar or sometimes he comes by here. That's all I know."

McCoy gave an exasperated sigh, ran his fingers through his hair and then looked back at Joey. "Why were you following me last night? Straight answer. No bullshit."

Joey shifted his weight and stuffed his hands in his pockets. "I got absolutely no idea what you're talking about." The smirk on his face sent a message of contempt.

With surprising quickness McCoy shot his arm out and grabbed Joey by the hair and dragged him out the doorway, bumping Otis out of the way. He flung Joey down the stairs of the short porch.

Joey rolled on snow covered asphalt but quickly sprung to his feet and walked directly back toward McCoy holding both hands, clenched fists straight out in front of him. "Go ahead. Put the cuffs on. Take me in. You think you got something? Arrest me. Damn it."

Otis had moved over to stand beside McCoy and both cops looked at Joey for a minute, then brushed past him and got back into their cruiser without another word. As they drove out of the trailer park, Otis looked over at McCoy and with a little laugh he said, "You sure didn't show much Christmas spirit back there."

"Christmas was yesterday," answered McCoy. "I got another three hundred and sixty-four days before I gotta be nice to people again."

Otis moved the cruiser out into traffic. "Did you get it?"

McCoy held out his open hand displaying at least a dozen of Joeys hairs. "A whole handful."

Otis laughed. "What's next? Billy's?"

"Billy's," said McCoy, "and then lunch, and why don't we have something decent for a change."

"No problem," answered Otis. "It's easy. Just tell 'em to super-size it."

Billy wasn't at the clubhouse, but someone else was. She was a mousy, undernourished looking little blonde in tight jeans and a very tight black tee-shirt with a bright green marijuana pedicel on the front. In spite of her provocative clothes, McCoy didn't find her sexy or appealing in any way. In his eyes, she was just another crackhead.

"Billy here?" McCoy had his head in the door and was looking around the big empty room.

"Naw. Who're youse guys anyway?" She sounded dull witted and the squeaky voice matched her scrawny physique.

"Police. I'm Detective McCoy and this is Detective Springfield. May we come in?' McCoy held out his identification badge for her to examine, although he was unsure if she could read.

She stepped aside. "I guess."

McCoy pulled the notebook from his pocket and occupied the young woman's attention with questions. He was gathering basic information like her name, address, and her connection with the Disciples.

Otis wandered slowly over to the bar where Billy's hairbrush was still laying since he set it down yesterday. Otis casually dropped the brush into the pocket of his sport coat and then walked back near the front door to join McCoy and the blonde.

"No, Miss, there's no emergency. We were just following up to see if Mister Bones had any information for us." McCoy fished a business card out of his wallet and handed it to her. "If you would, please just let him know that we stopped by."

"Sure." The mousy little blonde had not uttered one complete sentence in all the time that the Detectives were there.

Otis pulled the door shut behind him as he left. The sidewalk in front of the clubhouse had not been shoveled. There was a narrow trampled path through the snow out to the street. The two cops walked single file back to the car.

"She can't be anything important," observed Otis, "too dumb."

"You got that right," said McCoy. "She wasn't even sure of the name of the motorcycle club. Got her name right here." He fumbled with his notebook. "Shirley Klein. Lives on the west side out near Snyder Road. Says she just goes to the clubhoue to hang out sometimes."

"Let's grab some lunch." Otis set a course for his favorite Italian Restaurant on Six Mile Road.

Otis cringed when he heard McCoy order the spaghetti. History indicated that there would be sauce all over McCoy's shirt and tie by the time they left the restaurant. It was a pleasant lunch. They agreed that it had been a productive morning. Once back at the precinct, they would label the hair samples and submit them to the guys upstairs in forensics and then the afternoon would be free to catch up on all of the paperwork. The rest of their lunch break was spent discussing what sort of statement to come up with for Gregory Price, the newspaper reporter.

On the way out of the restaurant, Otis suddenly grabbed McCoy and spun him around to have a good look at him. "Hey. No spaghetti sauce on the shirt. No breadstick crumbs sticking to your tie. Nothing. That Ruby gal must have been teaching you some table manners."

CHAPTER 28

McCoy had just finished clearing the top of his desk and was getting ready to call it a day, when he got a phone call from Monica. "Officer McCoy? I'm on pins and needles waiting for something to happen. It's just a few days until Billy's deadline and I'm telling you that he's not bluffing. If I don't give him the money he's demanding, he will be coming after us and I guarantee that he will kill someone. I'm so afraid. Maybe I should just pay him. It would take every penny I've got but at least my friends would have a chance. Please. I don't know what to do." She was sobbing as her voice drifted off.

Otis had stood up to leave but McCoy motioned for him to sit back down. "Miss Wilson? Is it okay if I put you on the speaker phone so that my partner can help out with this discussion?"

She was still crying. "I, I suppose."

"Okay, we're both here now," began McCoy. "We anticipate that we will have the evidence that we need for an arrest warrant before noon tomorrow. We've already gathered the physical evidence and our lab is verifying it for us right now. We should have our answer tomorrow morning. Then it's just a matter of picking him up."

Monica seemed a little reassured. "How long will all of that take? Isn't there a lot of red tape involved in getting warrants?"

Otis answered her. "Not in cases where physical endangerment may be imminent. If necessary, the prosecutor's office will intercede on our behalf. Believe me, Miss Wilson, everybody at City Hall wants this guy off the street. We will get express service."

"I just wish I could be sure."

"You just go ahead with your plans for New Year's Eve," said McCoy. "I understand that you're playing at a casino up north. Is that right?"

Monica managed a shallow laugh. "Yeah. *Way* up north. We booked this one early last fall before our first video was shown. We were working a lot cheaper back then. These guys that own the casino got quite a bargain, but we didn't try to wiggle out of it. Bud insisted that it would look much better for the band if we honor all of our commitments, even on New Year's when we could have been playing New York."

"Our intention is to have Billy Bones behind bars within twenty-four hours, Miss Wilson. You should be able to enjoy your holiday weekend, worry free."

Monica sighed. "I needed to know that you were making some progress. I feel a little better now but I know that I'll feel a lot better once I'm sure that he's locked up. We're leaving for up north tomorrow morning. Bud wants the band to get away from Detroit and get our minds off of this thing. The band members are all inviting their families along but I don't think any of them are interested."

"Well, you just have fun and leave Billy to me. I've got your bandleaders cell phone number and I'll call him right away if there are any new developments. If you don't hear from me, you'll know that everything is going according to plan."

"If you say so, Mister McCoy. I guess it's…Oh well, good bye." Monica hung up without waiting for McCoy to reply.

The two detectives were still staring at one another when the phone rang again. This time it was Michael O'Conner. "Hey McCoy. It's me, Mike. I'm at Eddie's bar. Why don't you and Otis join me for dinner down here. I'm buyin'. It's one of my last couple of nights in Detroit and since you two guys can't make it up to my place to celebrate New Year's, I thought we could have our own little party tonight. We can break it up early so you can get home at a reasonable time. I know it's a school night. Whadda ya' say?"

Otis shrugged and McCoy replied, "Yeah, okay. We'll be there."

When McCoy and Otis walked into Eddie's Bar, they found Michael seated at the same table that they always used. He had his checkbook open on the table and a small pocket calculator sitting next to it. He was busy punching in numbers and then scribbling in the checkbook.

"Gonna have enough left over for dinner?" asked Otis "I'm mighty hungry tonight."

Michael looked up and grinned. "I just got my check from the State Corrections Department for the background checks that I did for them. I deposited it on the way over here so now I've gotta balance everything. They paid exactly what I invoiced. Maybe I should have asked for more."

"I should have such problems," said McCoy. "I usually put my paycheck in the bank and it brings my checking account all the way up to zero." There were three menus on the table. McCoy picked one up as he slid into the chair and turned to the last page where the dinners were listed. He silently wondered why the menus were already waiting for them on the table. Ruby was nowhere in sight either. McCoy assumed that she must be busy in the kitchen.

"So how's the case going?" asked Michael. "Think there's any chance you guys can wrap it up in time to get away for New Year's?"

Otis shook his head. "It would be a real stretch, Mike. Things are actually moving along pretty good but even if we make an arrest tomorrow, we'd still have to get ready for the arraignment, bail hearing, all that kind of thing. We'll probably be pretty tied up for another week, ten days, or thereabouts."

McCoy looked up from his menu. "Besides, maybe I got plans for New Year's. I got a social life too, ya' know."

Eddie, the bar owner made his way over to the table where the trio was sitting and addressed McCoy, "Hey, McCoy. What'd ya' do with Ruby?"

"Hell, I don't know where she is. I figured she'd be here. She's supposed to work tonight, right?"

"Absolutely," answered Eddie. "She shoulda been here over an hour ago. Didn't call. Nothin'. I tried calling her place and there's no answer. I figured maybe she was with you."

McCoy had a concerned look on his face. "Lemme use your phone, eh?"

"Sure thing," answered Eddie and he led McCoy to the telephone behind the bar.

McCoy dialed and the precinct clerk answered the other end of the line. "Yeah. Hey, this is McCoy in homicide. If you got any units in the area, can you have 'em check the welfare of a resident at ..." he dug his green notebook out of his coat pocket and read Ruby's address into the telephone. "Yeah, that's right. And when you get their response, give me a call at this number." McCoy recited the number of Eddie's Bar. "Okay. Tell 'em to hurry, will you? Thanks. Bye."

McCoy returned to the table, still looking worried. As he sat down, he said. "I don't know what to think."

Otis and Michael both ordered the roast beef sandwich special. McCoy declined, saying he was still too stuffed from lunch but he wasn't fooling anybody. He was worried and it was written all over his face.

When the telephone finally rang, McCoy bounded from his seat and was at the bar in three giant strides.

The barmaid was already holding the receiver out for McCoy to snatch it out of her hand. He recognized the voice on the other end as Captain Bice. When a Captain returns your call, it's never good news. McCoy closed his eyes and braced himself for the worst. "McCoy. Go ahead."

Captain Bice used his most soothing voice. "First of all, we have her and she's going to be all right. A few scrapes and bruises, that's it. No other physical concerns at all." Captain Bice was answering the question that he knew McCoy wouldn't want to ask. "We've got her down at Receiving Hospital. She's hysterical. She's too upset to talk coherently. I don't know what she's been through but whatever it was must have been terrifying. The doctor says that they're probably going to have to sedate her. Why don't you take a ride back over here and I'll explain it all to you."

McCoy gently hung up the telephone and walked out the door without saying a word to anyone, including Michael and Otis.

By the time McCoy got back to the precinct, the rage was beginning to rise within him. He was almost completely sure that this was Billy's doing. The outside chance that it might have been Joey Winters was the only thing that kept McCoy from driving directly to the Disciples' clubhouse and storming through the front door with his forty caliber in his hand and his finger on the trigger.

The Captain could almost read McCoy's thoughts. He knew that he needed to get the detective back in control of himself and thinking logically. A man with McCoy's capabilities would be extremely dangerous on an emotional rampage. "C'mon in and have a seat, McCoy. I'll tell you the whole story. Want a coffee or anything?' McCoy shook his head but walked over to the seat directly in front of Captain Bice's desk and sat down. He didn't say anything. He waited for the Captain to speak.

Captain Bice began slowly, wanting to make absolutely sure that there were no details omitted. The last thing he wanted was to compromise the bond of trust that McCoy shared with him. "You must have called the station to ask for someone to look in on your friend. When they got to her house, they found her little Volkswagon Beetle sitting in the driveway, running. There was nobody around anywhere and the front door to her house was slightly open. Our guys went inside and had a quick look around the place and found everything to be neat and orderly. It looked pretty undisturbed. The car doors were locked and even though it was running, there was no ignition key in it, That means it's got one of those remote starter deals where you can start it from in your house. We figure that she opened her front door to aim her remote at the car to start it and that's when somebody grabbed her right off of her front porch.

Our people were still on the scene when the call came in. A couple on their way to the Cineplex found a woman lying on the shoulder of Interstate 96, gagged and blindfolded with her hands tied behind her. An EMS unit was dispatched and we had a car there to meet them. The couple who found her thought that they had noticed a van pulling away from the shoulder when they were still quite a ways back, but they weren't really paying much attention. I would say that she was probably shoved out the side door while the van was standing still. If it'd been moving, she'd have probably been hurt pretty bad but her injuries are really minor."

McCoy now seemed in control as he asked, "Any idea what happened to cause the hysteria?"

"I think it was something she saw. Actually it was more likely something that she was forced to watch. When the medical technicians first pulled the gag out of her mouth, they said that she was screaming something like, 'You gotta stop them. They're killing her.' or something like that. She hasn't made any sense at all since. The doctor says that she might improve after ten or twelve hours sleep. Once they got her into the hospital, they gave her a shot to knock her out. It'll probably be noon tomorrow before she wakes up enough to talk. We'll have some therapists there when she comes to. We're going to do everything we possibly can."

"I know you will," said McCoy, "and you know that I appreciate everything. If you don't need me anymore, I think I'll wander over to the hospital."

Captain Bice stood up and McCoy rose along with him. They shook hands across the desk and McCoy left the office heading directly for Receiving Hospital.

Ruby looked terribly small and vulnerable lying in a deep sleep in the hospital bed. McCoy pulled a chair up to the bedside so that he could reach out and hold her hand. He looked at her fragile features for a long moment and then he said a prayer. With her hand safely in his, he leaned forward and laid his head on the mattress. As the cyclone that had ruled his brain for these past few hours began to subside, he became weary and eventually drifted off to sleep. For now, at least, they were both at peace with the world.

CHAPTER 29

McCoy wasn't sure if the voices were genuine or if it was just a dream. He decided that they must be real when he heard the unusually irritating giggle that one of them emitted. He opened his eyes slowly, one at a time in case he needed to close them in a hurry at the sight of whoever it was with the voice of a screech owl. He gazed at Ruby for a minute. She was still sleeping soundly. It looked like she hadn't moved at all during the night. McCoy was relieved to see her breathing relaxed and regular. He slowly raised his head and looked around the drab, dull green room. A young nurse in a very starched uniform appeared to be changing the plastic pouch for Ruby's intravenous device. He heard himself ask, "Whatta ya' doin'?"

"Oh," The nurse jerked around to look at McCoy. "You startled me. I thought you were asleep. I'm just trying to keep your friend here stable and relaxed until the doctor can be with her. Those are my orders."

McCoy fought back a yawn. "When will that be?"

The nurse studied her watch as she walked around the end of the bed. "Well, let's see. It's six-fifteen now and he's supposed to be here at nine according to the schedule I looked at. Almost three hours from now, I guess."

"And she'll be asleep all that time?" asked McCoy.

The nurse was standing by the door now, anxious to be on her way." Yes. Asleep." And then she was gone.

McCoy decided that he had enough time to run home, shave, shower and climb into some fresh clothes and be back here when Ruby woke up.

All the way home he was making mental notes; who to call, what he would need to bring back with him. Should he stay with Ruby all day? If she's still in a state of terror, maybe the doctors will keep her sedated. The last memo that he tucked away in his mind was to break down and buy a cellular telephone. He sure wished that he had one this morning. Perhaps they weren't just a novelty after all.

A hot shower and a giant size mug of instant coffee helped McCoy shake off the stiffness that comes along with a night's sleep where half of your body is sitting in a wooden chair and the other half is stretched across a mattress. He had made good time getting home because traffic was very light due to the holiday season. There would be ample time to stop in at the precinct and brief Otis on his plans. It was looking like it might turn into a very busy day.

Otis was at his desk going over the reports that he and McCoy had written in the last few days. He didn't look up as McCoy approached. There was an open box of donuts on the corner of his desk. "Go ahead. Help yourself. You buy next time"

"I'll be spending some time over at the hospital this morning," commented McCoy as he extracted a chocolate frosted cruller from the box.

Otis nodded. "Yeah, well don't get any ideas about tucking that box under your arm when you get ready to head over there. Tell the nurses to buy their own donuts. I'm gonna hang around here a little while and see how the forensic guys are making out with those hair samples."

McCoy turned in the direction of some new voices in the office. Captain Bice rounded the corner from the hallway accompanied by a friendly looking middle-aged woman in a soft brown business suit that complimented her golden blonde hair. She had an athletic and confident gait, a tall handsome woman who smiled and extended her hand as soon as she saw McCoy and then walked around the desk to shake Otis's hand.

"Hello, I'm Linda. You two must Detectives McCoy and Springfield. I feel like I already know both of you. Captain Bice has been filling me in all morning and I must say that I'm impressed with all he's told me."

Captain Bice stepped forward. "Miss Crawford is probably the best therapist in the city. We call on her when we need to get a statement or facts from severely traumatized victims. She works with a lot of children who have witnessed domestic assaults and on the really brutal rape cases. Her track record speaks for itself. I figured that she might be just the person to help you, McCoy."

Linda Crawford looked McCoy in the eye. "I understand that the victim is a friend of yours and we don't yet know what has caused her hysteria. Is that right?"

McCoy glanced at his watch. "That's about it. Right now, they're keeping her knocked out with some sort of drug. The doctor is supposed to be there in about a half hour and then bring her back. Hopefully, she'll be calmed down enough to make some sense. I want to be there when she wakes up."

Linda smiled. "Mind if I ride over there with you? You won't need to worry about chauffeuring me around all day. I can just call here when I'm done and they'll send a car for me."

Captain Bice nodded his approval and McCoy turned to Otis. "You gonna handle whatever comes up on the evidence?"

"Sure thing. If we get anything, I'll call you over at the hospital right after I get in touch with the prosecutor's office to request a warrant."

"Looks like you guys are all set," said Captain Bice. "You're in charge from here on out." The captain waved to the trio and disappeared around the corner.

Linda Crawford set a brisk pace as she walked with McCoy down the hall and out the door and across the street to the City garage. She didn't speak again until they were both in the car. "Is this lady someone special in your life?" she asked.

McCoy squirmed a little before he answered. "I don't think it's quite to that point yet. We're just now getting to know one another. Maybe someday."

Linda smiled knowingly. "Don't be concerned, I will be very gentle with her. I know what to do. Whatever happens, I'll try to make sure that you get all the information that you need."

McCoy didn't answer right away. He didn't really know how to answer. Finally, just barely above a whisper, he said. "Thank you."

Ruby had been moved into a private room. When McCoy got back to the hospital, he was told that he would be able to see her only after the doctor had finished. That didn't sit well with the detective. He'd wanted to talk to the doctor before Ruby was awakened and now he had no choice but to stand by and wait.

His constant pacing back and forth was a distraction for the nurse's station.

Linda rose from her seat against the wall and walked over to speak with the head nurse. McCoy watched as the nurse dialed the telephone and spoke into the receiver. As soon as she hung up, she came out from behind the desk and motioned for Linda to follow her. The nurse knocked gently on the third door they came to and it opened slightly but from where he was standing, McCoy couldn't see who was inside. Linda took what looked like a laminated ID card out of her purse and held it up to the partially open door. Then she turned to look at McCoy, smiled and winked and then entered the room closing the door behind her.

McCoy was waiting at the desk when the head nurse returned. "What was that all about? How did she get in there?"

The head nurse replied in a haughty manner, "That woman is a licensed therapist. She belongs in there and she is needed in there. The doctor welcomes her assistance." The two other nurses at the desk stared at the head nurse as she was speaking and when she finished, their attention quickly turned to McCoy to watch his reaction.

McCoy started to answer but then thought better of it and went back across the hallway to resume his pacing. At least Miss Crawford was in there with Ruby; McCoy had developed an almost immediate trust for the therapist. She was both personable and professional. Not the least bit intimidating. Ruby will like her too, concluded McCoy. The thought served to comfort him and free his mind enough to turn his attention back to dealing with Billy Bones and protecting Monica Wilson and the rest of the band.

This time, he was much more composed as he approached the nurse's station. "Excuse me. Is there a telephone that I can use for a little while? Official police business."

The head nurse still didn't smile. She wrote a few numbers on a sheet of paper and before she handed it to McCoy, she used it to point down the hallway. "You can use that one over there on the wall. Punch in these numbers to get an outside line."

McCoy took the slip of paper and didn't bother to thank her. He turned and walked over to the phone.

"Hello, Otis? Anything from forensics yet? It's after ten."

Otis sounded very sober on the other end of the line. "They said it would be around noon, maybe one o'clock before they'd have any answers. Something else came up though. I got a call from that bandleader and he says that there was a strange van with a couple of guys in it parked down the street most of last night. I contacted his local PD and asked them to have a look. It was still parked there when the black and white pulled up. They checked 'em out, and it seems that the van was registered to our buddy, Joey Winters. This 'Gizmoe' character was with him too. His name's Tom Sheridan. From what I know about him, he ain't much. He's a follower. Not very smart either."

McCoy tried to respond quietly, "Son of a bitch." All three nurses thrust condemnatory glances his way simultaneously.

Down the hallway, the door to Ruby's room suddenly opened and a nurse and an older man in hospital scrubs walked out. He's too old to be an orderly, thought McCoy. He must be the doctor. McCoy spoke quickly into the phone. "Hey look, Otis. I gotta run. Call me as soon as you hear anything, eh? Bye."

McCoy intercepted the doctor before he got to the nurse's station. With his identification card held in front of him, he asked, "How does it look, Doctor? Is she okay? I'm the investigating officer."

The doctor stopped and put his hand on McCoy's shoulder. He was one of those doctors whose face radiated character, a man who commanded respect and trust. "She's better than I expected. Miss Crawford is in with her now and they requested that they be left alone, so I would ask you to respect that. I know Miss Crawford from working with her before. There is no one more capable. Trust me."

McCoy's reaction surprised the doctor. "You got it, Doc. She can take all day if she wants. The important thing is that Ruby doesn't have to suffer any more." A huge weight had just been lifted from McCoy's shoulders.

CHAPTER 30

Linda Crawford zipped up the cosmetic bag and laid it next to her purse on the table beside Ruby's bed. There was no need to tell Ruby that the innocent looking little bag held a miniature tape recorder that would be transcribing their conversation. Adding another distraction would only complicate an already emotional situation.

"Detective McCoy drove me over here this morning," said Linda, "He's very concerned about you."

Ruby's hands went right to her hair and she glanced around the room in search of a mirror. "Oh, you can't let him see me like this. I must be a sight."

Linda chuckled. "Don't worry. I know exactly how you feel. I won't let him in until you're presentable." The smile faded only slightly as Linda reached over to take Ruby's hand. "You know that we have to talk about some unpleasant things, don't you? Whatever happened to you could easily happen again. You got away with only some really minor injuries. The next girl may not be so lucky. If we stand any chance of catching whoever did this, we're going to need every bit of information that you can provide. It's going to be hard. I know that. But you can make a difference."

Ruby closed her eyes for a moment, still a little unsteady from the medication. "I know. I knew it last night but I must have been in shock or something. I couldn't talk, couldn't pull myself together. I don't like thinking about it but I know it's got to be done. We might as well get it over with."

Linda breathed a sigh of relief. She had pegged Ruby as a strong woman who would do the right thing when it was laid in front of her in a matter-of-fact illustration. "What I'd like you to do," began Linda, "is to tell me the whole and complete story from beginning to end from the very first moment that you knew something was wrong."

Ruby propped herself up on a stack of pillows and reached over to the bedside table to retrieve a can of Vernor's Ginger Ale with a straw sticking out of the opening. She took a long sip of the soft drink and then began. "I didn't have to be to work until the afternoon but I had a lot of errands to run so I was trying to get an early start. It wasn't quite noon yet and I was just going to poke my head out the door and start my car with my remote starter. You know how they work?"

Linda nodded.

"Okay. Well, as soon as I stepped out on my front porch, somebody grabbed me from behind and pulled this really smelly cloth bag over my head. They must have been waiting right on my porch. There was nothing I could do. One of them picked me up, right off my feet and threw me into some kind of vehicle. I'm pretty sure it was a van. Anyway, we started moving but one of the guys stayed with me and tied my hands behind my back. I was sure that they were taking me somewhere to…who knows where? I was too scared to think at first, but then I realized that they probably weren't planning to kill me because they went to all the trouble of making sure I couldn't see who they were. Neither one of them said a word the whole time."

Ruby took another sip of her Ginger Ale. "It seemed like we drove for a long time, maybe a half hour or more and then the van stopped. Whoever the guy was, he must be pretty strong because he just lifted me up and carried me into some kind of building and then down some steps. He sat me down in a chair, tied my arms and legs to the chair so I couldn't hardly move and then they left me there for a long time. I'm gonna guess at least two – three hours. All kinds of horrible thoughts kept running through my head. I was getting sick from the smell of the bag that they had over my head. I cried for a while but then I just plain ran out of tears. I might have even dozed off once or twice. I wondered if they were ever coming back. And then…and then…"

She stopped talking for a moment and pulled a tissue from the box next to the bed. She wiped her eyes and then took several deep breaths. The hard part was coming up.

"Then I heard this voice. It was a woman's voice. She seemed happy, you know, giggling all the time. She was coming down the stairs but I knew that she wasn't alone because I could hear lots of footsteps, nobody else was talking though. She must've seen me because I heard her gasp a little bit. And then she asked what was going on. Nobody answered but then somebody came over to me and took that smelly bag off of my head. At first, I couldn't see anything. You know, bein' in the dark like that, your eyes gotta get used to the light. When I could finally focus, there were three guys, all wearing ski masks and sunglasses. They all had long sleeves on and were wearing gloves too. The girl didn't have her face covered at all. She was wearing jeans and a black tee-shirt with, I think it was a marijuana leaf on the front. She was all smiles and happy like everything was some kind of big game."

Ruby stopped again to catch her breath.

"Then one of the guys grabbed her and pinned her arms back while one of the other guys stuffed a big old rag in her mouth. They tied her to a post directly in front of where they had me sitting. She still thought that they were just playing around because she was still smiling. That's when it started happening. The biggest guy stepped up in front of her and punched her right in the face. He really hit her hard, too; her nose started bleeding right away. He hit her again about three or four times. And then the other two joined in, taking turns. First one and then the other. They just kept punching her and punching her. I couldn't watch any more. I just closed my eyes. That poor girl stayed conscious for a long time too. I could hear her trying to scream through that rag they had in her mouth but she couldn't make much of a sound. Finally it became quiet and when I looked up, she was just sort of hanging there from the ropes they had wrapped all around her. I couldn't even see her eyes anymore. They were completely swollen shut".

When Ruby stopped this time, the tears flowed freely. Linda let her cry until she had pulled herself together enough to continue.

"One of those guys walked directly over to me and I was sure that I was in for the same kind of brutal beating but he just walked around behind me and grabbed me by the head and held me facing straight forward so that I couldn't look away. And then one of the other two went around behind that poor girl in front of me. He stood directly behind the post that she was tied to and reached one hand each side and grabbed her by the hair. He pulled her head up tight against the post. She was out cold and didn't know what was happening. And then the biggest guy picked up this great big sledgehammer. He grabbed it with both hands and swung it with all of his might right straight into her face. The sound. Oh my God, that sound. Why did he have to do that?"

Ruby fell back into tears for several minutes. Linda was even having trouble maintaining her own composure. She got up from her chair and walked over to look out the window.

Finally Linda asked. "There were never any words spoken by any of these men and you never saw anything that you could identify? A shock of hair? Their eyes? Anything?"

Ruby dried her eyes again and then said. "There might have been something. I'm not a hundred percent sure but when that big guy picked up the sledgehammer and started to swing it, he had his back to me. The movement seemed to cause the ski mask to shift a little bit and it looked like he might have had a tattoo on his neck. I don't know what it was supposed to be, but it reminded me of a rat. There was nothing else. I only caught a glimpse of it."

With the worst of her ordeal behind her, Ruby explained how the guy who had been holding her head, pulled two towels from the waistband of his jeans crammed one of them into her mouth and secured it there with a wrap of duct tape and used the other one to blindfold her. They cut her loose from the chair but left her hands tied behind her. One of them tried to stand her up and make her walk, but her ankles had been tied so long that she had lost all the feeling in her feet and she couldn't stand. Somebody then had picked her up, carried her up the stairs, and then outside into the van again. She remembered riding for what seemed to be fifteen minutes or so and then the van pulled to a stop. She sensed a rush of cold air as the van door opened and was then aware of being pushed across the metal floor until she suddenly went over the side. It hurt when she hit the ground, landing on her side, but she knew then that it was almost over. When she heard the van drive away, she finally allowed herself to cry hysterically.

Linda Crawford walked over and sat on the bed next to Ruby. She took both of Ruby's trembling hands, looked into her eyes and said. "Ruby, you are one of the bravest women I have ever met. I am so, so proud of you. What you have done here today is more than anybody ever expected. Now get some rest and do the best you can to get it behind you and move on. Somehow, I just know that you'll be all right." Linda rose to her feet and without speaking again she leisurely gathered her belongings from Ruby's bedside table and turned to leave. As she reached the door, she glanced back to see that Ruby, emotionally exhausted had mercifully dropped off into a peaceful looking sleep.

CHAPTER 31

Linda Crawford found McCoy in the hallway with the telephone receiver glued to his ear. He was talking in very muted tones and using only partial sentences and one word answers, jotting notes in his little book and doing the best he could to carry on a private conversation in a busy public hallway. They made eye contact but McCoy's expression didn't change. Linda stopped and kept her distance until he finished and hung up the telephone.

McCoy stuffed his notebook into his shirt pocket as he walked over to where Linda was standing. "Everything go all right? Should I go in and see her now?"

Linda shook her head. "That lady has been through a pretty rough time and she has been doped up pretty good. Looks like the medication must have caught up to her again because she's sound asleep. It would probably be a lot better if you came back tomorrow after she's had a chance to clean up and put some make-up on. She knows that you're here and that seemed to be all she needed for now."

For a moment it looked as if McCoy was going to protest. He stood in front of Linda, silently studying her eyes. Finally he said. "It's probably just as well. I might be getting pretty busy any minute now. Looks like things might be beginning to pop back at the precinct. I was just on the phone with them. You ready to head back there? I can give you a lift and you can fill me in on what you found out."

Linda nodded and gestured toward the elevator. "Let's go."

Linda broke the uncomfortable silence. "A long time ago, when I started out in this business, I was working with kids who had just come back from Vietnam. Some of them had been prisoners of war and had been subjected to some extreme mental tortures. I thought that all of that was behind me, but this morning was like a cruel flashback. Your friend, Ruby, has been through an experience that could break down a battle hardened war veteran."

McCoy interrupted. "Did they? Did they touch her?"

"Not in the way you're thinking. Their object was to completely terrify her and they did that very well."

McCoy was just pulling into the parking spot at the precinct house. He left the car running and turned to Linda. "Tell me everything that happened."

Linda reached into her purse and extracted an audiotape cassette. She handed it to McCoy along with her business card and said. "When you have time, the whole interview is on here. It gets pretty intense in parts. If I were you, I wouldn't play it in front of an audience. You have my card. Call me if there's anything you need clarified." Linda turned and looked straightforward through the windshield of the Police car. There was nothing out there except the concrete block wall of the parking garage but she stared at it as she told McCoy the story. "She was kidnapped and blindfolded. She doesn't know where they took her except that it was in a basement. There were three of them and when they took the blindfold off of Ruby, they were all covered up. She couldn't see anything that might identify them, not even their eyes because they wore those mirrored sunglasses. They had this girl with them. She apparently had no idea what was going on because she seemed to be accompanying them willingly. Well, they grabbed the girl, gagged her and tied her to a post and then beat her to death and made Ruby watch the whole thing."

"Some people can take a pretty good beating and still survive," argued McCoy. "Maybe she's still alive. How could Ruby know for sure that they killed her?"

Linda swallowed several times before she attempted to answer. "Because. Because one of them hit her in the face with the full swing of a sledge hammer and crushed her skull into a building support post." Linda was crying now, her face buried in her hands.

McCoy leaned back in his seat and slid the tape cassette into the pocket of his sport coat. "The bastard." It was all he could say.

By the time they got into the precinct and were walking down the hall that led to the squad room, Linda had regained control and seemed remarkably unruffled. McCoy took the opportunity to ask some questions. "Miss Crawford, you said that the three men were completely covered but what about the girl? Was there a description of her?"

"Oh yeah. I forgot. Ruby said she was wearing jeans and a black tee shirt with a design on the front that looked like a marijuana leaf."

McCoy stopped in his tracks. "Shirley Klein."

Linda turned and looked at him. "Huh?"

McCoy answered her. "Yesterday, just before noon, Otis and me stopped over at the Disciples' clubhouse to talk to Billy Bones. He wasn't around but there was a girl there and she was dressed just like you described. Her name was Shirley Klein."

"According to Ruby," said Linda, "This all happened somewhere between three and five yesterday afternoon. And something else I just remembered is that Ruby thinks that one of the men, the one who swung the sledgehammer, might have had a tattoo on his neck. A rat or something."

McCoy grabbed Linda by the arm and with his free hand he took the tape out of his pocket and waved it in front of her face. "Is that all on here?' he asked.

Linda nodded, "Every word."

"Listen, Miss Crawford, I can't tell you how much help you've been to me. This is some powerful stuff here." McCoy still had the cassette in his hand. "I'm afraid it's gonna be police business from here on out so I won't be able to share everything with you while the investigation is ongoing, but I sure as hell would like to buy you a steak dinner when it's over."

"It's been my pleasure all along. You have been great to work with and yes, I will take you up on that steak dinner." Linda smiled and extended her hand. McCoy grabbed it and shook it so vigorously that Linda's hair bounced. He headed for his office and left Linda Crawford standing alone in the middle of the hall.

McCoy's mind was racing. The call that he got in the hospital was from Otis. Apparently Robert Bowen, the attorney from the prosecutor's office, had contacted Otis and summoned him to his office for an emergency meeting. He could only hope that the prosecutor felt that they had sufficient grounds to issue a warrant.

It was too late for McCoy to join the meeting but there were other things that he needed to catch up on anyway so his time wouldn't be wasted. To begin with he wanted to read all of the reports on Ruby's case. He was relieved to find that particular file laying on top of his desk when he walked into his office. He picked up the folder, looked at the open doorway and said. "Thank you, Otis." As he scanned the documents, he was pleased at how thorough the investigation seemed to be. There was even a copy of a note in Otis's handwriting, asking the forensic technicians to run a comparison between the rope that was used to bind Ruby's hands and the one that had been used to strangle Etta Kremer. He noted that the towels that had been Ruby's gag and blindfold had also been sent for laboratory analysis. Even the duct tape had been submitted and the whole package had been designated a "rush" with the Captain's signature.

"Are you McCoy?" A middle aged woman in a white lab coat and holding a manila envelope was standing in front of him, reading his name off the nameplate on the corner of his desk.

"That would be me." He replied with a smile.

"Here." She handed him the envelope and disappeared through the doorway immediately.

McCoy read the label on the front of the envelope. The first line simply said, HARTT in capital letters, and underneath, in smaller type, McCoy/Springfield. The contents were pretty bland. The report said that the towels were actually the property of Holiday Inn, the duct tape was from a producer who made millions of linear feet of that particular line, and that the rope was also the product of a high volume manufacturer. In the comparison test between this current sample and the one from the Kremer case, they were identical, coming from the same source and possibly even the same spool. But, again it was a common producer who made miles and miles of the same sash cord and it was sold at hundreds of outlets statewide and thousands more nationally.

If we get to a circumstantial case and can put this together with lots of other things, it might have some value, thought McCoy. But all alone, it's not much to get excited about. The Holiday Inn towels sounded like something that Billy Bones would have thought of. Virtually impossible to tie them to the Disciples. He tossed the envelope over on to Otis's desk. "Oh, well," he said aloud.

CHAPTER 32

Otis was walking fast as he approached the office, breaking into a trot more than once. He rounded the corner in time to see McCoy slide a bright yellow box into the top drawer of the old wooden desk. "What's in the box, McCoy? My belated Christmas gift?"

"Cell phone," said McCoy, "There's a place right across the street that sells 'em. I've decided to join the world of high tech living. Besides I want to irritate everybody on the road by having it up to my ear all the time I'm driving. I'll put it in the charger when I get home tonight and tomorrow I'll be in business."

"Looks like we struck gold, partner." As he walked around to his desk and before taking off his coat, Otis held up a sheet of paper that McCoy, even from a distance recognized as an arrest warrant.

"Billy?" asked McCoy

Otis smiled and nodded. "And in all likelihood we'll get Joey Winters and that 'Gizmoe' guy, Tom Sheridan, before the end of the shift. I thought you might want to execute this one first though. The forensics guys got a match from the hairbrush that I picked up over at the Disciples' clubhouse. The hard evidence, the DNA stuff will take a little longer, but the comparisons from our lab show enough similarities for us to proceed. I guess that our man Bowen in the prosecutor's office has been camping right on their back porch because, they sent a copy of their report to his office before they even brought it down here. He had this all signed and ready for me when I got there." Otis deposited the warrant on the desk in front of McCoy.

"My side of the house ain't been too quiet either," remarked McCoy. "We got another homicide to add to the puzzle here. Remember that little blonde who answered the door over at the Disciples' clubhouse yesterday"?

"Uh-huh. Shirley something, wasn't it?"

"Right. Looks like Billy and a couple other guys, probably Joey and Gizmoe, decided to send me a personal message. They snatched Ruby and dragged her down into a basement somewhere. Most likely the clubhouse. Anyway, they tied her to a chair and then murdered that Shirley Klein girl right in front of her. They made it as gruesome as they could too, just so that Ruby would be sure what the message was. We'll be awful lucky if we find a body for this one though. Billy's not about to take a chance on us picking up any unnecessary physical evidence. He made his point, so he doesn't need her anymore. She's probably at the bottom of the river or in an incinerator by now." McCoy stood up and put on his coat. Almost instinctively, he double-checked his sidearm. He wanted to make absolutely sure that everything was prepared. Being timid or indecisive when you're going after an adversary like Billy Bones could be fatal. McCoy wasn't one to leave a lot of room for surprises. "Ready"? he said to Otis.

Otis replied, "Let's move out." The two Detectives headed for the underground parking garage.

CHAPTER 33

"That's it." Bud lifted the guitar strap over his head and exchanged smiles with Monica before he gently placed his Gibson Ripper in its stand. "That's as good as it's gonna get. They're gonna love us up north. Let's all go home and pack and then get a good night's sleep and meet back here at six in the morning. I'll have the van all fueled and warmed up."

It was only slightly past noon but Bud wanted to give the equipment team a head start on the long trip to Michigan's upper peninsula. It would take the big two and a half ton, high cube equipment van at least twelve and maybe even fourteen hours to make the trip. Almost as soon as the band finished rehearsing, the crew began unplugging cords and dismantling the sound system to prepare it for shipment. Adding an equipment management group was an improvement that Bud had made just prior to their tour and it looked like it was going to be a very positive enhancement. Right now, there were only two of them but the crew would surely get larger as band added more effects to their performances.

Monica had seemed preoccupied lately and Bud knew that it was all because of the looming deadline set by Billy Bones. Bud hadn't told the other three band members all of the details of the extortion effort, so he waited until they were out of earshot. "Any news from the police?"

"I'm hopeful," said Monica. "I called prosecutor Bowen this morning and he said that the detectives had a warrant for Billy's arrest in a homicide case and that they would be taking him into custody today. I'll just feel a lot better when I know he's locked up. He won't be easy to arrest. He's gonna fight 'em, I know."

Bud had his hands on his hips. "Monica, don't give this guy too much credit. He's not super human. The police deal with guys like him all the time. He's nothing but another hood. They'll take care of it. Even if they don't bring him in today, he's gonna be too busy running and hiding to come after you.

Forget about him and let's have a good New Year's gig in the snow country."

Monica managed an unconvincing smile. "I sure wish I had your confidence. Maybe it's just that I know Billy so well and I've never seen anybody get the best of him. Not even close. Billy always gets things his way. Always."

"I'll give the detectives a call and let you know what's happening. Why don't you go on back to your motel and get ready to go. If it will make you feel any better, we can call back down here when we get there just to make extra sure. I've got Detective Springfield's card in my wallet. Oh, and another thing. When we get back, we're not going to be back on the road for over a month. You should start looking around for a house. You can afford it now. Living out of a suitcase is a bummer, even if you are staying in one of those long term motel rooms."

Bud's cool manner seemed to sooth Monica somewhat. She changed the subject. "I guess I'll stop at the sports outfitters on the way home and pick up some new outdoor winter clothes, long johns, and maybe a snowmobile suit. I'm not sure that I'm ready to try skiing yet."

After Monica left, Bud sifted through his wallet until he found the business card that read, *Sergeant Otis Springfield, badge 1440 – Homicide*. There were two telephone numbers, one for the precinct desk and one for the homicide unit. He dialed the homicide number. The voice on the other end simply said. "Homicide."

Bud cleared his throat. "May I speak with Sergeant Springfield please?"

"Not here. Can somebody else help?"

"Well, Sergeant McCoy would be just as good."

"Not here either. Is this in regard to an existing case? Maybe another officer can assist you."

"Ah. Yes, it is, and no, I don't think anybody else would work out. I really need to speak with one of them. Is there a good time to call?"

"Just leave your name and number and I'll put it on their desk. They'll call you when they come in. It's the best I can do."

Bud recited his telephone number into the receiver, not at all convinced that he would get a return call. He thanked the voice at the other end and hung up.

This Billy character sure has Monica intimidated, thought Bud. Maybe he is everything that she says he is. If that's the case, the police might even wind up having to shoot him. Bud wasn't in favor of killing anyone but he had to admit that it would probably make his life a whole lot simpler if Billy Bones would just cease to exist. He put the thought out of his mind and went to dig his suitcase out of the closet in the spare bedroom. It took the better part of three hours for Bud to gather up all of the socks, underwear and winter clothes that he figured he would need.

In his high school and college days, Bud used to compete in giant slalom races and although his skis were long gone, he still had a pair of quality boots and a colorful jacket with matching pants. He wondered if it was too far out of style but then decided to swallow his vanity and he packed it anyway. He was surveying his assortment of insulated gloves when the telephone rang, jarring his mind out of bygone times and into the present. His manner was almost casual as he picked up the receiver. "Bud, here."

"Hello Bud, this is Detective Springfield returning your call. What can I do for you?"

"Oh, hello, Sergeant. You remember me, right? From Monica and the Nephewz?"

"Sure I do," replied Otis. "I thought you guys would be gone by now. When are you guys heading up north?"

"Not quite yet, but all of our stuff, guitars, amplifiers, and things like that are on their way. Our set-up crew loaded it all up and left a couple of hours ago. Monica and the rest of us will be leaving before daylight tomorrow morning. It'll just be the band and Monica, so we're all riding together. None of the families are interested in going along. Look. What I called about earlier is that Monica, well, all of us really, would probably rest a lot easier if we knew that you guys had that Billy Bones character locked up. Is there anything like good news that you can pass along?"

Otis sounded confident in his reply. "It shouldn't be long. We have a warrant for his arrest now, issued earlier today. It's just a matter of picking him up. He'll probably be in custody sometime this afternoon."

Bud silently wondered why they hadn't already arrested him. "Monica is concerned that he will be really hard to arrest because he's so violent. I hope you guys are ready to handle whatever comes up."

Otis's laugh served to reassure Bud. "Our department knows all about Billy Bones. We've got a book on him that goes back almost to the day that he came to Detroit. We don't expect to take him down easy. We'll have plenty of back up when we move in for the actual arrest. We're getting set up right now."

Bud sounded as if he was still a little unsure. "Okay. But we'll be on the road pretty much all day tomorrow. How about if I give you guys a call after we get there, say seven, seven-thirty or so?"

Otis frowned at the lateness of the hour that Bud suggested but then noticed a slip of paper on his desk with a note scribbled in McCoy's handwriting. It said, "My cell phone number." Otis peeled the Post-it note off of his desk calendar and read McCoy's new cellular number to Bud. "We'll be out of the office after about five o'clock tomorrow but you can reach one of us at that number." He finished up with a big smile on his face.

Bud put the telephone receiver back in its cradle and went back to his bedroom to finish packing.. He was silently hoping that Monica would leave it up to him to stay in touch with the police. The cops seemed to really be on top of things. There was no need for worry.

CHAPTER 34

Otis was standing in front of his desk staring at the piece of paper with McCoy's cellular telephone number written on it when his phone rang. The voice on the other end identified himself as a technician in the forensic laboratory. "Sergeant Springfield?"

"Yes, this is Sergeant Springfield."

"That other hair sample that you brought up here? We've got a match on that one too. There were a couple of specimens on the victim's shirt and it was a Bingo. Do you want the results sent to Mister Bowen at the prosecutor's office?"

Otis thought for a moment. Chances were that the hair samples that McCoy had yanked out of Joey Winters's scalp would not be admissible as evidence because they were obtained without the subject's permission or a warrant. "That won't be necessary. Just forward the report to me or Sergeant McCoy and we'll take it from there. And, once again, thank you very much." He returned the telephone receiver to its nest.

Mace must have put up a pretty lively struggle, Otis thought. His body had produced the first hard evidence and that's the way it always seems to work. If the assailant has to physically grapple with his victim, he leaves his spoor.

It was after three o'clock and Otis was waiting for McCoy to return to the office. After a fruitless visit earlier today to the Disciples' clubhouse where they encountered nothing but a hefty chrome plated padlock on the door, the detectives had decided to come back to the precinct and discuss a contingency plan in the event that Billy Bones dropped out of sight. The first order of business back at the police station was a review of Linda Crawford's taped interview with Ruby. McCoy had kept his eyes shut during the whole tape but his face frequently changed expression with the intensity of the narrative. When it was finished he stood up, removed the tape cassette from the recorder and handed it to Otis. "Can you get this over to the prosecutor's office? They'll probably need it for evidence. God, I hope they don't ask Ruby to testify." McCoy stood looking at the floor and slowly shaking his head. He sighed, and then asked. "Can you spare me for an hour or so? I want to run over and see her for a little while." Otis waved his blessing to McCoy and said that he would take care of arranging surveillance at the Disciples' clubhouse and fill in the Captain on all of the developments.

When McCoy returned, his spirits appeared to be much better. "She'll be going home this afternoon. At first she was a little scared but I called out to the thirteenth and they said they'd keep a car right on her block all night. Made her feel a lot better. She's quite a gal, lots of spunk. I think she'll be just fine. I'll probably stop in at her place later tonight and see how she's doing."

Otis was glad to see McCoy's mood lifted. They both seemed to function their best when they were loose and unencumbered and they needed to be at the very top of their performance level when going after Billy Bones. "Nothing yet out at the clubhouse." Otis reported. "We'll have people keeping an eye on it around the clock until he shows up. The Captain wants to send backup when we move in. He's heard about this guy too."

"Yeah, it's probably best to have at least one more team there, especially if those other two are with him."

"Oh, and I called out to the Harper Park PD too," added Otis. "They're going to maintain surveillance on Joey Winters's mobile home for us. I guess he hasn't been around home all day either.

"I almost forgot to tell you about him. Forensics has linked him directly to Mace's murder too. That hair sample you snatched out of his head was a match to some hairs on the victim's shirt. Too bad it wasn't legally obtained, or we could use it to get a warrant for him too."

McCoy shrugged. "I've got a feeling that we'll be able to make a good arrest on Joey for some other reason and once we have him in custody, we can get a lock of his beautiful hair in accordance with all of the rules. But to be honest, I'm not very comfortable not knowing where the hell Billy and all his buddies are right now. By now, he's more than likely figured out that we've been setting him up on Mace's murder. He might be on the run or he might be just hiding behind a tree somewhere and laughing at us. If we can't find him, that puts him in control of the game and makes damn fools out of us."

Otis knew that it was a fair assessment of how things stood but didn't want to ignore any possibilities. "On the other hand, Billy's biggest weakness is his lack of patience, or maybe it's his ego. Anyway, I don't think that he can go more than a day or so without trying to send us some sort of message or challenge or something."

"Could be," answered McCoy, "But the morgue is beginning to fill up with all of his messages and challenges. When Monica Wilson told her story to the prosecutor, she said that Billy seemed to really enjoy hurting people. Talked about watching people die. It might be that he's getting a rush out of killing and now he's just looking around to see who's gonna be next."

"Speaking of Miss Wilson, I just got a call from her bandleader. He says that they're all leaving for up north tomorrow morning. I guess they want to get up there a couple of days early so they can play in the snow or something. At least they'll be out of harm's way."

McCoy sat at his desk, tapping his pencil on his telephone and staring off into space. Then he said, "Unless that's where Billy is headed right now."

Otis shook his head. "Don't even think it. That would screw things up royally. Man, you talk about your worst-case scenarios. But you know what? It's entirely possible. It probably wouldn't be a bad idea to alert the locals up there. You've worked with those guys before, haven't you? Maybe you could call them."

McCoy looked like he wished that he hadn't said anything then slowly began going through his Rolodex. He found the card he was looking for and punched the numbers into the phone on his desk. The conversation didn't take long. There were no recorded messages to navigate through. McCoy's call was answered by a Deputy Sheriff, who took down all of the information and politely thanked him. "Those guys up there are a lot more professional than you would think," Said McCoy, "They're always working in conjunction with the State Police, U.S. Border Patrol, and even the Coast Guard. Every officer in their department has had cross-agency experience. It sorta makes up for working in such a boring place. If we don't have Billy locked up by tomorrow night, we'll have to talk about what we need to do to provide some protection for Monica and the band. Probably need to send someone up north or maybe even go up there ourselves."

Otis had big smile on his face. He had been waiting for that suggestion. "Just what I always wanted. Chasing some guy through the north woods on a dogsled like Nanook of the North. I'll dig out my arctic wear when I get home, just in case. Maybe when we're up there, you can bring along your shotgun and pick off a couple of those 'fool hens' so I can see what they look like."

The clock rolled around to five p.m. with no communication from Billy Bones, Joey Winters, or Gizmoe. It was looking more and more like Billy was preparing to make his move. Otis wondered if there wasn't some sort of death wish somewhere in the mix. Billy had to know that Monica had been in contact with the cops and he had to know that he was marked as a special attention person by the police. Instead of derailing his course of action and keeping a low profile for a while, Billy seemed poised to continue in aggressive pursuit. Nothing was making sense. How could he expect to get away with this? Billy appeared to be openly challenging the police to stop him. Otis was still totally absorbed, struggling with the logic in Billy's thinking when McCoy's voice jarred him out of his trance.

"That's it pal. Your workday is over. Go on home to your wife and kids like a good father. I'll see you in the morning. Hopefully, we can make a couple of good arrests tomorrow. Keep your fingers crossed.

"I'm on my way. I'll be stopping by the hospital to give Ruby a ride home and then I'm gonna head straight to my place, plug in my new cell phone charger and sit down with a cold beer to read the instruction book."

Otis was still troubled by the disappearance of Billy and his buddies. "Yeah, I know. It's just that not knowing Billy's whereabouts doesn't sit well with me. I'd be a lot more comfortable if we had him."

It was obvious to Otis that McCoy had other things on his mind. With Ruby scheduled to be discharged from the hospital this afternoon, Billy seemed to be ranking a bit lower on McCoy's priority chart. "We'll get him." McCoy picked up the yellow cell phone box, saluted and walked out of the office.

CHAPTER 35

"The trouble with instant gratification is, it takes too long." he said aloud. McCoy stood in his kitchen, still in his bathrobe looking at the coffee maker and waiting for it to finish brewing his morning supply of energy. As he peered out of the window over the sink full of dirty dishes, he was surprised to see in the glow of his yard light, that it had snowed overnight. Not much, maybe in inch or so. He thought, good tracking snow. A little after five o'clock, it wouldn't be daylight for a couple of hours yet. He still didn't understand why he was awake this early. It seemed as if his eyes had just popped open and it was time to get up. Maybe it was the Billy thing that was bugging him. After all, he had promised to have Billy locked up by the end of December and today was the twenty-eighth according to the Lighthouses of the Great Lakes calendar on his wall. Four days, including today. Not much time at all.

He poured himself a large mug of steaming black coffee and went to take a hot shower and prepare to meet another day. He was still concerned about Ruby. On the ride home last night, she had insisted that she would be fine but the usual gusto was missing from her voice. He nevertheless had the feeling that she was confident in his ability to get the men who had forced her to witness that horrible nightmare.

There was plenty for McCoy to feel troubled about this morning. As he toweled off and climbed into his fresh clothes he assessed the circumstances. A lot of loose ends, unanswered questions, and the unknown location of at least one cold blooded murderer.

Wide awake now, he finished dressing and decided that he had enough control of his faculties to take on the task of programming a few phone numbers into the memory of his new cellular telephone. McCoy stopped in his living room to retrieve his address book from the desk drawer. He looked around the room thinking that it may be time to redecorate, get rid of the southwestern style furniture with all of its Navajo patterns inspired by a long ago vacation to Santa Fe. Maybe get something a little more traditional. He shrugged, stuck the phone directory under his arm, stared at the cell phone for a moment, and then retreated to the kitchen table to tackle his first chore of the day. McCoy didn't have many numbers to enter into the index. He put in the numbers for the precinct, Otis, Michael O'Conner's home and office, Eddie's Bar, and Ruby's. Feeling quite satisfied with himself, he deposited the cell phone in his shirt pocket and headed for the living room to return the phone directory to the desk drawer.

As he passed through the archway from the kitchen, a brilliant, powerful light suddenly came through the picture window in the front of McCoy's house, illuminating the entire room. The conditioned reflexes, cultivated through a lifetime as a cop, took over his moves. McCoy wasn't even thinking as he dove to the floor and drew his sidearm. It was all reaction. He avoided looking directly into the light and focused his eyes on a point slightly below the windowsill.

The first shot to come through his window was answered immediately by the bark of McCoy's own forty caliber automatic. The bright light suddenly went out. He continued to fire until the gun was empty and, with practiced precision, ejected the empty clip with one hand while the other hand snatched a fresh magazine from his belt. As he rammed the new clip home, he jumped to his feet and scrambled to a new position in the room where he could take advantage of the dim illumination of the streetlight. The intense ringing in his ears almost drowned out the sound of a car speeding away out front. Cautiously, he approached the shattered picture window in time to catch the fleeting glimmer of taillights as the shooter made his retreat. McCoy looked at his watch and made a mental note of the exact time. Five-fifty, just about normal wake-up time.

Lights began coming on in all of the neighbors' windows. One woman across the street actually opened her front door and wandered out onto her porch in her nightgown to see what was going on.

Edgy from just having been in a firefight, McCoy, called out to her. "Mrs. Franks, I'm going to have to ask you to go back inside and lock your door until I can get some help out here.

Please." He still had his gun in his hand, held down at his side hoping none of the neighbors would notice.

The telephone that had always sat on the corner of McCoy's living room desk now lay shattered on the floor. At least he knew where one bullet had gone. "Shit," he said, as he scooped up the pieces of broken plastic. His little artificial Christmas tree was on its side in the middle of the room surrounded by shards of broken glass sparkling like stars in the reflection of the streetlight. There was a seldom used extension telephone on the kitchen wall but then he remembered the new cellular phone in his shirt pocket. This was as good a time as any to make sure that it worked. The instruction book was still lying on the kitchen table. He hurried back there to make sure he was using the phone properly. "Piece o' cake," he mumbled when he heard it ringing on the other end. McCoy was surprised at how calm he had remained through this entire ordeal. In all his time on the force, this had only been the second time he had fired his weapon. The other time was over twenty years ago, back when the issued sidearm was a thirty-eight special, Smith and Wesson model ten revolver. He hadn't hit anything that time either.

"Hello? Homicide? McCoy here. Yeah, yeah, I'm fine. Hey listen. Send an investigating team and an evidence team out to my house. Somebody just tried to take me out, right in my living room. Send me somebody who won't have me locked down all day, will ya'? With this fresh snow, we could get some good physical evidence. I'll direct them when they get here. I'll call Sergeant Springfield and have him stop by too. I'm pretty sure that this is related to the detail that we've been working."

McCoy pressed the button to end the call and then poured another cup of coffee before trying Otis's number. He figured that Otis would probably be getting ready to leave home in about twenty minutes. No sense calling over there now. Otis was probably in the shower. He'd give it ten minutes.

He returned to the living room to assess the damage and see if he could begin to piece together the details of the attack. He had no idea how many shots had been fired into his house. His own retaliatory barrage had been at least ten rounds. Looking out the broken picture window, he was somewhat relieved to recall that all of his shots were fired from a position laying on the floor and shooting upward toward the window. The trajectory would have taken the projectiles over the roofs of all of the neighbors' houses.

He flicked on the porch light and noted one set of footprints in the fresh snow on his front porch. They came up the stairs but apparently exited over the railing. The shooter had obviously been surprised by the rapid return fire.

The investigating team would be here any minute now. McCoy punched in Otis Springfield's number and got an answer on the first ring. After reassuring Otis that all the shots had missed him, McCoy suggested that, since he'd have to hang around home while the investigation was going on, they could use his house as a field office this morning. And then he added. "Oh yeah, and can you stop at one of those twenty-four hour department stores on your way and pick me up a new phone? Well, mine's not working anymore. I'll show you what I mean when you get here. Hey, get me one of those cordless jobs, eh? Yeah, a black one. Okay. Bye."

McCoy's ears were finally beginning to tune in normal sounds again as he came down the stairs from his bedroom with two new, fully loaded ammo magazines from the gun cabinet. The one that he had emptied in the gunfight still lay on the living room floor where he had ejected it. No sense messing things up for the evidence guys. He was about to return the pistol to its holster when he heard a car pull up outside. He flattened himself against the wall at the bottom of the staircase, all of his systems on high alert. From what he could see of the car that had pulled up outside, it was not a police vehicle and it was not a car that he recognized. He held the Glock in the "ready" position while he waited for the driver to emerge from the car.

McCoy relaxed a little when the car's dome light came on as the door opened. No assassin would expose himself like that. There was something distinctly familiar about the lanky form that unfolded from behind the steering wheel. He returned the gun to its hoslter but didn't snap the thumb break, then opened the front door. "Gregory Price. What the hell are you doing here? I thought that all you newspaper reporters slept until noon."

The man froze in place with an amazed expression on his face. "I was told that you'd been killed."

McCoy didn't respond immediately. He collected his thoughts. That kind of information could have only come from one source. Finally, he said, "C'mon inside. You and me have got one hell of a lot to talk about. By the time we're done, you're going to have the best story of your career."

As he came inside, Gregory Price stopped for a moment to take in the destruction in the living room and then followed McCoy into his kitchen where he accepted a cup of coffee and a seat at the kitchen table. From Price's stunned demeanor, McCoy assumed that he had expected to encounter a taped-off crime scene populated with technicians, cops, witnesses and spectators, but instead found himself the first to arrive. The reporter was clearly unnerved by the situation. Price waved his arm back toward the living room. "How long ago did all this...?"

"About fifteen minutes," McCoy was looking directly into his eyes.

"But the call just came in about... Well, let's see. I've got the printout right... here." Price fished a sheet of paper out of his shirt pocket. "Five-forty-one. That's what time the machine took the message."

"Lemme see that," McCoy reached out and took the report out of Gregory Price's hand. "Are you sure that this time is right?"

"Absolutely. It's off a computerized system that is kept right on the second. I set my watch by that computer every morning."

"Did you set your watch this morning?"

"Yes sir. As a matter of fact, I was setting it when that report came in. I have a password so that I can log onto the system from my home computer. I was getting ready to head downtown when this came through."

McCoy leaned over to read Price's watch and compare it with his own. They were the same.

McCoy read the printout from the anonymous tip line. "Police Sergeant Albert McCoy killed at his home this morning by an unknown assailant."

"Is this exactly the way the anonymous tipster said it?" Asked McCoy.

"No, there is a person assigned to answer the tip line. Those would be her words."

"Mr. Price. I'm going to ask you, as a citizen, to work with us on this case. Forget you're a reporter until I give you the okay. I promise that nobody will get ahead of you on this story."

"Well, all that sounds good but whoever is sending me these anonymous tips is expecting to see something in the papers. If I don't deliver, he'll go to somebody else."

"We'll give you some prime bait for the hook. Trust me."

CHAPTER 36

The police cars arrived at the same time, all four of them. McCoy cautioned Gregory Price to move his chair back away from the table so that his whole body was visible at a glance and to place his hands on top of his head. "Just a precaution," said McCoy, "in case somebody got an 'Officer in Trouble' message."

McCoy met the officers at the front door and then yelled back to the kitchen. "It's okay Mister Price, you can stand down now." Gregory Price very tentatively entered the living room, his arms stretched out wide and his face as pale as the lonely birch tree on McCoy's front lawn.

Otis Springfield was the next to arrive. He presented McCoy with a box containing a two-point-four gigahertz titanium case cordless telephone. "Nothing but the best for my partner," he announced. "Only trouble is that, being a cordless, you're gonna have to let it sit in the battery charger all day before you can use it."

"That's all right," said McCoy. "We can use the one in the kitchen until it's ready. About the only call that I've got to make is to get some contractors out here to take care of that front window. I'm damned lucky that there's no wind. It'd be freezing in here. It's a good thing that I got a buddy who owns a glass shop. I can get top priority and if that evidence team is any good, everything can be wrapped up and we'll be able to lock this place up and be outta here by ten o'clock." McCoy read the number of the window replacement company off of a business card stuck to his refrigerator, dialed the number and left a message on their answering machine.

Otis looked over at Gregory Price. "How long's he been here? Who called him?"

"It's kind of a long story, but I'm actually glad he showed up. He brought me some pretty good stuff to work with. I'm going to give him something for the afternoon edition and send him on his way." McCoy turned back to the reporter. "I'm going to have to hang on to this report from your tip line. I need it for the investigation and it will probably be held as evidence." He waved the paper in Price's direction. "You can run the story about the attempt but I don't want you to divulge what is on here. Including the time that it came in."

"Whatever you say. Is it okay to put it in today's edition?"

"Sure thing. You can even say that you were following up on a tip when you came out here and that you personally interviewed me. I just don't want you to be too specific about anything."

McCoy watched as Gregory Price climbed into his car and drove away, then he turned to Otis. "That reporter doesn't know how lucky he is. If he'd have been fifteen minutes earlier, those guys might have wasted him."

"How'd he know about it so quick?" asked Otis.

"Anonymous tip line. About ten minutes before the shooting started, the newspaper had this report that said I was dead." McCoy held up the sheet of paper that he'd gotten from Gregory Price. "One of those untraceable lines like we've got for our snitches."

"At this point," began McCoy, "I'd be damned surprised if we see any sign of Billy or his two pals. My guess is that they wanted to cause a major diversion here so that nobody'd notice that they slipped up north to collect some money from Miss Wilson and her band. But, y'know, I doubt that it's about money anyway. I think that he just wants to ruin her career or maybe something even worse. Just to prove that nobody ever outgrows him."

"So what are you saying," asked Otis, "you think he's planning to kill her too?"

"Naw, that'd be too direct," suggested McCoy. "I figure he'll try to bump off the band and leave her alone with no place to turn except to him. This guy is a real head case. I don't care what his IQ is. In my book he's just plain wacko."

Otis poured the last cup of coffee from the pot, and held the empty container up for McCoy to see. McCoy took it out of his hand and busied himself making a fresh supply. Otis sat at the table, took a sip from his cup and said. "One thing I can't figure out is why they're going after you and leaving me alone."

"I'd say it's probably a matter of resources," answered McCoy. "He can't spread himself out too thin, so he's only taking on one of us. More'n likely, it wasn't a coin flip decision either. He probably sees me as the easier target. There's what? Five people living in your house? That's a lot of eyes. I'm here all alone and I gotta sleep sometime. If I'da been on my normal routine today, I woulda been still in my skivvies and bathrobe when the bullets started flying. I just happened to get up about an hour early today and so I was all dressed including my holster, so I was able to return fire. If I hadn't had trouble sleeping last night, that news tip about me being dead, might have been right."

A uniformed officer walked into the kitchen carrying a very bulky looking black and blue plastic flashlight. The light was suspended from a heavy wire hook to preserve any fingerprints that might be on it. "This was on your front lawn. It's an 'Ocean Pro'. SCUBA diving light. I've got one like it, only a newer model. These things have tons of candlepower."

"Tell me about it," responded McCoy. "That sonuvabitch was pointed right into my eyes. No wonder I couldn't see what the hell I was shooting at. Any bullet holes in it"?

"I'm afraid not. Looks like the guy must've just dropped it. The back cap was loose and the battery had lost contact. After I put it back together, it worked fine."

"Any kind of a blood trail out there?" Asked McCoy.

"Nothing that we've found yet. There must have been at least two of them, though, because we followed his tracks in the snow and he exited and entered the passenger side of a vehicle. They're out there working on the tire tracks right now. The fresh snow makes it easy. We'll be inside to start looking for slugs in your walls an' stuff within an hour or so."

"Whatever," McCoy replied. He opened a drawer under the kitchen countertop and withdrew a clipboard full of blank incident reports and returned to the table to sit across from Otis and begin filling in all the details. It wasn't even daylight yet and McCoy felt like he'd already put in a full shift. The adrenaline was beginning to subside and he wished that he could just go back to bed. It was going to be a long day.

A new voice drifted in from the living room. It was the familiar growl of Captain Bice. McCoy rose to meet him. "Geez,

Cap'n. You didn't need to come out here. Looks like the whole damned department's here. I ain't sure I got enough coffee for all you guys. Who the hell's watching the city?"

"Don't push your luck, McCoy. I could order you into the hospital for a physical checkup and place you on leave until we have a psychological evaluation. You know what can happen when you've been in a shooting. I'm going to go easy on you, though. I brought along a paramedic to check your blood pressure and stuff and if she finds everything normal, I'll waive all the other crap."

McCoy sat back down while the young lady from the EMT team busied herself wrapping the cuff around his upper arm and pumping it up with the rubber squeeze bulb. It really didn't much matter what the results of this quickie exam said, he had already made up his mind that nothing would stand in his way. This was his case and it had become very personal. He was determined that he would continue the investigation. It would be nice if his blood pressure cooperated but he had no intention of sitting out. The pretty young technician finally looked up at Captain Bice, smiled and nodded.

"Okay, McCoy. I'll let you go on this one. What've you got so far?"

"Well, Captain," said McCoy, "I'm putting my report together right now but the evidence team is still sifting through things. Can you give us a few hours?"

Captain Bice sighed. "Yeah, I suppose. Just make sure that you call me as soon as all of the reports are available. It's that Bones guy, ain't it?"

"Pretty sure," replied McCoy. "He's got a couple of elves helping him too but we know who they are. I'm not sure who the shooter was. I honestly don't think it was Billy himself. He cut and run too easy."

The Captain seemed like he was about to say something more, but then just shook his head and waved. He left without another word.

McCoy returned to finish filling out the incident report and when he had it done, folded it and stuffed it into the inside pocket of the gray tweed sport jacket hanging on the back of the kitchen chair.

The evidence team was working with the investigating officers in his living room. They had recovered two bullets. One was lodged in a stud in the wall and the other had passed through the telephone and had been deflected downward into the oak baseboard behind the desk. A third appeared to have gone through the drywall ceiling and then through the roof of the house. From all indications, the shooter had fired twice from the front porch and once more after jumping over the railing. There were no shell casings on the porch or in the snow on the front lawn, leading the investigators to theorize that the weapon had been a revolver.

"I could have told you that," said McCoy. "There was a big ball of flame when he fired. I could see it even with that bright flashlight because the gun was behind the light. Revolvers always look like that when you fire them in the dark. It blows out from the space between the cylinder and the barrel."

The sun was finally making its way into the eastern sky and promising a bright and clear day. McCoy stood in the middle of the room, looking out his shattered picture window at the crime scene tape stretched across his lawn and the long shadows on the snow covered street, and realizing that it was only by some amazing coincidence or perhaps divine intervention that he was alive to witness another sunrise. His thoughts were interrupted by Otis. "I'm gonna slide over to the precinct and pick up a City car and our radios. I'll check for messages and see if there are any surveillance reports and then I'll probably stop back here. Sound okay to you?"

McCoy didn't respond. He was staring into space as if mesmerized by some non-existent object off somewhere in infinity.

"You okay?" asked Otis.

McCoy slowly broke from his trance and finally answered softly. "Yeah. Yeah, I'm fine."

Otis patted McCoy on the back and said, "Don't worry about a thing, partner. We're gonna get through this."

McCoy nodded, "Sure. We always do. I was just thinking that I'd better call Ruby and tell her about this before she sees it on television or reads it in the paper. I'll play it down a lot though. She's been through enough lately. Poor girl."

Otis smiled, winked, and went out the door.

CHAPTER 37

Nobody had been seen at the Disciples' clubhouse and a query with the Harper Park PD returned the same results from Joey Winters's place. Otis dropped the reports on his desk, gazed at the calendar hanging on the wall. December twenty-eighth. Only three more days to find and collar the elusive Billy Bones.

Monica and the Nephewz would be on the road for the north country about now. Bud would be calling later today to see if any arrests had been made. Otis shook his head. He didn't even want to think about the disappointing answer that he'd more than likely have to give to the nervous bandleader. Otis glanced at his watch. Almost nine o'clock. There was still plenty of day left. Enough time for something good to happen. But then, a lot of bad things could happen too.

When the phone on his desk rang, Otis somehow knew that it would not be welcome news. It was Sergeant Godfrey, one of his old friends out at the thirteenth precinct. They'd found another victim along the side of an outbound expressway. This one was different though. He was still alive. Practically disemboweled but the EMT's had been able to stabilize him and keep him alive long enough to transport him. He was now in the ICU at Receiving Hospital. There was no news from the hospital yet but the paramedic had said that the victim's vital signs were fairly strong.

"Do you have an I. D.?" asked Otis.

"Not yet, but they're working on it. Got some really good prints though, so I'm sure we'll have a name pretty soon. I'll make sure that it gets passed along to you."

Otis's mind was racing. "Do you know if he's conscious? Would he be able to talk?"

"The last I heard, the doctors had just finished putting him back together. That's about all I can tell you."

"That's okay," said Otis. "I appreciate the information. Can you run a little interference for me with your guys? I don't want to ruffle any feathers by sticking my nose into someone else's territory. Thanks again. I owe you one." Otis hung up the phone and sat down to think. The last thing he wanted to do was to leave McCoy in the dark. Better call him first, Otis thought. He dialed McCoy's number and leaned back in his chair.

"Yo, McCoy. I don't know if this is one of our guys or not, but Godfrey from the thirteenth just called and said that they found up a guy all cut up on the freeway shoulder about an hour ago. Yeah, outbound lane. They're trying to get an I.D. right now. He's gonna call me back as soon as he has a name. Oh yeah, and this one's still breathing."

McCoy's voice still had a trace of distress in it as he answered. "How about swinging by here before you go to visit the victim. The guys from the glass shop are here fixing my window right now and I expect most of the investigating to wrap up any minute now. I should be able to get out of here in under an hour. I want to see this one myself."

"Roger that," responded Otis. "No one has showed up at any of our stakeouts either. Sounds to me like they're following some sort of plan right now."

"Yeah, well, they stumbled a little bit this morning. I'm still here."

Otis answered, "I'm thinking that's what this guy they found on the expressway might be all about. I don't know how bad off he is but I'm hoping that he'll be able to talk. From what I hear, he could be pretty far gone. We'll have to see when we get there."

"Well, c'mon by and pick me up and we'll talk about it in the car." McCoy hung up the phone.

When Otis pulled up in front of McCoy's house, there was only one police cruiser still there and it appeared as if the glaziers had finished their work on his picture window. The place looked normal. The front door was partially open and a uniformed officer was about half in and half out of the house, his head bobbing up and down as he talked to someone inside. He turned to look at the sound of Otis flinging his car door shut. Otis recognized him as one of the veteran sergeants from the general investigations section of the homicide division. They waved and nodded to one another while the cop in the doorway continued to talk. As Otis ascended the three short steps to McCoy's porch, he heard the uniform say, "Well, bye. Take care." He held the door open for Otis to enter.

"They find anything good?" asked Otis gesturing toward the cop who was just climbing into the police car in the driveway.

"Yeah. Wadcutters." said McCoy. "Can you believe it? Some dumbass, would be hit man tries to take me out with target ammo. Not what I'd call a professional attempt."

"Well, they'd probably do more damage than full metal jackets if they've got a full powder load," answered Otis. "If it had really been a pro, he'd have used a shotgun. Maybe it was all they could get their hands on. Makes it sound kinda, 'spur of the moment' don't it? Were they thirty-eights?"

"Yeah, the slugs measured up at thirty-eight with the calipers but they were definitely target loads. There's still plenty of power in 'em to kill someone but the first round was probably deflected pretty bad when it broke through the glass. I agree. It probably wasn't something with a lot of planning behind it. Maybe they're getting desperate."

"I'm sure they are," said Otis. "We'd better keep our eyes wide open, 'cause there's no tellin' what they might try next. I'll betcha they don't even know what they're gonna do, but I know that they're gonna be awful interested in our moves."

"Strange, isn't it?" observed McCoy. "Over twenty-five years on the force and this is the first time I've ever been stalked. Now I know how some of the bad guys feel when we're getting close. No doubt in my mind, I'd much rather be the hunter than the hunted."

McCoy stepped into his kitchen and grabbed his sportcoat. "By the way, I called Ruby. She's quite a trooper. Took this thing in stride pretty good. She just said to be careful, that's all."

"Could be, she's just plain sick of your ass too. Maybe she don't care. Ever think of that?" offered Otis as they walked out to the car at the curb.

McCoy didn't answer.

The two detectives walked into Receiving Hospital to find Sergeant Godfrey waiting for them. "We've already ordered a paraffin test. Just waitin' for results. I heard what happened over at your place this morning. Gives me the chills. Coulda been any one of us. The docs are giving this guy better'n fifty-fifty. Said that none of the vital organs had been cut. They had to sew up some intestine and some stomach but I guess the liver and all that stuff wasn't involved. He'll be out for a while though."

"How about if we just have a look?" asked Otis. "There's a good chance I might recognize him."

"Yeah, sure." said Godfrey. "Just follow me." He turned and walked quickly down the hallway stopping at a door about halfway to the nurses station. He opened the door tentatively at first, but then swung it all the way open for Otis and McCoy to walk into the room.

"Gizmoe." said Otis "Just what I figured."

Sergeant Godfrey asked, "You know him? Is he part of the case you're working on?"

"That's right." answered Otis. "His name's Tom Sheridan. They call him Gizz or Gizmoe. He's one of Billy Bones' sidekicks. Or at least he used to be." He turned to look at McCoy. "I'll bet that he was the one who came after you this morning. He's always been a follower. Takin' you out would have made a name for him. He probably wanted to impress Billy." Otis made a sweeping motion across the unconscious body. "This is the price of failure."

"Wonder how long before he'll be able to talk?" said McCoy. "I'd sure like to find out what's going on in his head. It'll be interesting to see his reaction if he wakes up and sees me standing over him."

A nurse appeared in the doorway. "Don't get your hopes up, guys." Her tone wasn't arrogant, but it had a confident flavor. "He's drugged up pretty good. I'd say he'll be out for at least twenty-four, probably closer to thirty-six hours. He's gonna have one helluva belly ache when he wakes up."

All three of the police officers just nodded. It was as if none of them were willing to challenge the validity of the nurse's declaration. She didn't seem to notice as she inspected the intravenous apparatus and checked the readings on the monitors. "Doing as good as can be expected," she said and swiftly walked out the door.

"What next?" asked McCoy. "Ain't it about lunch time?"

"If you say so," answered Otis. He looked over at Sergeant Godfrey. "Wanna go along? We're probably going for fish and chips today."

Godfrey shook his head. "Nah. I wanna gather up all the reports that I can on this guy so I can figure out what to do with him."

Otis turned to him. "Well, if that paraffin test comes back positive, better get an attempted murder warrant on him. We'll stay in touch on this. He ain't goin' anywhere right now."

CHAPTER 38

It was almost one-thirty when the two detectives got back to the precinct. Traffic had been light today because most of the city was still enjoying the Christmas holidays. The regular routines wouldn't resume until after the New Year. The desk pad on Otis's desk had three notes stuck to it and McCoy's had seven.

All of the notes on McCoy's desk were calls from television stations and newspapers asking for statements and interviews, except for one and that one was from Captain Bice and it simply said, "See me before releasing anything to the media."

The messages for Otis had much more interesting information. The paraffin test on Gizmoe showed that he had recently fired a gun. Another note was from Robert Bowen, the prosecutor, telling Otis that the hair samples that McCoy had snatched out of Joey Winters head could be used as evidence in a pinch under the "plain view" evidence guidelines, but it would be a bit of a stretch.

It was the third note that caught Otis's attention, though. The Harper Park surveillance people had a sighting on Joey Winters's Mercedes. They had tried to set up a tail but the vehicle had gotten away before they could get it organized. The note said that there were two subjects in the car and the time recorded was twelve thirty-six, less than an hour ago. "Looks like they're still in town," said Otis. He reached across the desk to hand the information to McCoy.

"I wonder why they're hanging around," pondered McCoy. "Their quarry headed up north this morning. But then, he's got a couple of days before he said he'd be coming after her and it's not as easy to stay out of sight up there. But then, he's not exactly a man of honor either. Who's to say he won't show up a few days early and say he's changed his mind and wants his money now. I wouldn't put it past him to pop his face out in front of us every once in a while just to keep us planted here. I think I'll call the Superior County guys tomorrow morning and bring them up to speed on what's happening so that they can do whatever they need to get prepared. I'll even send 'em a couple of pictures. I figure that we ought to stay put until the last minute. If we're gonna drive up there, it's about a twelve hour run. We'll have to keep that in mind."

"Gotcha," said Otis. "Here's another one for you to look at. They got a positive on the paraffin. Looks like Gizmoe was your shooter."

"I figured," said McCoy

The phone rang and Otis picked it up. "Springfield, Homicide. Yeah, how you doin'? You did? No shit? Okay, if you can't send it over, I'll have a couple of our guys come and get it because it sure sounds like it's the one we're looking for. All right. Thanks. Bye."

Otis looked at McCoy. "I think they've found the weapon too. The guys from the thirteenth found a Taurus thirty-eight special all wrapped up in a plastic bag about a quarter mile from where they found Gizmoe. It's a five shot with three spent casings in it and the two live rounds are wadcutters."

"Bingo," said McCoy. "At least a part of this thing is coming together. Now, if only we could wrap up Billy."

"Hey, McCoy." The voice came from the open doorway of the lieutenant's office. "The phones have been ringing like crazy all day. The media people all want something from you. I told 'em that you'll be holding a press conference at four-thirty. You can use the downstairs briefing room. A couple of TV crews are gonna be there so you might wanna comb your hair."

McCoy rolled his eyes. "Man, I hate this shit."

Otis was grinning. "Don't say 'shit' on camera."

McCoy made his way to the Captain's office to find out what he would be allowed to say. Captain Bice was brief. "Just watch what you say about the investigation itself. You know the drill. Don't mention any evidence or clues and especially don't say anything about that guy they found on the e-way with his guts all over the ground. I haven't released anything on that yet and I just might want to sit on it awhile to see if it'll bring your guy within reach."

McCoy didn't normally like it when the brass began to micro-manage his cases but he decided not to object to the

Captain's involvement. He tried to be as tactful as possible. "Whatever you say, Cap'n. I just ask that you keep me up to the minute on anything that you want to personally direct. We're playin' with a really dangerous animal here. I just don't need any surprises."

Captain Bice frowned. "I'm not trying to run it for you. It's still your case. You and Otis are in charge. I'll stay out of it from now on. I wasn't trying to step on your toes."

"Oh, no, Cap'n. That was a good move. I agree with it a hundred percent. Wish I'd have thought of it. I didn't mean to imply…"

"Never mind, McCoy," The Captain cut him off. "I should have talked to you guys first. There is absolutely no reason to second guess a couple of old timers like you guys. Now, get out of here and go smile for the cameras."

McCoy got up to leave.

As he opened the door, the Captain said, "Oh, and McCoy? You can't say 'shit' on television." Captain Bice had a broad smile on his face.

McCoy looked dumbfounded. Otis had set him up again

The press conference was less painful than McCoy had expected. The reporters had been briefed in advance by a public information officer and she had laid down the specific guidelines that typically govern the types of questions that are allowed in ongoing investigations. When asked the obvious questions about whether he had any idea who would want to kill him, the press seemed to be content with the standard answer that policemen, by the very nature of their work, will sometimes make enemies and that nothing and nobody had been ruled out at this time. McCoy was convinced that they really didn't care what his answers were. All they were looking for was something to fill blank pages and dead air time in the relatively uneventful days between Christmas and New Year's.

By the time the last reporter had left the precinct house, it was after five o'clock. Otis had pretty well wrapped up all of the day's paperwork and had checked in with the surveillance teams. Everything had been quiet since the mid-day sighting.

"Ready to call it a day?" asked Otis. "I gotta drive you home, y'know. Or do you remember anything about this morning?"

"Don't remind me," said McCoy. "Feel like stopping by Eddie's Bar for a beer or anything? I'll buy."

"Ruby must be working today," commented Otis.

McCoy just smiled and said, "Naw. It'll be a few days yet."

Michael O'Conner was sitting at McCoy's favorite table devouring a cheeseburger when the detectives walked into Eddie's Bar. McCoy slid into the chair opposite Michael. "Thought you'd be gone by now," he commented.

Michael swallowed, wiped his face with the napkin and said, "Tomorrow morning. Five o'clock at the latest. I'd like to get there with a little bit of daylight left. Looks like the roads should be clear, we've only had a little bit of snow in the past couple of days. Sure you guys can't shake loose and join me?"

"Well, Mike. It looks like our case is beginning to heat up. There's just too much going on right now," said McCoy.

"I got a surprise for you," said Michael. "I picked up Ruby on the way over and brought her along. I know she's supposed to be home resting up but she called me and said she was going nuts. Besides, she wanted to see you. She's in the ladies room right now. She told me that you had some kind of trouble this morning, said you'd explain when you saw me."

Otis pointed to the big screen television at the end of the bar. "Shh. The six o'clock news is coming on. You can see for yourelf, Mike."

Ruby emerged from the rest room and spied McCoy. She hurried to where he was standing and gave him a big, unexpected hug. "Thank goodness you're all right. I've been praying for you all day."

Michael looked at the scene with a puzzled expression just as the TV newscast began.

"An early morning assassination attempt was foiled by a quick thinking Detroit police detective with an even quicker trigger finger," began the reporter. "A would-be hit man bit off more than he could chew a little before five o'clock this morning when he fired shots through the living room window of Detective Albert McCoy, drawing a volley of return fire that was more than a match for him. The gunman fled in a waiting getaway car and remains at large at this hour."

Ruby squeezed McCoy's hand and said, "I'm so scared. I don't want them to hurt you. Will you have someone watching your street tonight?"

McCoy tried to reassure her, "Yeah, we'll have patrols all over my neighborhood and yours too, but I'm not really too worried. We've got one man in custody right now and I'm pretty sure that he was the main player. I'll be fine and so will you."

"But the television just said that he's still out there," protested Ruby.

"We don't always tell them everything," answered McCoy. "Hey, we gotta keep a few secrets, y'know."

"Wow," said Michael, "It sure is heating up. You must be makin' someone awful nervous for them to come after you like that. You think you got the right guy? Sure didn't take you long to find him. Was it one of those guys who followed you the other night?"

"Well, we had a little help," said Otis. "You might say that somebody sort of handed him to us."

A telephone began ringing and McCoy grabbed at his shirt pocket dragging out his new cellular telephone. He held it in his hand and stared at it as it rang. "How do I answer the damn thing?" he asked.

Michael took the phone from McCoy and pressed the "send" button and said. "Hello?" Then he handed the telephone to Otis, saying. "It's for you."

"What the hell is going on?" asked McCoy incredulously.

Otis held up his hand while he answered. "No sir, the arrest has not been made yet but it could come at any time. The situation is under control and you have no reason to worry. Yes sir. Goodbye." He pressed the "end" button and handed the phone back to McCoy. "That was Bud Huber, the bandleader. Wanted to know if we'd picked up Billy yet. I gave him your cellular number yesterday. Sorry, I forgot."

"Who the hell else did you give it to?" McCoy seemed agitated.

Otis held his hand to his chin. "Well, lemme see. I left it with the precinct desk, the Lieutenant, the Captain, and our contact at the Harper Park PD."

His indignation deflated, McCoy nodded his approval. "Yeah. Yeah, okay. Thanks. Now I just need to know how to work it."

"I'll show you," joined in Ruby. She snatched the miniature telephone out of McCoy's hand and quickly went over the basic functions with him.

Michael rose from his chair and leaned over Ruby's shoulder. "Hey, how about programming my cellular number into the memory?" He recited his number as Ruby entered all the digits. Then he announced that he was headed home, planning to get to bed early so that he would be fresh in the morning. "Got the Tahoe all packed and gassed up. I'm traveling kinda light 'cause I gotta do the last twenty miles by snowmobile and I'll have my dog with me. The road is pretty well plugged up. Probably forty or so inches of snow on the ground up there."

"What'd I tell you about dogsleds?' commented Otis.

"No, no. He won't be pulling it," Michael grinned. "He'll be riding in the cutter behind the snowmobile."

"Whatever," said Otis. "Drive careful and we'll see you when you get home."

CHAPTER 39

Monica and the Nephewz were an instant hit at the Copper Sky Ski Resort and Casino. Sid, the stage manager, seemed thrilled when Bud told him that the group had talked it over on the ride up here and had agreed to throw in a couple of complimentary performances. This was their first appearance since Kelly, the lead guitarist, had returned to the band and they wanted to work in front of an audience a time or two before their main gig on New Year's Eve.

Bud was surprised to see that their group would be sharing the billing with the Johnny Vitale Orchestra, a sixteen piece up and coming swing band. Sid apologized saying that he had expected Monica and the Nephewz to try to break their contract now that they were a hot property, so he had booked the other band as insurance.

The situation presented Bud with a good opportunity to negotiate and so he was able to strike a bargain. Monica and the Nephewz would take the nine o'clock show and the Swing Orchestra could have the Auld Lang Syne slot at midnight. Bud knew that his group would welcome the chance to join in the midnight festivities, a rare treat for musicians. The stage manager appeared glad that he was being let off the hook, as if he didn't like making delicate decisions. Bud told him that if the leader of the big band objected, he could always plead that he was pressured by the other group and, after all, they held the original contract.

The band had two full days to enjoy the winter sports and activities or maybe even the slot machines before settling down to serious work. Bud and his younger brother Kelly took to the slopes, knocking off the rust and showing much of the skill that they had developed in their energetic younger years when they both skied competitively. Bud insisted that they not try anything too risky until New Year's Day though. It wouldn't be prudent to sustain some sort of injury and not be able to perform on stage.

Monica tried taking a few skiing lessons but eventually said that even the bunny hill looked too much like one of the Rocky Mountain widow-makers and opted for a snowmobile instead. It seemed like a good choice. Monica could putt around the resort at tortoise speed, staying on the well marked, groomed trails and it gave her the perfect opportunity to show off her pretty, electric blue snowmobile outfit. Her smile inferred that she didn't have a care in the world. To all appearances she was having the time of her life.

When the sun finally settled in the western sky on their first full day in the north woods, the group met in the dining room for a traditional meal of "Yooper" pasties. All of their appetites had been supercharged by the winter activities. The combination of strenuous exercise and the body's natural struggle for warmth burns calories at a rate generally reserved for stampeding longhorns. The steaming hot, platter sized blend of tender beef chunks, potatoes, carrots, onions and a few secret vegetables wrapped in a flaky crust, were devoured with Viking-like enthusiasm. Even Monica, who usually picked at a salad and almost always left at least two thirds of her servings on the plate, attacked tonight's supper like a starving timber wolf. When Bud pushed back from the table, he declared. "I don't think that any of us will have any trouble sleeping tonight." The rest of the group murmured their agreement.

The next morning was a lot more like business than pleasure. The group spent several hours setting up their equipment, testing things like the sound projection, getting the lights and special effects just right. All in all, it was a simple set, not nearly as elaborate as some of the concoctions that were in the plans for the next tour. It would take a full staff of technicians to make everything function when they got to that point. For now, however, along with just two assistants, they could handle it all by themselves.

At high noon, the group gave their first performance. The entire band was pleased at just how smoothly it all rolled out. The only announcements for the impromptu matinee were a half dozen posters set on easels at the Casino entrances, but that seemed to be enough because they played to a full house. The acoustics in the small theater were very compatible with the music style of the group. The audience was easily able to hear and understand every word that Monica sang. With the return of Kelly to lead guitar, the lighthearted banter among the band members between numbers had begun to reappear. Everybody in the group looked as if they were relaxed and enjoying themselves. That feeling radiated to the audience and brought them into the performance. It's the kind of magic that all entertainers strive for. When they had finished their final encore and had all taken their bows with beaming faces, Bud turned to the band and said, "Perfect."

This afternoon's show was just the kick-off the band needed. It brought the smiles back. Although only Bud and Monica knew all of the details of the dark cloud hanging over them, the three other band members couldn't help but notice the gloomy faces and even gloomier dispositions that had been so devouring in recent weeks. What happened today had been a healthy change.

Bud called a meeting in his hotel room before dinner to lay out the schedule for the New Year's Eve shows. "We'll do a one hour show at noon and then our main go will be at nine. Sixty minutes later, we'll be partying just like the rest of the guests. Management has even offered to let us stay and play for a couple more days if we like. I figure that we can make up our minds about that on New Year's Day."

The meeting only lasted a few minutes and nobody seemed interested in lingering. Monica was the last to leave and she paused at the door. "Any news from Detroit?"

Bud wouldn't look her in the eye. "Detective Springfield told me that they're close to making the arrest. He said that things are under control."

Monica lowered her head and walked out into the hallway.

CHAPTER 40

"We're runnin' out of time," agonized McCoy. "If we don't get him today, we'll have to go to plan B."

"I thought that this was plan B," said Otis.

Things were uncomfortably quiet at the precinct this morning. All of the surveillance reports said the same thing. No Activity.

Otis sat at his desk holding a small strange looking electronic device in his hand, pressing buttons while constantly referring to the open instruction booklet in his lap.

"What's that thing?" Asked McCoy.

Otis held the instrument up so that McCoy had a better view. "Christmas gift from the wife. They call it a GPS, stands for Global Positioning System or Satellite or something like that. Anyway, it reads signals from a bunch of different satellites and it can tell you right where you are, within a few feet, anywhere on the planet. I'm just learning how to use it. Michael O'Conner gave me his coordinates last night so I was programming them in here. I guess that he's got one of these gadgets too. Says they're great. Keep you from getting lost in the wilderness."

"You mean to tell me that you could find Michael's place up north just by using that?"

"You got it. Right to his front door," answered Otis. "Kinda makes you wonder just how different the world would be if say, Moses would have had one of these babies."

"Looks like a garage door opener to me," said McCoy "I'm going to call up to Superior County and let them know what we've got so far. I wanna make sure that they're aware of just how dangerous Billy can be. If this guy gets loose up in that neighborhood, no telling what might happen." He reached for the phone.

While McCoy was talking to the Superior County Sheriff's Department, Otis picked up a call from Sergeant Godfrey at the thirteenth. It was looking like their suspect at Receiving Hospital might regain consciousness fairly soon, at least that was what the doctor told them. "If you guys want a crack at him, get your asses over here," was the official message. Otis thanked him, hung up and waited for McCoy to finish.

"Godfrey says we should get over to the hospital." said Otis. "He thinks that Gizmoe might wake up soon. I sure hope we can get something out of him. There's no doubt he knows where Billy's been hiding out. It'd be awful nice to get that sort of information."

"Damn straight about that," said McCoy. "Let's see, it's nine o'clock now. With any luck we could have Billy in a nice warm cell by lunchtime."

Otis shoved his little GPS unit into his coat pocket as he stood up. "Don't expect too much. Gizmoe's gonna have to spill his guts first."

"He did that yesterday. That's why he's in the hospital," McCoy smiled. "Let's move." McCoy grabbed his coat and headed for the door.

The last person McCoy expected to find waiting outside Gizmoe's hospital room at Receiving Hospital was Gregory Price the newshound. "Don't tell me that you got an anonymous call on this one too." said McCoy.

"As a matter of fact, I came up with this incident all by myself," answered Price with an embarrassed sounding giggle. "This isn't even a case out of your precinct. I generally have a look at all the ones that come in here as assault victims. I have to admit that I was wondering about this one though. I mean it came across my scanner only a few hours after that guy shot up your place and I sorta smelled a connection. Can you help me out with anything?"

McCoy sighed. "Well, I suppose. So far you've been pretty good. As long as you understand that we're gonna ask you to hold back anything that might jeopardize the investigation. We got a deal?"

"You know I'll work with you. I got a conscience." Price's words sounded sincere.

"You'd never make it on the police department, then," commented Otis.

The door to Gizmoe's room opened and a surprised looking nurse froze in the doorway. McCoy immediately held up his police identification tag to put her at ease. When her breathing resumed, she said. "The doctor is in there with him right now. He's still pretty groggy. Wait here and I'll let the doctor know that you're right outside the room." She disappeared back inside.

When she returned, she said. "The doctor will be with you in a few minutes and he'll give you the guidelines for interviewing the patient."

McCoy laughed. "Thanks."

If Gizmoe was surprised to see that McCoy was still alive, he didn't show it. Perhaps he was still under the influence of whatever it was that they had sedated him with, but he displayed no sign of recognition. The thought occurred to the detective that Gizmoe may not even be sure who McCoy was. After all, they'd never been formally introduced and Gizmoe had only seen him from a distance and for only a few brief minutes.

"Do you know who I am?" Nothing like starting out with a basic question, reasoned McCoy.

He could see that Gizmoe was having difficulty trying to focus. He didn't look terribly comfortable either, with the needle taped in his forearm and the clear plastic tubing running into his nostril. McCoy didn't feel particularly sorry for him.

The pitiful looking man in the bed quietly shook his head from side to side and then closed his eyes and went back to sleep.

McCoy stood looking at him for several minutes and then said. "Shit." He turned around and left the room saying to Gregory Price, "He's all yours, but not one word in the paper without my okay. Understand?"

"It's your call," answered Price.

"Ready for lunch?" asked Otis.

"Yeah. Lunch," replied McCoy.

On the way out of the hospital, they encountered Sergeant Godfrey at the main entrance. "Got a warrant. Attempted murder in the first," he said holding up a folded sheet of paper. "Some guy in the prosecutor's office. Guy by the name of Bowen. Said he knew all about it. I didn't even have to ask. I'm figuring that it will be at least a few days before he poses a flight risk. By then, I can have him transferred. In the meantime, we probably don't even need a guy outside his door."

"Good enough," said McCoy. "He ain't going anywhere for a while. Right now he thinks he's waiting to talk to Saint Peter."

McCoy and Otis opted for one of the medium price range businessmen's restaurants near downtown. The crowd was light because of the holidays so they had the chance for a leisurely lunch and some extra time to sit and discuss strategy.

"I've been thinking," began Otis, "We've got this Gizmoe guy who Billy thinks is dead. Should we put out the word that he's alive and conscious and singing like a bird? Or should we tell the press that he's too ripped up to talk?"

McCoy didn't look up from his menu. "Now that Price is involved, I suppose we'll have to release some kind of statement. We can't say he's dead, that's for sure. When the guys from the thirteenth are able to execute that warrant, it'll make the six o'clock news and it would be tough to explain why he ain't still dead."

The detectives took advantage of the slow afternoon to enjoy their working lunch and plan for the next day. "I'm gonna throw all my winter stuff in the car tomorrow and haul it along to work with me," said Otis. "Just in case we've gotta go up there. Did you mention that possibility to the God's country Sheriff?"

"Yeah. He said to c'mon up. Always enjoys the company. I really like those guys. Great attitudes. People are so much more laid back when you get away from the big cities. But if Billy gets up there, all that will change in one hell of a hurry. Why don't we go for a little ride. Check out the clubhouse and the trailer park. I know we probably won't see anything but I feel like we're doing absolutely nothing, sitting around and waiting."

"Agreed," said Otis "A second look can't hurt a thing. You never know what we might have missed the first time around."

A drive past the Satan's Disciples' clubhouse was all they needed to confirm that nobody had recently visited. The only tracks in the snow had been made by some small animal, possibly a squirrel or maybe a rat. Likewise the snow that covered Billy's van remained undisturbed in the field beside the clubhouse and the big padlock on the front door was clearly visible from the street. They continued on to the corner and turned north, headed for Harper Park.

"I think I know what bothers me about that rusty ol' van that Billy drives," said McCoy. "It's like he's making a statement that shiny new cars and things aren't important to him. He's saying that life ain't about money, it's about power."

There was more of the same nothingness at the Tranquil Estates Mobile and Modular Community. Joey Winters's banged up old van was still parked in the same spot, the left rear tire beginning to go soft. There were no tracks in or out of Joey's place either.

"Nothing new here," commented McCoy. "But I guess we really didn't expect anything. Figure they're still in town?"

"Geez. I wish I had an answer for you," said Otis. "I guess that all we can do is be ready to jump whichever way we have to when the time comes. We might as well head back to the station."

The fax waiting for McCoy indicated that all of the preliminary information gathered from the gun that was recovered from the expressway and the ballistic reports on evidence taken from the scene at McCoy's house, pointed to a match between the gun, the physical evidence, and Tom Sheridan AKA Gizmoe. Things didn't normally move this fast and, of course, the official test results were not expected for a while yet, but with Prosecutor Bowen pushing, it sure gave the investigating officers a lot to work with. McCoy was convinced that he was getting full support from City Hall.

The day ended with the same surveillance reports that it began with. No Activity.

McCoy arrived at work the next morning with the trunk of his Bonneville packed full of his outdoor gear. He had left his blaze orange hunting clothes at home and had packed the black arctic weight Carharts instead. The suitcase held a couple of flannel shirts with quilted linings, his polypropylene long johns, and two pair of wool socks. The LaCrosse IceMan boots sat on the floor in the back seat.

Otis was waiting when McCoy entered the office. "Not one damn thing new this morning. Looks like a repeat of yesterday."

"Better not be," said McCoy, "We need to make some progress by noon or we'll have to head up north to play bodyguard.

I'd just as soon make the arrest right here in town and then go home and get a decent night's rest for a change."

"The way I see it," began Otis, "our best bet will be getting something out of Gizmoe at the hospital. He's had another twenty or so hours to clear the fog out of his head and he's far and away our most hopeful shot at finding Billy and Joey. Wanna have another go at him?"

McCoy grimaced slightly and said, "I guess there just ain't much else. What the hell, let's give it a whirl."

Gizmoe looked very much like a high school science lab experiment this morning. He was surrounded by and wired to electronic equipment and there were tubes going into his arm and his nose. The hospital bed had been cranked up slightly so that he was in a position that loosely resembled sitting. His eyes were open and they followed McCoy's movement arount to the foot of the bed.

"Morning, Giz. We just stopped by to see if there's anything we can get for you."

For the first time, it seemed like Gizmoe actually recognized McCoy, his blank expression slowly turning to fear. His head moved back and forth rapidly as if he were looking for something. A gun maybe? Or was it just a panic response.

"Relax, Gizmoe. You keep jumping around like that, you're liable to unplug yourself and I'd have to hook you all back up. I'm not sure I could get all the tubes back in the right holes. We're not here to hurt you. We just want some information. Now, that shouldn't be too hard, should it?"

Gizmoe stopped moving but the look of terror remained etched into his face. He seemed to be trying to speak. Nothing would come out at first, but after several attempts, he was able to say, in a very hoarse voice, "He'll kill me. You can't stop him."

Otis joined McCoy at the foot of the bed. "You're wrong, Gizmoe. We already have. You're proof of that. And you can help us finish it off. All we need to know is where he is."

Gizmoe became animated again. He was obviously in a state of total panic. The electronic monitor above his head was beginning to emit high-pitched sounds and had evidently set off some sort of alarm at the nurses' station because two nurses came rushing into the room as if they were on a commando raid. "What are you doing to him?" screeched the taller one.

"Not a thing," said McCoy. "We haven't even asked him a question yet."

"Don't lie to me," she demanded. "People don't get this upset for no reason."

McCoy wasn't sure how to respond to her but Otis, with a big smile, seemed to be enjoying his partner's quandary.

Finally, McCoy looked at the nurse and asked. "Have you ever thought of becoming a nun?' Then he turned to Otis. "Let's get out of here. Maybe we'll try again later."

McCoy checked the time on the ride back to the precinct. Ten o'clock. "I'm thinking that if we don't have anything concrete to work with by noon or so, we'd better check out a car for a couple of days because we're gonna need it."

"We'd better talk to the lieutenant as soon as we get back, so he knows what we're planning," commented Otis. "I was hoping to have this thing all taken care of by today, but it sure has turned into one helluva mess."

By twelve o'clock, McCoy and Otis had pretty much accepted the prospect of a long drive this afternoon. The plan was to run out for some fast food and then load their gear in the big black, unmarked Crown Victoria and get on the road. Neither one of them was much in the mood for a heavy lunch so they were back in the office wrapping up the last minute paperwork when the phone rang. The surveillance crew had just sighted the red Mercedes and was in pursuit. "Well, I'll be damned," said McCoy.

"There's radios in the cruiser," yelled Otis. "Let's move."

It took less than fifteen minutes for McCoy and Otis to reach the grid where the two suspects were supposedly hemmed in. It appeared that there were squad cars everywhere you looked. There was a lot of help on the scene. Along with the Detroit cars were the black and white vehicles of the Wayne County Sheriff's Department as well as the bright blue Fords of the Michigan State Police. Seems as if the word was out that they were after the man who had ordered the attempt on a cop's life.

McCoy pulled up to the car that looked like it was serving as the command center. "What's the scoop?" he asked.

The Captain in charge responded, "Well, I just got here a few minutes ahead of you but I'm being told that they're in this vicinity and couldn't possibly have slipped out. If we can't find 'em on the streets, we'll start checking driveways and if that doesn't turn anything up we'll do a door to door search of every garage."

Otis was leaning on the door of the cruiser. "How long you figure it'll take?"

"Six-seven hours at most," replied the Captain.

"Right up against the wall," said McCoy, "The bastard has us right up against the wall. I'd be willing to bet a week's pay that we won't find him in here. He's gone. I just know it."

At nine-thirty in the evening, the search was concluded and had netted a total of one arrest, a bail jumper who gave himself up. McCoy and Otis talked it over and decided that they would have to leave for the upper peninsula in the morning, after a good night's sleep. They couldn't take the chance of leaving Monica and the band unprotected. They agreed to meet back at the station at seven o'clock in the morning.

There was someone sitting in McCoy's chair when he walked into the station but he jumped to his feet at the sound of McCoy's voice. "Price. What the hell are you doing here?"

"I've got something for you." The expression on Gregory Price's face was as serious as a heart attack. "I was afraid I'd missed you. This is really important."

McCoy didn't sit down. He heard footsteps and turned to see Otis approaching. Motioning for Otis to join them, he returned his attention to the newspaper reporter. "Okay, go ahead."

Price began. "I get called down to Receiving Hospital at about four o'clock this morning to check out a couple of accident victims. Turns out to be nothing. Treated and released. Anyway, as I'm passing this Tom Sheridan's room, you know, the knifing victim? Well, I hear him in there talking but there's nobody around so I wander inside. You guys know me, I'm always after a story and I know that this character is a special interest type.

"He's like having a bad dream or something so I shake his shoulder a little bit and he wakes up. All sweaty and such. Well, we get to talking and he thinks I'm a priest. I guess I remind him of his old parish pastor or something like that. So I go along with it and he proceeds to tell me about this murder that he's been helping to plan. I guess that the guy behind it all is the leader of some motorcycle gang.

"It's some big rock star that they're planning to hit. A female singer. He says that they've been telling her that they want money but that ain't true at all. The plan is to kill her. And he says he's gonna do it right at the stroke of midnight on New Year's Eve."

CHAPTER 41

The Mercedes three hundred-two horsepower V-eight hummed as it cruised northward on interstate seventy-five. It had been a close call last night with the cops. Billy had insisted on being seen so that the police would keep their attention focused on the Detroit area. It damn near backfired though. The cops responded a lot faster than Billy had thought they would and he had to run for his life before they closed off the area. He had considered ditching the Mercedes and using a stolen car for the ride up north but then thought better of it. The Mercedes had been part of the plan from the beginning and he wouldn't start changing things now.

Joey was sleeping in the passenger seat. Billy planned to wake him up and switch places when they got to the Mackinac Bridge. Then it would be Billy's turn for about a four-hour nap before they pulled in at the Birch Motel, just down the road from the Copper Sky Casino. Billy had never been there before but as long as he stayed on the main road, it couldn't be too hard to locate. According to his map, there was only one paved highway in the area and everything was on it.

They were lucky to find a room available on New Year's Eve. Billy had booked the room several weeks ago. He got the last room left at the motel. It had just been freed up by a cancellation. It was the deluxe Jacuzzi "getaway weekend" suite complete with a pair of complimentary snowmobiles.

They could come in handy, speculated Billy.

The sun, rising into a cloudless sky over Billy's right shoulder, promised a beautiful and bright day to end the year. His thoughts drifted to the sparkling blue eyes and exquisite red hair of Monica Wilson. He could picture her delicate features. "I sure hope she's enjoying the sunrise," mumbled Billy, "It's the last one she'll ever have the chance to see."

He kept the cruise control set at seventy-three miles an hour. The northbound highways would be seething with speed traps on this New Year's Eve. Billy didn't really expect to encounter any this early in the day, but he wasn't about to take any foolish chances. The mobile police scanner clipped to the overhead sun visor had been broadcasting relatively few traffic calls. The route looked clear. He calculated that they would land in Superior County at about five o'clock in the afternoon, just before dark.

It was near mid-day when Billy shook his passenger awake. "C'mon, get up. We'll stop for lunch as soon as we cross the bridge and get out past the town and then you can drive for a while."

Joey yawned, his foul smelling breath causing Billy to back away. "Holy shit, we're way up here already? Seems like I just closed my eyes a few minutes ago."

Billy eased the Mercedes into the driveway of the old trucker style restaurant and drove around back to a less conspicuous parking spot. The pair walked into the half empty sandwich shop and chose a booth next to the back door that offered a good view of the main entrance. Billy ordered a soup and salad. Joey just had a bowl of soup. The lunchtime conversation turned to the subject of Gizmoe. "It kinda bothers me that there ain't been anything in the papers or on TV about Giz," said Joey. "There ought to be something about it somewhere. You don't suppose ... nah, forget it."

"Forget what?' Asked Billy. "What don't I suppose?"

"Well, what if he's still alive? I mean ... geez."

"It's them two cops playin' games again," said Billy, "They like bein' cute. Always tryin' to confuse me. They're likely holding all the news back, tryin' to make me curious. I wouldn't worry too much about it."

"Whatever. Just a thought." Joey went back to studying his soup.

Billy picked up the meal tab and then led the way out to the parking lot. He opened the trunk of the Mercedes and had one last look at the two AK-47's laying up against his gear bag. Satisfied that everything was in order, he slammed the trunk lid, tossed the keys to Joey and slid into the passenger seat.

The pleasant weather held its ground all day, making it a problem-free drive for the last two hundred and eighty miles of surface highway.

Billy didn't sleep well on the trip, possibly because he was anticipating the precarious nature of tonight's mission. He had still not finalized the plan. A good look at the casino layout and its surroundings would help but the lack of highways in the immediate vicinity posed a logistical problem. The getaway would require meticulous preparation and military precision. The key would be to create enough confusion so that they could get a substantial head start and then possibly slip out by heading west through Wisconsin. Billy had confidence that he could work it out. He lived for challenges like this.

The billboard on the side of the highway read – *Copper Sky Casino and Ski Resort - One hundred and thirty luxury rooms - Slots - Black Jack - Entertainment - Exciting Downhill Slopes and Groomed Cross Country Trails - Snowmobiles available - Twenty Five Miles - Straight Ahead.*

Billy rolled back in his seat and opened his eyes to read the sign. "What time is it?" he asked.

"Four thirty."

"Good. That'll give us about a half hour of daylight when we get there. I want to drive around the place a little bit before we check in at the motel."

The Ski Resort/Casino didn't try to masquerade as a Swiss Chalet like so many of the others further south. It put on the rugged log cabin countenance of the regional culture and heritage. It was a huge imposing structure looking as if nobody less than Paul Bunyon himself could have built it. The traditional covered porch must have been at least two hundred feet long. The parking lot was jammed full of a wide variety of vehicles ranging from compact pickup trucks to full size luxury sedans. Almost as many snowmobiles were scattered in no organized fashion around the front and sides of the building. The brightly lit sign out by the road was huge and garish, almost to the point of being vulgar.

"Lively looking place," commented Billy as they drove by. He was glad to see how built up the area was. That would make the escape a little easier. There were several secondary and residential streets on two sides of the lodge and even more on the other side of the highway. To the north lay the ski slopes with their breathtaking view of Lake Superior. The western edge of the property disappeared into the hardwoods and pines through a maze of snowmobile trails that splayed out across the expansive clearing behind the lodge. "This'll work." He added. "Let's go check in to our honeymoon suite."

In their motel room, Billy dumped his pac-boots on the floor and threw his gear bag onto one of the two queen size beds. He hung the camouflage parka on the back of a chair. "As soon as you get your shit put away," he said to Joey, "let's go check out the snow machines."

Joey nodded and dropped his old, imitation leather suitcase on the table next to the television set.

"Arctic Cats, not a bad sled," said the motel clerk. "They're a lot more peppy than the machines you'll find at the other motels. These are adult models. You guys know how to ride, don't you?"

"All my life," answered Billy. "Where you got 'em parked?"

"There's a shed along the back edge of the parking lot and there are slots in there that correspond with your room number. They're all fueled up and ready to go. Here's your keys." The clerk held out two cardboard tags with little brass pendulums swinging from them.

"Thanks," said Billy. And took the keys.

Billy and Joey parked the snowmobiles side by side near the rear entrance to the Copper Sky lodge. Billy took the bundled up AK-47's and jammed them into the snow in between the two Arctic Cats so that they were completely out of sight.

"Why we gotta lug these damn things around?" asked Joey, holding the gym bag.

"For chrissake, Joey. Use your brain. We need to blend in with the crowd. We can't wander around in there lookin' like a couple of Eskimos in these parkas. And what would you figure on doin' with 'em? Checking them at the coat room and then go stand in line to get 'em back on the way out? When we get inside, just put your coat in the damn thing and set it on the floor under your chair. What time is it anyway?"

Joey looked at his watch. "It's twenty past nine."

"Cool. Let's go in and catch the early show."

CHAPTER 42

In times like this, Otis was glad to have a partner like McCoy. They were a perfect blend because they thought alike and neither had an ego that would cause problems. McCoy had seemed a bit edgy this morning. Perhaps it was just the stress beginning to catch up with him. Otis figured that the long ride ahead would help settle him down.

McCoy told Otis that he had hoped to get an earlier start from Police Headquarters. It took time to load all of their gear into the cruiser and gather up everything that they might need. He copied all of the telephone numbers that he thought might be useful into his address book and then made another call to the Superior County Sheriff to pass on the latest news. On the way out of town, he stopped and picked up a car charger for his cellular phone.

"What time do you figure we'll get there?" asked Otis.

McCoy checked the digital clock on the dashboard. "Well, my best guess would make it around nine thirty – ten o'clock tonight. Not a whole lot of time to spare."

"Thank goodness the roads are clear. Let's just hope we don't have a flat tire or get tied up anywhere. Do you know where the place is?"

"I've actually been there once," answered McCoy. "I was there with Michael O'Conner in the summertime. His place is only about six or seven miles from there as the crow flies. Of course it's closer to thirty if you have to take the roads. We came in the back way, on four wheeler ATV's. Lots of folks up there travel that way. Seems sort of a shame to come all the way up here within spittin' distance of Mike's place and not even be able to stop in and say 'Hi'."

"Well, I'm sure he'd understand. After all, it's business." Otis had his GPS unit in his hand, staring at it. "I think I've got this thing figured out well enough to calculate a thing or two."

"Good. We just might need the damn thing. Between your 'Dan'l Boone' gadget there, and my new cell phone, we're movin' right on into the next century of law enforcement."

Otis laughed as the big Ford roared northward on Interstate Seventy-five. They still had a long way to go but they were making good time. Then his thoughts turned homeward and the smile faded. He had let Marla down once again.

God knows, a man couldn't ask for a better wife or just plain friend. When he told her that he'd likely be working and they probably wouldn't be able to attend the big New Year's Party at the Athletic League, she smiled and said. "Just go and do your job and you know that you'll always be my hero. It's no more sacrifice for me, than it is for you." After all these years of marriage, she still treated him like an idol. He often wondered why he deserved such a wonderful woman.

The trip totaled slightly over six hundred miles. Michigan is a pretty big state when the upper peninsula is added in. They would be going from the southeast quadrant all the way to the northwest corner. The cruiser pulled into the parking lot of The Copper Sky, at twenty minutes after ten. Eighty minutes to zero hour.

CHAPTER 43

Monica was beginning to get the hang of this snowmobile thing. She was surprised at just how much she enjoyed gliding over the snowdrifts. Following her noon performance, she had tagged along with one of the guides from the lodge, a good looking blond guy. They embarked on a trip that took the small group off the trail and onto a frozen, snow covered small inland lake. The guide provided some off road riding instructions, and soon Monica was smitten by the feeling of freedom as she traced a zigzag pattern across the lake. Her enjoyment was so complete, she had managed to push the thoughts of Billy Bones and his dark shadows completely out of her conscious mind ... until she returned to her hotel room.

It was only a silhouette but the profile was unmistakable. Monica reasoned that there must be a standard posture that went along with a County Sheriff's uniform. They all assumed the same pose no matter what county they were in. It was a cross between confidence, arrogance, and intimidation but almost never friendly. Perhaps that was why she was surprised by the gentle tone in the voice. "Good afternoon Miss Wilson, I'm Undersheriff McBride. Welcome to Superior County." Monica could see that he was holding a copy of the latest Monica and the Nephewz CD and a felt tipped pen in his left hand. He held it out to her. "For my daughter. She thinks you're great."

Monica smiled a relieved smile. "And what's your opinion, officer?"

"To be honest," he began "I'm not even sure I've ever heard you guys. I don't pay a whole lot of attention to music. But if it's important to Chrissy, it's important to me."

"Pretty name, Chrissy," Monica opened the case and slid the paper photograph out of the cover. She checked the spelling with McBride, signed it "to Chrissy from Monica" and handed it back to the tall lawman.

"And I have a message for you too. Some police officers from Detroit are on their way up here to help us make sure that everything goes okay for you tonight."

Monica's smile instantly evaporated. "What are you expecting? Do you have any reason to think there might be a problem?"

"Oh no, ma'am. Nothing at all. They just wanted to make sure that you were completely comfortable."

"Nothing more to it?" she asked.

"Nothing."

The nine o'clock show was undoubtedly going to be the highlight of the evening. It was a standing room only affair, by far the biggest crowd ever to attend a performance in The Copper Sky ballroom.

Bud appeared to be in his glory in the intimate setting of the room. The rest of the band seemed taken by the contagious enthusiasm he radiated. It was the type of performance that created legends. Monica belted out the lyrics in a voice that hinted at angelic inspiration and counsel, every number ending with a standing ovation. The band played for a solid hour without a break. At the designated pause, a quick poll showed that they would all rather remain on the set. Magic rarely happens and it is to be savored. It was after ten o'clock when the audience finally allowed them to take their closing bows.

Monica was so intoxicated by the spirit rising in her that she almost missed him. But there he was. Standing against the back wall next to the door. He had been applauding and cheering with everybody else and now he was going to kill her. She tried to exit the stage and head directly for her room but he was too fast for her and intercepted her at the door and grabbed her arm. "Great performance," he said. "I'll try to be in the front row for the midnight show." Without another word, he released his grip and let her go.

She rushed down the hallway, ran into her room and double locked the door. Her heart was pounding so loud, she could hear it and her breath was coming in short bursts. Monica had never been this terrified in her entire life. She knew that she had to calm down and think. Her days on the streets had taught her that lesson. Something that Billy had said didn't make sense. He'd mentioned the midnight show. That was it. Billy thought that Monica was going to be on stage at midnight. He didn't know about the new arrangements with Johnny Vitale's swing orchestra. Maybe it was a break. She had information that Billy didn't.

Where were those Detroit policemen anyway? They were supposed to be here to protect her. And how about that local deputy with the daughter named Chrissy?

There were signs posted all over the casino and dining room, advertising the swing band for the midnight show. Sooner or later Billy would be able to figure it out. There was no time to start making phone calls hoping to find the right cop. She needed to escape.

Monica really didn't have a warm coat or shoes so she climbed into her snowmobile suit and pulled on the heavy boots. The extra keys for the van were in her purse. She dumped the contents of the handbag on the bed and fished the keys out of the pile.

Moving through the hallways of the hotel was harrowing for Monica. Fear numbed her and tears streaked down her face. She envisioned the pretty smile of Etta Kremer and the lurid sneer of Ronnie Murray, both dead by Billy's hand. And now he was after her.

The rush of arctic air brought her back to the moment as she opened the door. She hurried around to the side of the lodge where the van was parked only to have her heart sink to see the vehicle parked in solid. Blocked by no less than four other cars.

The sound of nearby voices drove her into the darkness up against the building. Right now, every voice sounded like Billy and every shadow was his form. Afraid to venture back into the light, she inched her way along the wall and around the corner where the bright moonlight defined the shape of a snowmobile tucked under the old lean-to that had once served as a woodshed. It was her snowmobile, the brilliant yellow Ski-doo that she had enjoyed so much earlier today. Monica wondered if she still had the key in her snowmobile suit. Yes. It was there in the right hand pocket. Without another thought, she bolted for the machine, fired it up and pointed it to the endless forest to the west.

There was no insulating layer of cloud cover tonight and the clear skies meant that the temperature was falling rapidly. Monica had not planned on facing the merciless cold and, although she wore her heavyweight snowmobile outfit, she wasn't protected by the normal layers of warm clothing underneath. Fortunately, she had stuffed the wool lined nylon gloves into one of the pockets of the suit so her hands had at least some protection.

At first, all she could think of was to get as far away as possible. She struck out on a trail that took her deep into the hardwoods. After about a half hour of riding the winding and twisting path, she pulled the machine to a halt in a small clearing. She would need some sort of plan for escape. By now, she was shivering uncontrollably from the cold. The night wind was knifing through her clothes and she was beginning to lose feeling in her fingers. She needed to find the highway, maybe seek refuge in the home of one of the locals.

Surveying the clearing in the moonlight, Monica could see at least a dozen trails leading off into the forest as if they had been charted by a scattergun. She wondered if they all had destinations. At least one of them, and maybe more would lead back to the ski lodge. The thought of running right back into Billy's gunsights brought her to the verge of panic.

The icy cold reminded her of the immediate challenge of finding some kind of refuge, or at least a main road of some sort. She recalled that she was looking directly at the moon as she fled the Ski Lodge. Her reasoning told her that, if she kept the moon in front of her, she would at least be heading away from danger and sooner or later she would find some kind of civilization.

Monica chose a trail that pointed straight toward the lunar beacon and gunned the snowmobile forward. She could feel the path rising as she rode, the track heading into hill country. At times, she would reach a crest that would offer a view of thousands of acres of absolute wilderness with no human sign whatsoever.

The cold was becoming unbearable. Monica knew that if she didn't find shelter and warmth soon, she would run the risk of freezing to death. The trail was becoming much less defined and harder to follow. There just weren't any alternatives though. She had to press on.

Now she was on what seemed to be the steepest grade so far, almost to the top. Maybe she'd be able to see something from up there. A light, anything. The snowmobile began to falter. It sounded different and it was slowing down. Slowing, slowing and finally nothing but silence.

Monica buried her face in her hands and cried. "Oh God, forgive me," she wailed, "I don't know what else to say."

When the tears finally stopped, the thought struck Monica that anyone could follow her trail right up to the back end of the snowmobile and there was only one person who might be that determined to find her. She had to get away from the sled. But then there would be her footprints.

Her mind racing now, she spotted a tree branch overhead and found that she could reach it by standing on the snowmobile seat. Swinging hand over hand, she was able to get just beyond a snowdrift about dozen feet away from the Ski-Doo before losing her grip and falling to the ground.

Her senses were failing her now, and reason had given way to hallucination. She was no longer of this world, but drifting through space not even noticing the cold anymore.

It was time for a rest. Monica curled up at the base of a tree and, with a fool's smile on her face, she went to sleep.

CHAPTER 44

Undersheriff McBride met the two Detroit Police Detectives at the registration desk in the main lobby. "Welcome gentlemen. You'll be glad to know that the show went off without a hitch. Everything is as smooth as can be."

McCoy looked at the big clock behind on the wall over the door. "What? Are you guys in a different time zone or something? I don't figure the show should even start for at least another hour and a half or so."

"Oh, well they changed all that. Monica and the Nephewz finished up less than five minutes ago. They're all done. That is, unless they decide to jump in later, but nobody mentioned anything like that."

The speaker mic that the undersheriff had clipped to his crisp looking, chocolate brown uniform shirt unexpectedly sprang to life causing him to flinch ever so slightly. The woman's voice instructed him to call the station. The officer excused himself and slid around the end of the sign-in desk, disappearing into one of the two small private offices a few steps away. He emerged a few minutes later with a scrap of paper in his hand.

"You guys looking for a Mercedes Benz, Michigan license number WD thirty-four fifty?"

"Sounds right.," answered Otis, "what've you got?"

"Birch Motel. About four miles northwest of here on the right side of the highway. It's in the parking lot."

McCoy leaned over to the desk clerk who seemed to be listening intently to the conversation. "Gimme the number of that motel."

The clerk pulled a directory out from under the desk and scribbled the number on a pad then tore off the sheet and handed it to McCoy. McCoy pointed to the same office that the undersheriff had used and the clerk nodded. He hurried inside to call the Birch Motel.

"Two men checked in on one registration earlier today. They put the room on a credit card. Thomas Sheridan was the name."

"Gizmoe," said Otis.

"Who?" asked undersheriff McBride.

McCoy waved it off. "Just one of their associates. Look. We've got arrest warrants on both of these guys. We're gonna run over there and pick 'em up. You want a piece of the collar?"

"I'd better call the station," answered McBride, "but as far as I'm concerned, we can back you up, but it's your show."

"Sounds fine. We'll head on over there and wait for your guys to show up and then we'll move in." McCoy was already zipping up his parka.

It didn't take the Sheriff's department long to get there. Two cruisers showed up and took up positions blocking the only two driveways in the parking lot.

McCoy nodded his approval as Otis emerged from the manager's office with a master key in his hand.

The Birch Motel was a fairly new place sprawling along the highway frontage, all on one level. There were no interior hallways and all of the rooms had outdoor entrances.

The Mercedes was there all right. Parked next to the dumpster and well out of sight. A light coating of frost on the windshield suggested that it had been sitting there for a while.

A stubby little fire-plug of a man hurried toward the detectives from the office. He was sixtyish with a worried look on his face. "Was one of youse guys just in talkin' to my clerk and gittin' a pass key?"

"That would be me," said Otis.

"Well, before you go messin' anything up, lemme tell ya' I don't think they're here."

McCoy pointed toward the Mercedes.

"Yeah, yeah. That don't mean nothin' I think they took the sleds. I seen 'em leavin' maybe three hours ago. Don't do nothin' yet. Lemme check the shed." Without another word, the fireplug scurried off in the direction of a structure that looked like a covered carport. He disappeared around the corner of the building but then emerged almost instantly and headed back toward the detectives shaking his head vigorously. "Nah, nah. They're gone. Just like I said."

"That's fine," said McCoy. "We want to have a look in the room just the same. Would you like to see the warrant?"

"Nah. Go ahead. I just don't want nothin' broke. Okay, guys?"

McCoy waited until the man had vanished through the office entrance before opening the door. Otis stood by with his sidearm drawn and at the ready. The room was vacant.

McCoy looked over the room. "Looks like they were only here long enough to drop off their gear. The beds don't look like they've been disturbed. Only one hand towel has been used. Must've been just in and out."

Otis holstered his non-issue Ruger P90. "I'm thinkin' we'd better hightail it back to the casino. Billy's there and Monica's there and we've got all the cops with us."

"Right," answered McCoy. "We'd better haul ass."

CHAPTER 45

"Yes sir. I'm the trail guide and safety instructor for all of the snowmobile activity at the lodge. Sometimes I even have the chance to teach celebrities how to ride. As a matter of fact, I had a big singing star out there today." The blond haired, athletic young man gulped down the remainder of the Heinekens and slammed the bottle down on the bar.

"You don't say," commented the curly haired man in the turtleneck sweater with the movie star smile, "and who would that be?"

"Well, I'm not supposed to say. But she's a well-known star. I can tell you that much. Took right to it too, just like a natural."

"Does she have her own machine?" inquired the movie star smile.

The blond shook his head. "One of ours. Ski-Doo. I like the bright yellow paint job. Makes it a lot easier to keep track of 'em."

"This...singing star. Is she working here by chance? Gonna help us welcome the New Year?"

"I don't think the orchestra has a singer for the midnight show," answered the blond, "but she was singing here earlier tonight."

"You mean she's all done? She won't be on stage at midnight?"

The blond was busy trying to attract the bartender's attention. He just nodded and said, "Right."

Joey hadn't said a word. When Billy looked his way, he just shrugged.

It was after eleven o'clock. Not much time to find her. Just because she wouldn't be on stage wasn't going to change anything. Except it might be a lot easier to get away if he didn't have to contend with the crowd.

There were three bars in the lodge. The shot and a beer place where he'd talked to the snowmobile guide. The main ballroom where Monica and the Nephewz had presented their show earlier and the skier's lounge where all of the one night stands were arranged. Billy checked them all along with the swimming pool area and the exercise room. Not a sign of Monica.

She wasn't the type to stay in her room on New Year's Eve, Billy thought. She's gotta be out here somewhere. He pulled on his heavy parka and headed outside to the sledding hills and ski lift area with Joey following along like a puppy.

Billy found the blond guide out near the bonfire where a group of pretty girls were gathered for a little warmth before challenging the slope. The blond wore his tailored snowmobile suit that gave him the look of an Indy Car Driver. He was doing his best All-American boy impression.

"Oh say," The blond turned in Billy's direction. "That lady who you were asking about earlier? A couple of guys said they saw her leaving on her Ski-Doo for a moonlight ride an hour or so ago."

"Any idea where she might be headed?" asked Billy.

"Not a clue. Just...out there." The blond pointed to the forest.

Billy and Joey tried to appear casual as they strolled back toward the two Arctic Cats that were parked just a little ways off of the well-traveled trail.

"We need to do this thing right," said Billy. He was strapping the two AK-47's to the side of his snowmobile as inconspicuously as he could. "It could take a while so we'd better be prepared. Follow me." He fired up the machine and made a sweeping U-turn, heading toward the combination gas station/sporting goods shop across the highway. After topping off the fuel tanks in both snowmobiles, Billy went inside and purchased a small pair of binoculars, a compass and two five gallon gasoline cans, which he filled up as reserve. "Look at it this way," explained Billy, smiling as he lashed the red plastic can to the rear passenger seat of his Arctic Cat. "If we don't need the extra gas, we can always use 'em as fire bombs."

Joey cackled his endorsement. "What's our plan?"

"Well," said Billy. "I'm sure that she started out on the main trail, but if she's running away, she's probably found a path that nobody's used lately. The snow's a few days old so most of it's been run over quite a bit. All we gotta find is where the track kinda peters out and only one or two snowmobiles has followed the route. That's gotta be her."

"Gotcha," answered Joey. He pulled up the rabbit fur lined hood on his parka and tugged the drawstring tight. "I'm ready."

CHAPTER 46

"She's not answering the phone, sir. Is there anyone else you'd like me to try?" The desk clerk at the Copper Sky was doing everything she could to be helpful.

"Yeah," replied Otis. "Try Bud Huber."

The clerk had her eyes downcast while Bud's number was ringing but when she suddenly looked up with a triumphant smile on her face, Otis knew that someone had answered at the other end. She held out the phone to Otis.

"Yeah, Bud. Detective Springfield here. I'm in the lobby. I need to see you and Miss Wilson. She doesn't seem to be in her room at the moment, so I guess I'll start with you. Can I come up? Okay. One seventy-one. Got it. Be right there."

"After eleven o'clock," said McCoy. "We better find 'em soon. Billy's got big plans for midnight."

As they rounded the corner to the long corridor, they spotted Bud with his door open and standing partially in the hallway. The look on his face was sober. "Does this mean that our maniac is still on the loose?"

"I'm afraid so," answered McCoy, "and he's somewhere in the neighborhood. Do you know where Miss Wilson is?"

"Her room is right down there," Bud pointed to his right. "One seventy-nine, I think. I haven't seen her since the end of our show. I was just gonna call her to see if she wanted to get together with us at the midnight show. The stage manager has a table reserved for us down there."

Otis brushed past Bud, saying, "Excuse me. I need to call the desk and get someone up here to let us into Miss Wilson's room."

McCoy was afraid of what might be waiting behind Monica's door. His mind flashed back to all of the victims that they'd found along the expressways, and that brutal scene that Ruby had been forced to watch still burned in his consciousness.

The room wasn't exactly trashed but it was a mess. It had the look of someone leaving in a hurry. One bureau was open, a pair of patent leather high heel shoes were on the floor, one by the bathroom doorway and the other next to the bed. A purse lay on the bed with its contents strewn across the bedspread. It certainly didn't look like a burglary. There were crumpled up dollar bills scattered among the array of cosmetics and manicure items.

"She's on the run," said Otis. "It's all that it could be. I don't see any car keys in this pile. What was she driving?" He looked at Bud.

"Uh, we all rode together in a Chevy van," answered Bud. "I'm pretty sure that she did have a set of keys too. Seems to me that she used the van to run out for some shampoo the day after we got here."

"Where's it parked?" asked McCoy.

Bud started to point, but then said, "Follow me." He wheeled around to hurry toward the exit.

"Still here." He stood in the middle of the parking lot and pointed off to a corner. "Looks like you couldn't move it if your life depended on it. Blocked in solid."

"Gimme the keys and lemme take a look inside," said McCoy holding out his hand.

Bud surrendered the keys and McCoy worked his way through the maze of cars to the van, opened the drivers' side door and looked around. Satisfied that there was nothing to learn here, he flipped the keys back to Bud and said, "Let's get back inside. I'm freezing."

Back in Bud's room, they discussed the situation. McCoy asked Bud if he'd seen Billy here at the resort and Bud responded that he'd never met Billy and had no clue what he even looked like. McCoy was feeling helpless and out of ideas when a thought struck him. "Hey. What about snowmobiles? Do you know if Miss Wilson can handle one?" He was looking at Bud.

"Oh sure," replied Bud. "She's been having a ball riding the damn thing all over the place. The resort gave her one to use all the time she's here. I'm expecting her to buy one of her own after this gig."

"Any idea where she's got it parked?" asked Otis.

"Put your coat on and I'll show you," shot back Bud.

"She must be on it," remarked Bud. He pointed to the run down lean-to. "This is her parking spot. She picked it out and she always leaves it right here. It's a bright yellow Ski-Doo."

"Man," said McCoy, "we must've passed a hundred of those snow machines on the way here. Most of the riders are either wearing ski masks or they've got a scarf wrapped around their face. You'd never recognize 'em in the daylight. There'd be no chance at all in the dark."

"All we can do is ask the Sheriff's Department to start checking all the restaurants, gas stations, and bars up and down the road. Bein' New Year's Eve ain't gonna make any easier," said Otis, "I'll go inside and call 'em. Maybe we can get the State Police to throw in a couple of cars too."

The search continued through the night with no results. In addition to McCoy and Otis, there were five more teams of policemen searching every road in the County. Scores of snowmobilers had been stopped and interviewed, every yellow machine received special attention.

At seven o'clock in the morning on New Year's Day, the two Detroit detectives sat down at a table in the Copper Sky dining room to have a coffee and decide their next move. "I suppose that this is a classic case of no news being good news," said Otis. "If he'd have caught up with her, she'd be laying on the shoulder of a road by now."

McCoy was about to comment when he was distracted by loud voices laughing and singing. He turned around to see a group of die-hard party goers stumbling into the dining room. Leftovers from last night, still celebrating the holiday. They were all pretty young women except for one athletic looking blond man in a very fancy snowmobile suit. He was the one singing. He stopped short when he noticed the two cops sitting quietly at the table.

"What? You don't like my singing?" The blond man seemed to be having trouble focusing his eyes. "Well, I'm all you got, man. The real singer, you know, that pretty redhead? She lit out for the woods on her sled last night. Still ain't back."

Both detectives were in the blond man's face within seconds. "Sit down a minute," said McCoy. "We need you to answer some questions."

The blond man acted like he had been caught stealing cookies. He pulled his arms in close to his body with his hands guarding his face. "Who are you guys?"

"Police," Otis flashed his identification tag. "Tell us about this lady singer on the snowmobile. What time did she leave? Was she alone? And which direction did she go?"

"I didn't see her leave," said the blond man. "But, I'm pretty sure that she was alone. She took that middle trail right there." The man pointed out the dining room window at an opening between the trees. "I think it was just after ten o'clock. Yeah it was. I remember now because those other guys were asking about her at somewhere around eleven. That's before I knew she was gone. I think they went looking for her but I doubt if they'll catch up to her. Hell, she had over an hour head start."

"Tell me about these other guys," said Otis

"I only talked to one of 'em. Big guy. Curly hair. Smiled a lot."

"Where does that trail lead?" asked McCoy, pointing out the window.

"Lot's of places," answered the blond. "It's sort of a trunk line. Must be thirty – forty different trails branch off of it. I don't even know where some of 'em go. A lot of the more popular ones just loop right around and come back here but some of 'em go off to some real wild country."

McCoy stood at the Casino Hotel check in counter. "I don't care who okays it but I need two good snowmobiles for police business. What have you got available?"

The woman behind the desk was unruffled. She looked like she might be close to fifty and was probably the night time manager, just wrapping up her shift and not overly happy about having to work through the New Year holiday. She pulled out two file cards. "These are what you want. They're more of a touring machine. Extended range sleds. You know, oversize fuel tank. That sort of thing."

"Perfect," said McCoy. "Are they ready to go?"

She nodded. "We keep 'em ready. Full of gas. Maps, everything you need."

McCoy signed for both snowmobiles and hurried back to the dining room where he found Otis and a Sheriff's Deputy studying a county map. "None of the secondary trails show on here. Makes it look like we won't see another road in this direction for over ten miles." Otis traced his finger in the general direction that Monica had headed.

"That's about right," said the deputy. "Big haystack; little needle."

Otis was already bundled up in his cold weather gear. He smiled at McCoy as he took the snowmobile keys from him. "I'm all set, just show me where the dogsled is."

McCoy chuckled. "I'll get my stuff on and meet you outside."

Otis had his GPS unit in his hand when McCoy joined him in the parking lot. "You know what?" he said. "According to this thing, she headed straight toward Michael O'Conner's place. Maybe we can get him and that Indian buddy of his to help us cover some of this ground. He's got snowmobiles at his place, doesn't he?"

"Good idea," said McCoy. "And I got his number programmed right in here." He pulled his cellular phone out of his pocket and highlighted his address list.

CHAPTER 47

Michael tossed and turned all night. He may have dozed off for a half hour at a time but he certainly hadn't had a restful night's sleep when he finally gave up and reconciled himself to the conscious world. But then, the reclining chair didn't exactly offer the same comfort as his normal king size mattress. His bedroom was at the other end of the building and he wanted to be nearby in case the young woman recuperating in his guest room should happen to wake up. He wondered who she was and how she happened to be so deep into the woods. She looked young but she wasn't a child. There were no rings on her fingers so Michael couldn't be sure if she was married. Surely, somebody must be looking for her. His cellular phone had been in the charger all night and should be usable again, so at least he'd be able to contact the outside world. He looked at the clock, almost eight. The sky would be taking on a grey hue about now, gently edging its way into daylight.

Too much thinking, he said to himself. A cup of coffee would taste good right now. He plodded into the kitchen, started up the coffee maker and watched the dark liquid trickle into the glass pot. He was staring at the brewing French Roast when he heard Clancy come pattering in behind him. It was just about the right time for the dog to go outside and take care of business. He turned around to look at the dog and there she was, standing behind the dog in the archway, rubbing her eyes. Michael could see hundreds of questions written all over her face.

"Are you okay?" It was all he could think of to say.

The girl stood in the doorway looking around before she answered. "I think I am. This isn't the Casino. I'm in a house somewhere. How did I get here? Where am I anyway?" She reached out and steadied herself against the doorjamb.

Michael crossed the room and led her back to a kitchen chair and sat her down. "You're still a little woozy from the hypothermia. You'd better sit here for now. The coffee will be ready in a minute." He fished a carton of half and half out of the refrigerator and set a bowl of sugar cubes in front of her.

Michael watched the girl for several minutes without speaking. She seemed to be struggling with her thoughts. At one point, she looked as if she were about to burst into tears but then seemed to recover. It was obvious that she was fighting some internal demons, real or imagined.

The girl slowly got to her feet and walked to the window, leaning forward so that she could see as far as possible in both directions. "We're not in town."

Michael laughed lightly. "No, we aren't. I found you out there, up on top of that hill over there. You were almost frozen to death. You said something about a Casino. Is that where you came from? Copper Sky?"

"I had to get away. I was in danger."

"Husband? Boyfriend?"

The girl just shook her head. "Nothing like that. It's complicated. I'm not sure I can tell you about it." Then she looked Michael directly in the eye. "You don't recognize me, do you?"

"You look familiar as hell," said Michael honestly. "But I can't recall where I've seen you."

"Just as well." She walked back to the table and sat down just as Michael pushed a large mug of coffee in front of her.

"Is there someone you want me to call? Parents? Friends? Somebody must wonder where you disappeared to."

She sighed. "I'd better explain all of this. I suppose I owe it to you anyway."

Michael settled into the chair across the table from the girl.

"To begin with, my name is Monica Wilson and I'm an entertainer, a singer with a band that's beginning to make a name for itself. That's where you've probably seen me before."

Michael nodded.

"I was sort of stupid in my younger years and I got mixed up with some bad people. The drug crowd, to be specific. Well, anyway there's this one guy from back then who won't let go. He thinks that I've betrayed him and now he wants to kill me. That's who I was running away from last night. He was there, at the Casino. He won't stop until he finds me. He's crazy. I know he's out there looking for me right now." Tears began welling up in Monica's eyes. She sipped the coffee slowly.

Michael didn't speak. He got up and walked to the door and let Clancy out into the morning sunlight. He stood with the door open and watched the dog sniffing the same area he had sniffed hundreds of times before. Then his eyes took in the horizon and the distant tree line. If anyone were to come from the Casino, they would most likely come from the direction in which he was looking. The forest was peacefully quiet this morning. Michael whistled once and the dog bounded toward the open doorway and into the kitchen tracking snowy paw prints behind him.

Monica laughed at the sight. It was the first time Michael had seen her smile. "Cool looking dog," commented Monica.

"Not a brain in his head," said Michael, "but he's got a great nose. As a matter of fact, he's the one who found you. If he hadn't been there, I'd probably still be searching."

"Is there anyone else here? Is it just you? I mean, do you live alone?"

"I'm the only one and yes, I live alone but not here. This is just my hunting cabin. I actually live in Detroit."

Changing the subject, Monica said. "You know, last night I gave the performance of my life. The audience was so great. Really, I think it was the venue. You know, with the people up close where you can see their eyes. We've been playing in big concert halls and hockey arenas where the crowd never gets closer than twenty feet or so. Last night was so different. I just hope and pray that I can live to do it again some day."

"Maybe I should call the Sheriff's office and have them come out to pick you up," said Michael.

"I'm so scared," pleaded Monica. "I feel safe in here. I'm afraid to go outside. I'm not sure what would be the best thing. I don't even know if the cops are aware that he's around here. They might not even be looking for him."

The conversation was interrupted by the sound of a telephone ringing. Michael stood up with a puzzled expression on his face. "What the hell? Nobody around here knows my number. Well, only Harley Charlie but he never calls. Can't be more than ten people in the world got it."

Michael was surprised to hear the voice of Detective Albert McCoy on the line. "Hey Mike. Looks like me and Otis might get together with you today, after all. Only, it won't be like you think. We got a missing person somewhere out in the woods in your area and we're looking for some searchers to help us out."

"Would this person be a pretty young woman?" asked Michael

There was a long, uncomfortable silence before McCoy's voice returned to ask. "What are you telling me, Mike"?

"I think I've got what you're looking for right here in my kitchen. We were just having coffee and discussing breakfast. Care to join us?" Michael winked at Monica.

"Mike. Lock all of your doors and don't go outside until you see me and Otis pull up. Otis says he can get us there with this junior radar thing that his wife gave him for Christmas. Know what I'm talkin' about?"

"GPS. Yes. I gave Otis the information to plug into it and if you let him lead, he'll bring you right to my door. I assume you're on snowmobiles, right? Are you guys at Copper Sky?"

"You got it. We're right in their parking lot."

"Okay, if you leave right away, you should be here in say thirty, maybe forty-five minutes. We'll watch for you."

"Who was that?" asked Monica. "Is someone coming here? Someone you know?" The look on her face told Michael that her terror was still with her.

"They're old and trusted friends," reassured Michael, "and besides, they are both Police Officers. Good guys. They're on our side." Michael discreetly wandered over to the door and turned the deadbolt lock. He had only used this one entrance and the big garage door downstairs. He knew that all of the other doors were secured.

"There are towels and all that stuff in the bathroom attached to your room if you want a shower or anything. I'd offer you some of my clothes too but I'm afraid they'd be kinda big."

Monica smiled. "Good idea. A hot shower might be just the thing I need to perk up my mood this morning." She walked over to the coffee maker refilled her cup and carried it off toward the guest room.

As soon as she was out of sight, Michael ran downstairs and slid the big security bolt into place on the garage door and then rushed back upstairs into his living room and unlocked the big gun safe. Reaching way into the back, he pulled out two rifles, his Remington model 7400 and the older model 742 that had been his father's gun. Michael hadn't used either one of these rifles in several years, preferring to hunt with the more accurate bolt action type rifle. But this wasn't hunting. He was preparing for combat and the two rifles he chose were both semi-auto's chambered for 30-06 ammunition. Somewhere in the bottom of the cabinet were a half-dozen ten-round magazines. He found them and loaded up all six with military surplus, full metal jacket ammo.

When Monica returned to the kitchen, she found Michael leaning out the door talking to someone. She walked to the window where she could see two shapes wearing parkas, just climbing off of snowmobiles and walking toward the house.

When McCoy came through the door and threw back the hood of his parka, Michael couldn't help but notice the look on Monica's face.

"Sergeant McCoy." she blurted out.

McCoy just waved.

"You two know each other?" asked a surprised Michael

"Sure do," said McCoy. She's one of the star witnesses in the case we've been working on."

"The biker warlord," said Michael.

"Worked like a charm," proclaimed Otis, holding up his GPS unit. "Only thing had me worried was that it's still got the same battery in it that it came with and I was afraid it might just quit on me."

McCoy rolled his eyes.

"Well, what have we got?" asked Michael.

"Billy and his buddy are out there somewhere," said McCoy. "The locals have done a pretty good job of tracking their movements right up to the time they entered the woods. We know that they've got extra fuel and are probably prepared for a long search. We don't know if or how they're armed."

"These woods are full of little pockets of Chippewas," offered Michael, "maybe one of them has seen these guys."

"Got any way to contact them?' asked Otis.

Michael thought for a moment. "Only one I know's got a phone is Harley Charlie. He has a cell phone. Probably got it with him. He's supposed to be part of a pageant over at the council community center today. He's probably already over there. I'll get hold of him and see if he's heard anything." He picked up his cell phone and walked into the other room.

"I thought that you were going to arrest Billy a few days ago," said Monica, looking at McCoy.

"Well, we've had the warrant for a couple of days or so but he dropped out of sight. Been lookin' for him but haven't found him yet. We're doin' the best we can."

"I know. I think that Billy honestly believes that he can't be caught. Once, a long time ago, he told me that he's been questioned a bunch of times but has never been arrested."

"That's right," chimed in Otis. "I was in charge of investigating him for a long time. I've read his record forward and backward and, up until now, there has never been enough evidence for any kind of indictment."

Michael returned to the kitchen, sliding his cellphone back into the case hanging from his belt. "I just talked to Charlie. He hasn't heard a thing. Said he'd try to drop over as soon as he can get away. So what do you think is going to happen next?"

McCoy answered. "Billy will more than likely find us. And then we'll have to take him out."

"Geez," said Michael. "There's over thirty thousand acres of nothing but forest here. Finding this place isn't going to be all that easy."

"Think about it," answered McCoy. "All he's gotta do is come across one of our snowmobile tracks and follow it. Once he gets away from the casino, it gets a lot easier."

Otis looked out the door. "If we're gonna make our stand here, I'd better go grab my duffel bag off the snowmobile." He hopped down the steps toward the two snow machines parked out front.

"Get mine too," yelled McCoy.

CHAPTER 48

Billy and Joey stopped around five o'clock in the morning and built a medium size fire in a small clearing.

"Think we're doin' any good?" Joey sat in front of the fire, the reflection of the dancing flames bringing a sinister quality to his features.

Billy threw another armful of of brush on the fire. "Yeah. I think we are. I came across something when I was looking for firewood. Take a look at that track over there." He shined his flashlight on a singular track that broke off from the others, crossed the clearing and entered a narrow gap in the trees. "I'll bet that's her right there."

"So, what's the plan?"

"Nothing too complicated. Even you should understand it. We follow the trail until we catch up to her and then we do her. Simple."

"What about the body?"

"I haven't made up my mind about that yet. I'll have to think about it."

"Shouldn't we get moving? I mean she's just getting farther ahead of us, right?"

"Wrong. She can only ride until she runs out of gas. We can go a lot farther than she can. I'll bet she's already walking. Sound probably carries for miles in these hills and I don't hear anything that sounds like an engine running out there. It's just as easy to follow footprints as it is a snowmobile track." Billy smiled his big movie star smile at Joey across the bonfire. "We're in control now, my friend. In control."

The pair fired up the two Arctic Cats just before dawn and struck out following the solo track through the dense forest, Billy leading the way. As the sky began to brighten, a marked change in the terrain became quite visible. They seemed to be steadily climbing in altitude and there were a lot more huge granite boulders everywhere they looked. It appeared they were in the foothills of a mountain range. The trail zig-zagged a lot, almost doubling back several times. It seemed to take an awful long time to cover a few short miles, but they had no choice but to follow the trail.

It seemed to appear out of nowhere, just as they crested an unusually steep rise. There it was. A bright yellow Ski-Doo.

Billy stopped ten feet short of it and shut off his engine. Joey followed suit.

The scene was a little bit confusing, There were footprints and snowmobile tracks everywhere. There were even tracks left by some sort of animal. Maybe a big dog. It looked like there had been another snowmobile here too and another set of tracks that followed the second snowmobile looked like they were left by a set of skis. A cutter, no doubt. It had all the earmarks of a rescue. Billy had a disappointed expression on his face. "Well, Let's see where the hell these tracks lead to." He walked back to his snowmobile and unstrapped the long slender canvas wrapped package from the side of his Arctic Cat. Carefully unwrapping it, he picked up the AK-47 and slapped the thirty round clip into it. Then he slid his arms into the khaki vest that held ten more magazines.

Joey, following Billy's lead, did the same thing.

With the Russian made rifle slung over his back, Billy climbed back aboard his snowmobile and settled into the deep track left by whoever had rescued the girl.

Billy held up his hand in a "halt" signal as they broke out of the trees at the top of a hill. Something in the valley ahead didn't exactly fit with the landscape. He dug out his binoculars to have a better, close-up look at things.

If it wasn't for the two snowmobiles parked out in front, he might have missed the place altogether. After close inspection through the glasses, it took the rough shape of a building. A big one with a river just beyond it. Eventually he could make out the shape of a door and then a window. "Well, what have we here?"

Joey came up and stood beside him, his rifle at the ready. He studied the scene silently for several minutes before he began to understand what he was looking at.

The door in the building abruptly opened and a man appeared. He bounded down the three steps from the concrete porch and started untying something from the rear seat of one of the snowmobiles. Billy watched him intently through the binoculars. "Well, I'll be damned." he said.

"What?"

"It's Springfield. One of those cops from Detroit. One of the two that have been harrassing me. I'll bet the other one's inside. Gotta be. Shit."

"The other one McCoy?" asked Joey.

"You got it."said Billy.

Otis Springfield walked over to the second snowmobile and removed a bag from that one as well. Then he headed back for the porch.

"Son of a bitch," said Joey. He raised the rifle to his shoulder, aimed it at the man walking up the steps and squeezed off a burst just as Otis opened the door.

CHAPTER 49

Otis dove through the open doorway rolling on the floor as the spray of concrete and dust followed him. He got to his knees, spun around and pushed the heavy steel door shut with all of his strength. "Everybody down," he shouted.

Monica screamed and then sprawled behind the kitchen table. She was sobbing. "Oh God. Please, please, please. Somebody stop him. Please."

Michael spoke. "You're safe as long as you stay away from the windows. This place was built to withstand an armed assault. Don't forget, it was originally part of a defense facility."

"How about the doors?" asked McCoy

"Steel. Three layers. No problem as long as they don't have anything bigger than rifles."

"Kalashnikov," said Otis.

McCoy looked across the room. "How do you figure?" he asked.

"Nothing else sounds like them. They've got a very distinctive voice. No doubt about it. Kalashnikov AK-47 or AKM. Just hope that they don't have grenade launchers."

"Hey, Mike," yelled McCoy, "call the Sheriff's department and find out if they've got a helicopter they can send out."

Otis had crawled back over to the door and had it open a few inches, trying to spot where the shots had come from. There was still a trace of smoke drifting out of the pines at the top of a hill about two hundred yards out in front.

"See anything?" McCoy was right behind Otis now, looking over his shoulder.

Otis pointed up the slope. "There. I think I saw some movement. Wish I had a decent long range weapon to shoot back with."

"I've got something," Michael retreated into the living room and reappeared carrying a Remington semi-auto with a three to nine power variable scope. It would have looked like a hunting firearm if it hadn't been for the oversize clip hanging out of the bottom.

"Aha. The poor man's assault rifle," commented McCoy

Otis took the rifle and fired four quick shots in the direction of the trees, watching the puffs of snow mark the hits. His plinking incited an immediate return volley and then another series of shots from a source about ten yards to the right of the first salvo. Nothing came close to hitting its mark. "That's one of the problems with those Russian rifles," said Otis, "They've got a hell of a trajectory because of the heavy bullet they use. Not too accurate at this range."

Michael finished his telephone conversation and reported that a chopper would be dispatched by the State Police but the nearest one was at least an hour away. It would probably be closer to two hours before they could expect to see any air support because a SWAT team would have to be called in.

Otis said, "As long as we use our heads, we're not in any immediate danger. We should easily be able to hold out a couple of hours. I'll keep them busy. You know, wake 'em up every fifteen minutes or so."

Another burst of full-auto fire broke loose from the woods, chipping the edges of the front porch. This time, it came from a different position. "I wonder how many of 'em are out there. Should only be two of 'em," said Otis. "Could be they're just moving around to keep us from getting a fix on 'em." He leaned out the door and answered with six more shots in rapid succession. Otis looked back at McCoy and grinned. "Gotta keep their heads down."

Monica had her hands over her ears. "Why is he shooting if he can't actually see them?" she asked of nobody in particular.

"Keeps 'em from getting ideas and tryin' to move in closer," answered McCoy.

Michael brought up the other semi automatic rifle and a military surplus ammo case full of thirty caliber ball ammunition. He leaned the rifle against the wall behind McCoy and opened up the case of cartridges and announced, "Just doubled our firepower. I've got a 77E Stevens riot gun loaded with five rounds of double O too, if we need a close quarters weapon."

"How about binoculars or something like that?" asked McCoy

Michael looked a bit thoughtful and then disappeared around the corner. He returned with a pair of pair of rubber covered binoculars and a powerful, tripod mounted spotting scope. "You'll be able to count his whiskers with this."

McCoy set up the small, powerful telescope well back from the window, on a kitchen counter. He scanned the tree line but came up empty.

CHAPTER 50

Billy wasn't happy with Joey after his impulsive barrage aimed at Otis Springfield. Billy liked things more planned out and organized. To start out by just blasting away was foolish and it tipped their hand way too soon. But the damage had been done and now he'd have to make the best of it. He grabbed Joey by the collar and dragged him back out of the line of sight from the building. "You're gonna have to listen to me and do exactly as I say. Got it?"

Joey had a surprised look on his face, as if he couldn't understand why Billy was upset. "Hey. We came here to kill 'em didn't we? That's what I was tryin' to do."

"Yeah. I know, but it didn't work did it? We're gonna do it my way and we won't have a lot of time. Remember they're cops and every time cops get in trouble, the first thing they do is holler for backup. So we gotta get this done and get the hell out before the cavalry arrives. Understand?"

The sounds of a high-powered rifle shattered the silence. Somebody in the building was shooting back.

Billy looked in the direction of the shots and set off a quick burst of return fire then turned back to Joey. "Here's the plan. I'm going to start moving to my right and I want you move out to your left. I want us to change positions about every five minutes or so. Move maybe twenty yards and fire one burst, and only one burst from each position. Keep working your way around to the left. Don't just move in one direction though. I want you moving back and forth but keep widening your pattern until you're quite a ways over. Got it?"

Joey nodded.

"Now listen close. When I think your position is about right, I'm going to fire three bursts in rapid succession. That's your signal to stop shooting and work your way right up to the side of the building. There's plenty of cover so you should be able to get in real close without being seen. Understand?"

Joey nodded again.

"They'll get curious as to why we've stopped shooting and eventually they'll come out. Now, once they're outside, I don't want you to fire any shots at all until after I start shooting. I'll decide when it's the best time to take 'em out."

"Whatever you say." Joey seemed to understand.

"You stay right here for a minute and I'm gonna go a little ways over here and throw a few shots down that way and then I'll have to duck. But they won't be looking over your way so I want you to watch and tell me right where their shots are coming from. The door or the window. Got it?"

"Got it."

Billy took up a new position thirty yards to the west and touched off a quick series of shots at the building. The return fire was close enough to make him drop to a crouch behind a tree stump. Whoever it was down there, seemed to be a pretty accurate rifleman. Billy backpeddled down to the safety of the shallow gully behind the hill and then sprinted through the snow to rejoin Joey. "Well?"

"Doorway," said Joey. "Looked like the guy was laying on the floor while he was shooting. I could see the barrel of the gun but couldn't quite make out who was behind it."

"Good. That's what I wanted to know. Okay, let's get started and remember. Only one burst from each position and aim at the doorway. And make 'em short too. You only got three hundred rounds besides what's left in your gun right now and in these rifles, that's only thirty seconds worth in full auto. It should take us about an hour to get this done. Now, go."

Joey seemed to be following Billy's instructions very well. Much better, in fact than Billy had expected. The plan was coming together beautifully. The volleys were frequent enough to keep them on edge down there in the building and were only drawing sporadic return fire. Billy surmised that they probably didn't have an abundance of ammunition.

The temperature had risen to the mid thirties in the brilliant sunlight and Billy was no longer conscious of the cold. As a matter of fact, he was beginning to sweat under his heavily layered clothing. He was working faster now, running back and forth between positions and spotting his next destination before firing a few rounds and quickly moving on.

From his current location behind a gnarled old oak tree, he spied a large granite rock that would provide great cover for his next round of shots. He covered the distance at a dead run and slid in behind the rock feet first. There must have been some sort of hole in the ground behind the rock because Billy dropped into it all the way to his armpits, jarring the rifle out of his hand, kicking up a plume of powdered snow as it skidded away from him. Momentarily stunned, Billy looked around for something to grab onto to drag himself out of the hole. That was when he felt something moving under his feet.

CHAPTER 51

McCoy and Otis were taking turns firing back at the intermittent gunshots coming from the ridge near the top of the hill. Michael was acting as their spotter. The plan was to alternate so that the rifle barrels would not get too warm, preserving their accuracy. It also gave them plenty of time to keep the magazines loaded with fresh ammunition.

Monica sat on the floor in the corner of the room hugging her knees, her face buried in her arms, looking very much like a pigeon-toed ball in pink socks. At least she had stopped crying.

"I'm seeing a pattern develop here," commented Michael. "I'm sure now, that there's only two of them and they're spreading farther and farther apart. There are no shots at all coming from their original location."

"I think we've all noticed the same thing," said McCoy. "Right, Otis?"

"Right. And you can bet there's a strategy to it. Pretty soon, they'll be so far out to the sides, we won't be able to get a shot at 'em without going outside. The thing is, they're going to have to get a lot closer before they make a move. Right now they're just trying to spread our attention out. I don't know what they're thinking but everybody keep an eye out for any changes in what they're doing."

"And you can just about bet that it will be a strange move, too," added McCoy "Billy likes to be an original thinker. Always gotta do things a little bit different and it's always gotta have a little flair."

Even though the rifle muzzle was outside of the building, the constant sound of loud gunfire inside of Michael's lodge had dulled everyone's hearing. It was Monica who first lifted her head and said, "What's that sound?"

The gunfire from the hill out in front, seemed to have subsided. Otis was lying in the doorway straining to hear. McCoy and then Michael crowded into the partially open doorway to listen intently. It was a chilling sound. It was the sound of someone screaming but not from fear. It was a scream of agony, of pain, and of torture. It was the blood-curdling scream reserved for someone in the throes of the most unimaginable horrifying death. Even at a distance, it was the kind of sound that burns itself indelibly into one's soul. The kind of sound that haunts for life. And then there was silence.

The dog had wandered into the room from his sanctuary in the basement, his ears perked up as high as he could raise them. It started as a whimper and then a low, throaty growl and finally became a troubled, mournful howl, a requiem in his own language.

McCoy turned to the rest of the group. "What do you make of it? I mean, we were just talking about Billy's unusual style but, I dunno. Sounded awful real to me."

"You think it was Billy?" asked Otis

McCoy shrugged. "I don't know what I think. If it wasn't him, who the hell was it? And more important, what caused it?"

Otis stood up and strained for a better view in the direction that the cry had come from. There was nothing but trees. No movement and no sound. "I don't see how we can take the chance. Going out there now could be suicide. I say we stay put until the chopper gets here. Anybody got any other ideas?"

Michael and McCoy shook their heads and Monica pulled herself into a tighter ball, not offering anything.

Otis pushed the door shut and locked it. Twenty minutes passed with no shots fired, no sign of life at the edge of the forest, and no sound whatsoever, not even a songbird.

Looking up at the clock, Michael commented. "That helicopter is still probably at least an hour away. The way those two guys were spreading out wider and wider has me concerned. I'm thinking we'd better keep our eyes on the tree line for any trace of movement. If that screaming was some sort of trick, they might be making their move now."

McCoy turned and began walking toward the living room. "Otis, you can stay right here and watch to the north. I'll take the west side."

Michael glanced in Monica's direction. She was beginning to uncoil herself and quietly said. "I'm the one who brought all of this down on us. I suppose I should at least be willing to offer some help. I'll take the back bedroom."

McCoy occasionally left his post to circulate between the other three, making it a point to visit Monica more often than the others, offering reassurance and appreciation for her help. Although it still echoed in his ears, almost an hour had passed since McCoy had heard the frightening outcry. He settled back into a crouch near the west window.

Monica's gasp was loud enough for all of them to hear. "Oh my God," She moaned.

The three men rushed to the room where Monica was stationed, causing a momentary logjam when they all hit the doorway at the same time.

The scene that awaited them through the bedroom window could have been cut directly from a Hollywood classic western.

Emerging from the trees astride a beautiful Appaloosa stallion was a tall Indian brave in full battle war paint with a single eagle feather rising from the narrow beaded headband that circled his raven black hair. A man in a camouflage parka with a fur-lined hood was at the end of a long rope, being led by the mounted native. The man's hands appeared to be tied behind his back and he seemed to be concentrating very intently on each step, trying to maintain his balance so that he wouldn't fall and be dragged through the snow.

"Charlie," exclaimed Michael.

Otis whistled. "Shit, he's even scarier in that outfit."

Charlie continued to lead the man around to the front of the building at an unhurried pace. He stopped in front of the porch, swung his long buckskin clad leg over the Appaloosa's head and slid off his back, dropping the reins, ground-tying the horse. Turning and pointing a finger at the man on the end of his rope, he said. "Don't move."

The man acknowledged with a nod. The face on the man belonged to Joey Winters.

Otis cracked the door open slightly and yelled. "Careful. There's one more out there."

Charlie looked up at the door, slowly moving his head from side to side. "He's gone." The Indian gestured toward the trees with his huge hand. "Bear got him. From the looks of it, somehow he got into a den with a sow and a couple of cubs. You don't want to see it. She tore him to pieces. Not much left except a head full of curly hair."

CHAPTER 52

Ruby Hartt took extra care getting ready this evening. Most of the day had been spent at the beauty salon getting a new, youthful looking hairdo and having her nails done. She didn't often pamper herself that way, but this was special. This was going to be her first real date with Detective Sergeant Albert McCoy.

She was so relieved to hear that the nightmare was over. Two men had been arrested and all the rest of them had been killed in one way or another. She didn't know any details, just that those devils were gone and her man was safe and that was enough for her. Now the biggest quandary she faced was whether it should be White Shoulders or Sortilege.

McCoy picked her up at seven o'clock on the dot and was clearly impressed and pleased by the vision that he found waiting for him. "You're more gorgeous than I had even remembered," he said. Ruby blushed like a schoolgirl.

"Where are we going?" asked Ruby.

"It's a nice place way out on the west side of the City. It's sort of an upscale bar. More like a nightclub, actually. You'll see."

McCoy had seen to it that his Bonneville was meticulously clean for the occasion. He wouldn't want Ruby to find fast food hamburger wrappers stuffed into the seams in the seat cushions. On the cross-town ride he mentioned that Otis Springfield and his wife Marla planned to join up with them for dinner.

Ruby didn't mind. As a matter of fact she had always found it easier to keep the conversation going if there was a group. "That's wonderful. How about that young O'Conner fellow? It would be nice to see him again too."

"He could show up. He knows that the rest of us are getting together out there and it's on his side of town. We'll see."

At the entrance to The Aardvark, McCoy turned his car over to the valet parking attendant, took Ruby's arm and escorted her into the club. Inside, they found Otis and Marla already occupying a table, smiling at one another and sharing a bottle of wine. Otis stood as they approached and McCoy introduced Ruby.

Michael popped in and joined them just as the waiter showed up with the menus. McCoy ordered the Cornish hen and Otis immediately asked if that would be also known as a "fool hen." Ruby wondered what the men found so funny. It was a relaxed and enjoyable dinner.

At nine o'clock, the master of ceremonies took the stage with an important announcement. "Ladies and gentlemen. It is my great pleasure to announce that tonight and only tonight, The Aardvark will have the privilege of presenting to you, a band considered to be the fastest rising pop music group in the nation. They are honoring us with a special appearance to commemorate their origin and very first performance together right here on this stage. It is with pride and tremendous enthusiasm that I present to you, the world famous, Monica and the Nephewz!"